Revealed
The Found, Book One

CAITLYN O'LEARY

© Copyright February 2015 Caitlyn O'Leary
ISBN-13: 978-1-508855-91-0
ISBN-10: 1508855919

All cover art and logos © Copyright February 2015 by Caitlyn O'Leary
Cover by Charity Hendry

Published by Passionately Kind Publishing, Inc.

All rights reserved.

No part of this book may be reproduced in any form or by any electronic or mechanical means, including information storage and retrieval systems—except in the case of brief quotations embodied in critical articles or reviews—without permission in writing.

This book is a work of fiction. The characters, events, and places portrayed in this book are products of the author's imagination and are either fictitious or are used fictitiously. Any similarity to real persons, living or dead, is purely coincidental and not intended by the author.

Published in the United States of America

DEDICATION

I want to thank my posse. These ladies have been my partners throughout this process and I couldn't have survived without them. Bryce Evans, Elle Boon and Lynne St. James.

To the wonderful ladies who held my hand and read portions of my book, Karen DiGaetano, Jenna Perlin, Vanessa Guillard and Marie Brown, thank you!

To Kelley from Smut Book Junkie Book Reviews who has been a mentor to me. She has helped to guide me through this process. She has also done a tremendous job of encouraging me to step out and believe in myself. I wouldn't have taken this step without her. Kelley I can't thank you enough.

Sure, I'll thank my husband again, well because, he is John, and even after eighteen years, I really dig him.

Chapter One

"Tell me where you came from."

It always started this way. First the question, then the excruciating pain as the electric paddles were held against her temples. The smell of her burning flesh. Then they would take the rubber bit from her mouth and ask another question. Another question she couldn't answer.

"How many of you are there?"

She prayed to all the saints her mother taught her that this time she would pass out. It was the only thing to ever stop the questions. Stop the pain.

"I don't know!" she wailed, as the bit was shoved into her mouth. She squeezed her eyes so tight she saw stars before the shocking red flames took over her very being.

"Where did you come from? Where are the rest of you now?" They yanked the bit from her mouth, making her lip bleed.

"Just tell me what you want me to say…" her

voice didn't sound like her own. For hours or months, she wasn't sure how long she begged them to tell her what they wanted her to answer. The paddles were again placed on her temples. Fire exploded behind her eyes and her teeth actually tore into the rubber bit.

She wasn't strapped down. She stretched and it felt wonderful, until the pins and needles started. Where was she? She wanted to see if they noticed they forgot to buckle the straps. She tried to look around. She couldn't. She was blind. They'd blinded her, the shock therapy had blinded her. Oh God. She trembled in horror for long moments before realizing it was her eyelids, they were swollen shut. She tried to touch them to make sure it was the only thing wrong but pain seared her arm.

Moving slowly to restore some circulation to her limbs, she realized she was lying on something soft. Rolling just a little so she wasn't lying on her arm, she fell on to a hard cement floor. It hurt, it was cold, but at least she could move. Trying to stand up, she used the cot as leverage, but her legs wouldn't support her.

She crawled and bumped her head against a wall. Using it as a guide she followed it around the small room with cement walls, basically a cell. Mostly empty except for the cot and the toilet, there was a tray with something that felt and smelled like bread and cheese. She wolfed down some of the food, but there wasn't anything to drink. Crawling over to the toilet she flushed it, then greedily drank handfuls of water.

"Good to see you're back with us Kelly." She hadn't heard any door open or anything else to indicate she wasn't alone.

"Who are you? What do you want from me?" Cringing at the desperate edge in her voice, she clamped her lips tight. God, how she wanted to beg for water that didn't come from a toilet, for food, or a blanket, or to go home.

"Who are we? You don't get to ask the questions, we do. We want to know who all of you are. We know about you and the four others. You all showed up twenty years ago. Why did you come here? Where did you come from?" The woman's voice was calm and soothing. It was like they were having a polite conversation, but Kelly knew the horror awaiting her at the woman's command.

"I told you, I don't remember anything before waking up in Dad's police car." Kelly's voice was raspy from all the screams, but at least it was even.

"But Kelly, Mike Wachowski isn't really your father now is he?" Again the woman's speech was calm and soothing. "You appeared out of thin air twenty years ago and were adopted into his family, isn't that right?"

It wasn't a question, and Kelly didn't reply, but

suddenly realized what was coming next. She'd forgotten. This wasn't the first time she'd woken up in this room and drank from the toilet bowl. Doubted it was even the tenth time. It had to be the shock treatments. They were messing with her memory. She didn't remember when she'd been kidnapped, but it had to have been well over a month, *oh God*, could it have been a year?

She sat there, turning her head away from the direction of the voice. She waited, and then heard more people entering the cell, knowing what came next. Holding up her arms she didn't have long to wait, they were there, grabbing and dragging her out.

"Noooooo-aaaahhhhh!"

"Shove the bit in again. I don't want her biting through her tongue. Hopefully this new dosage will break down the damn barrier."

Whatever chemicals they gave her burned as they made their way into her system. She moaned around the rubber bit and struggled with the restraints as the paddles were placed against her temples. Maybe they'd finally kill her and her suffering would end.

First black, then white, and then the red of fire and pain. Coursing through her like molten fire, through every molecule, forcing her to lose control of her bodily functions.

REVEALED

The colors burst in front of her, yellows, purples, pinks and blues. Ripping the head off one wildflower she pushed it against her nose and inhaled the fragrance, and then threw back her head and laughed. The sun was up and warm against her bare shoulders. Charging forward, she giggled as the flowers brushed legs, the soft grass squishy between her toes. She soared over the log in her path, and then she saw him.

Noah was her best friend. She knew he wanted to be alone, but he needed her. Tiptoeing behind him, she jumped up to surprise him as he turned around. He gave her a dark look but she smiled at him and flung her arms wide, watching as his face suffused with laughter. He scooped her up and twirled her around. He was nine and she was five, but their age difference didn't matter, they were best friends. Grabbing his silky black hair as he twirled her, she hugged his neck, and Kali was content. Nothing was better in her world than loving Noah, he belonged to her.

"Don't be sad anymore, Noah."

"I'm not sad, Kali."

"Don't lie."

"I'm leaving with the others." She'd known. But she didn't want him to leave. "Kalani, you need to understand, let me show you." He touched their foreheads together.

"No, I don't want to see."

"Open up Kali, you need to see. Let me show you."

Kali relaxed and let him share the other universe needing their help. He revealed everything. So many things didn't make sense, but the pain and suffering was easy to comprehend, and more, she could see what it was Noah and the others were supposed to do. It was simple, they were to be themselves and just help a little.

He was right, he had to go, it was important. Kali started to cry. She knew it meant she would have to leave everything she loved, her Nana, the meadow, and everything else, because there was no way Noah was leaving without her.

Chapter Two

This time when she crawled over the floor to the toilet, she somehow remembered not to flush it. She sniffed then she cupped handfuls of water. Hopefully not flushing the toilet would allow her a longer respite. Of course her captors might have cameras in the cell. Kelly was thankful this time, even though her eyes were still swollen, she could open them a little.

As she scooped up the water it hurt her wrists. She traced a finger close to the pain and almost screamed in agony. There were huge gashes on her wrists. How in the hell had that happened? Then she remembered the zip ties biting into her flesh and holding her down. After gulping water she carefully crawled around the cell. Every part of her body hurt, her head most of all. But Kelly had some instinct, some drive deep inside, insisting she not give up.

Her knees snagged on the gown she wore.

Pulling it out of the way, she realized it was a hospital gown and the back hadn't been tied. Wonderful, she was crawling around bare assed for the world to see, she thought bitterly.

She finally found the food. Oatmeal. Of course there weren't any utensils. Using her hands to eat, she was grateful to put something in her stomach. For a moment she thought she wouldn't be able to keep it down, and then she remembered why she was so hungry. She had lost control of everything. Her cheeks heated with shame, but she ruthlessly shoved it aside. At least someone had been nice enough to clean her. All things considered it served them right. They deserved to literally clean her shit since they were the assholes torturing her. She grinned at the thought.

For a moment she felt normal again. No helpless damsel-in-distress for Kalani, nope she was a hard-core cop's daughter. Oh God, what the hell? Her name was Kelly. Kelly Wachowski, and by God her Dad would be on the warpath. He'd find her. She stopped after four handfuls of the mush. She tried to make her way to the cot, but she didn't have the strength. Giving up, she curled up on the floor and tried to rest instead of passing out.

Kelly said a quick Hail Mary and smiled, knowing her mom would be so happy she was finally saying her prayers. She missed her mom, and most especially she missed her big dad. They must be so worried about her. Her last thoughts before she fell asleep were about her parents.

The stealth Black Hawk helicopter was taking too long. Sam felt her pain. It had been getting worse the closer they had gotten, and now it was agonizing. His training allowed him to compartmentalize, to push it to the side and still function, but he knew she couldn't survive much longer. He couldn't set aside that knowledge, even though he needed to in order to get the job done.

Sam never heard of Kelly Wachowski before, but as soon as they'd been shown her picture he'd had a visceral reaction. He *knew* her. Hostage rescue was one of the things his team did. But normally they weren't pulled out of a live mission to go recover a school teacher, even if her father was a captain in the Chicago Police Department.

Sam looked around the interior of the helicopter at the five members of his team. All of them had been pissed when they were taken out of the jungle, until the Admiral briefed them, then they all wanted in. Sam had been a little uncomfortable having his background explained. Only one of his team knew he was one of the *found* children who had shown up out of thin air twenty years ago. It was not something Samson Noah Kukailimoku readily shared. The Admiral explained another one of the *found* had recently been killed in a botched kidnapping attempt. It was obvious to everyone the reason Kelly had been taken was because she too was a *found* child.

It took the team three days to get the necessary intel to figure out where Kelly was being held. Even after that was done, they only narrowed it down to an abandoned business park with four empty structures. All of the buildings contained basements, and even with their heat seeking equipment they weren't likely to find their targets if they were holed up in one of the lower levels. They were still two hours out, and Sam had a bad feeling they were cutting it close.

"Hey Lieutenant, think you can do your voodoo?" Nate asked. Sam winced but nodded. He again looked at his team, but they all seemed relaxed.

"No need to get weirded out Sam, we aren't," Riley said with a laugh.

Sam looked at the youngest of the bunch and saw nothing but a kid who looked up to him. What's more, he knew Riley was more religious than the rest of them.

"You've saved our asses time and time again. I talked to my Dad about you. He said yours is a gift from God."

"Everybody has gifts. I talk women into bed. Mine is a much better gift." Nate said winking at Sam. "But Sam can definitely tell us where the bogeys are, and he will be able to find Kelly, so this is one lucky girl. Especially because I can give her my gift when she's recovered." Everybody laughed. Sam, laughed along, but gritted his teeth — Nate really wasn't that funny — then another jolt of pain shot through him.

Jerked awake, Kelly thought her arm was being ripped from the socket. Another set of hands lifted her from the other side. Her head lolled against her chest, swaying, and the nausea roiled and she gagged. Needing to puke she clenched her teeth, making her head hurt even more. Then she was flung onto the familiar metal table.

"The bitch is going to end up killing her."

Kelly couldn't hold back her scream as the raw skin on her wrist was scraped when they pulled the zip tie restraint tight.

"Yeah, that'll be a shame, I'll miss the paycheck." Someone yanked open her jaw and shoved the rubber bit into her mouth.

"I don't get why she keeps at it. It's obvious this girl doesn't know anything. Nobody could have withstood this much pain and not cracked."

Kelly moaned around the rubber in her mouth as her other wrist was slammed down and tied.

"It's what the Iron Lady wants, she wants her to crack. I heard her talking to someone on the phone saying the pain was a stimulus and would help dig out buried memories or some such shit. Not the nicest cure for amnesia if you ask me." The talking abruptly stopped as Kelly heard the click of heels on cement.

"Lester, hook her up to the monitor, you're in charge of watching her vitals. I'm sick of her passing out, if she does, it's on you." They ripped off the bandage on her upper arm and adjusted the shunt on her shoulder, connecting it to the machine. They were using some technology she didn't know about. It all seemed too surreal. "Axle, here's a new solution I want you to administer in quarter doses throughout today's session. I'll tell you when to inject the second dose, and you'll do it immediately, do you understand me?"

"Yes ma'am," he stuttered on the word ma'am.

Kelly jerked away as soft fingers caressed her cheek. "Sweetness, your job today is to absorb the pain, let it take you far away from here. Can you do that for me? Can you go far away and tell me about it?" They applied the gel to her temples.

"Tell me where you came from. Just drift back and remember."

Spasms wracked her body as Kelly tried to block out the smell of her burning flesh, and the tearing sensations in her wrists as she pulled against the restraints. She smelled copper from the fresh blood oozing from her wounds, and her nose. Would she ever get rid of these smells of pain and torture?

Oranges and vanilla. She smelled oranges, vanilla and cloves. Nana was baking a treat! Jumping out of bed, the rubber soles of her sleeper keeping her from sliding

across the wooden floor, she scrambled to the kitchen. She burst into the room and shrilled with glee as her grandmother caught her from behind and gripped her in a tight hug.

Kalani breathed in the scent of flour, vanilla, cloves, and something distinctly Nana. She was safe. For a moment she clutched the woman tighter, not wanting to leave, knowing she wouldn't always be safe where she was going.

"It's okay baby, I feel it too. I know this is right. It's not always going to be easy, but remember I'm always with you. I'll always love you and you can always reach me." The words drifted across Kalani's mind as reassuring as the smell and the warmth of her grandmother's arms.

Chapter Three

"Are you fucking stupid!?" Kelly shook from the ice water dripping off her body.

"Even if you get her to remember, you have her gagged, how in the hell is she going to tell you anything? I told you to wait for just two weeks, but you couldn't, could you? Jesus Tara, go get a cat from the pound to torture if you need a fix that bad. We need this girl alive and talking."

"Jared, I…"

"Shut up! You two, unstrap her. Get her cleaned up. Get her warm. And you, you dumb bitch, follow me."

Kelly tried to breathe through the pain as the wrist and ankle restraints were removed from her raw flesh. The cell, *thank God*, she was going back to her cell. This time she wasn't dragged, someone carried her like she was a child. It must be because of the yelling man, Jared, his name was Jared. Trying to figure out the reasons for changes in her routine were just little ways she tried to stay sane, ways she tried to remain connected to the here and now. No matter how happy those hallucinations made her, no matter how comforting she found them, she had to remember they weren't reality. *They were not real.*

The vibration of the Black Hawk at his back kept him centered, kept the pain at bay. Helped to stop the rising panic. Two images merged in Sam's mind. He saw the glossy picture the admiral had passed around of Kelly Wachowski, a family photo, showing her laughing at a family gathering, her straight white blonde hair flying around her face in the wind. She had the fair skin of a Scandinavian, but in this picture she was pink from the cold, and her eyes were a navy blue. Sam had another image of Kelly in his mind, it was of her as a small child, laughing up at him, teasing him, calling him Noah. Another jolt of pain, and he closed his eyes, knowing he needed to rest before they landed.

"Noah, are we going to a good place?"

"Yes, we're going to a good place." He crouched down and hugged the little girl who was his best friend. She was so bright and happy, and even though she was

five and he was nine, she was still his favorite person to play with, to spend time with. His older brothers teased him for having a little girl as his best friend, but he didn't complain. She always made him smile.

"I'm going to miss Nana but you'll be with me, right?"

"Not to begin with. For a long time you won't even remember me. But one day we'll find one another. Remember, they told us. We have to wait until we're grown-ups."

"But you promise, right?"

"I do." Noah looked around the stadium. It was filled to the brim with people to see them off. Looking at the other children, many of them mirrored his expression—sad to go. He would miss his family, but was excited for the adventure and opportunity to help. Noah squeezed Kalani's hand, and as their damp palms touched he finally admitted he was also scared. It was the right thing to do, and he needed to be strong for Kali. One of the older children came over and put his hand on his shoulder.

"Are you ready?" Noah nodded, reminding himself he would have a good home, a good life. He would make a difference, and in twenty years he would find Kali again.

"I'm ready."

With a flash of white light they were gone.

Sam's eyes shot open as the helicopter touched down.

"Did you see any heat signatures from the air?" he asked Nate.

"Negative. We're blind. Do you have any ideas?" Sam nodded. He knew exactly which building they needed to go.

They disembarked in silence. It was twilight, the helicopter hardly made any noise, and what noise it did make the tree line muffled. Sam looked at his team and pointed at the building closest to them. "That one."

The Black Hawk hovered just above the canopy of trees. The team rappelled to the ground. The helicopter would be able to land in the clearing or on the rooftop after the enemy was eliminated, but for now they needed to go in unseen. Sam and Nate took point. As they ran, Sam stumbled, pain shooting through his temple.

"Are you all right?" Nate whispered.

"We've got to hurry, she doesn't have much time." Nate gave him a sharp glance and they both sped up, the others following at breakneck speed.

When they made it to the door of the building it was secured.

"Back up," Sam shouted. Shooting through the lock, he didn't care who heard them, they had to get to Kelly.

Pain. Needle hot spikes of agony sliced through her brain. Tentacles slithered underneath the soles of her feet. The pain curled around her toes, and spread to the top of her foot. It would to keep on coming, she knew this from past experience.

"Explain it to me Kelly," the voice came from the dark, the dispenser of the pain. If she could focus enough on it maybe she could get it to stop.

"Explain what?" How often had she asked that question in return? Had it ever really stopped the pain? The fire raced higher, stroking around her ankles, her calves.

"Where did you come from? Where were you before Mike Wachowski found you?" It was the same question, and no answer had ever been right. This pain was going to continue until she died.

"I don't know, for the love of God, I don't know." The flames were spreading, crawling past her knees. This time she really begged for death, *please let this be the last time*. No more questions, no more pain, just let her go. If there was a before she couldn't remember, maybe there would be an after where she wouldn't have to feel this agony. She concentrated, not on trying to bring up those long forgotten memories, she searched for the after.

The darkness behind the voice, behind the pain, she spiraled away from all of it. She was flying and looking at the softest pink. In front of the pink sky, she saw herself, arms spread wide in welcome.

"You're safe now, you can come home Kalani. We missed you."

Kelly walked on her feet, surrounded by wild flowers, in glowing air. She saw something sparkle, shimmering to her right, but she couldn't keep her eyes off the vision that was her, but not her.

"Where am I?"

"You're wherever you want to be, wherever you need to be."

Kelly let herself be enveloped in a hug smelling of orange, vanilla and cloves. After some time, they linked arms and walked across the soft green grass towards the others who were waiting.

"I need you to wake up now. Come on honey, please Kelly, wake up. Please, open your eyes. You're here, I can feel you. I need you to open your eyes and look at me, and then I'll let you go back to sleep, but you have to come back from where you are. Please Kali, please."

It hurt, it was too far to go. Kelly didn't want to leave knowing there was going to be more pain and she couldn't take it. She couldn't survive any more, it would kill her very soul. If she didn't stay hidden they would kill everything that made her Kelly, and then she would never be able to put herself back together.

"Please baby, just for a minute, I need you to open your eyes for one moment, then you can go back to sleep I promise. Just for this one instant, I need you here with me, back here with me."

It was the voice, she'd never heard it before, but...she'd been waiting for it. Just that voice. She took a deep breath, and tried to open her eyes, ready for the pain to start again. They fluttered open. There was hardly any light in the room. At long last, the bright overhead lights were gone. Soft brown eyes looked at her, filled with pain and concern.

"Thank God. She's awake, we haven't lost her."

Kelly groaned at the newest voice that was pitched too loud for her sensitive ears.

"Kelly, this is going to hurt."

Oh no, now he was going to hurt her too? Too tired to struggle, a tear leaked down her temple.

"No, baby, it's okay, we're going to get you out of here." Maybe this man wasn't lying to her, she wanted to believe his voice, those eyes.

Sam couldn't believe the shape she was in. Her eyes were almost completely swollen shut. He'd been lucky to get her to open them just that little bit. Her wrists and ankles were meaty pulps where she had struggled against the restraints. If he could kill the three people in the room again, he would, only much slower.

"We gotta move man." Sam watched Rydell cut through the last of the ties holding her down.

Sam gently lifted her off the table, trying to block out her scream of pain. As he stood, she spasmed and then went limp.

"Jonah is landing the helicopter on the roof, it'll touch down in two. We gotta move, Son. We found the communications room and they sounded the alarm. People are on their way."

Holding his special cargo, Sam followed Rydell, easily keeping up with his fast pace. As they crashed through the door to the stairwell, Sam threw a quick thanks to the universe that Kelly was unconscious and didn't feel anything as he repositioned her over his shoulder into a fireman's carry. It was four flights up to the roof and it wasn't until they hit the cold night air that she started moaning.

Mathers and Kota were already onboard and pulled her into the belly of the helicopter. They placed her on the cot and Kota started to strap her in. Then all hell broke loose. Sam watched in horror as her bloody hand shot up and contacted the side of Kota's face. Her panic and rage must have blocked what had to be excruciating pain as Kota grabbed her wrist to stop her from hitting him again.

Sam dove to the first aid kit under the bench seat and pulled out one of the pre-filled syringes with morphine. When he got to her, Rydell already had her arm pulled and prepped so he could administer the medication. Within seconds the chemicals rushed through her system, alleviating her pain and calming her down.

Tearing his friend's hand away from Kelly's wrist, he nodded at the horror on Kota's face when he saw the shredded flesh he had been holding. Both men looked closer to examine Kelly's injuries, realizing they could actually see to the bone. The kind of pain she must have suffered to fight her restraints to that extent must have been unimaginable.

A movement caught his eye, and for just a moment, Sam thought he saw a flash of blue through the swollen slits.

"Noah," she whispered, reaching for him before passing out.

Chapter Four

Noah. Had her dream been true? Everything was a blur. She was in and out of consciousness during those first days in the hospital. Her mom later told her they were worried about her eyesight and potential brain damage. What happened if the doctors were right and her visions of Noah were a sign something was wrong with her brain? But it was all fuzzy. Then there were the surgeries done on her wrists and ankles to repair tendons and ligament damage. It was over a week before she was coherent enough to speak with the authorities, but as soon as she was, it was like a cork had exploded out of a champagne bottle.

Every imaginable arm of law enforcement came in to question her, wanting to know why she had been kidnapped. She told them everything she could remember. She'd been grabbed as she'd been leaving work, and she must have been either knocked unconscious or drugged, because the next thing she remembered was waking up strapped to the metal table.

The more people who questioned her, the more agitated she became. It was like she was back there, being held against her will. Finally, her dad kicked them out. He told them to quit with the stupid questions, it was obvious she had been taken because she was one of the *found* children, and now it was their job to *find* the people behind her kidnapping. She loved her father.

"I can't believe some of the idiots I work with, Kelly. Now, your job is to get well." He immediately roared for one of the doctors to come into the room. Kelly laughed, and it hurt her head but it felt good at the same time. Her mom was in the corner of the room pretending to read a book and winked at her. The doctor who was handling her case came in with a surgeon. They discussed how well her grafts had taken, and the remarkable rate of recovery she was experiencing. Her doctor was extremely pleased, but the surgeon seemed distant. He asked about her family history, but her father asked them to leave.

"Dad, you don't have to be so protective," she admonished.

"Yes I do. Whenever anyone finds out you're one of the five *found* children, they treat you differently, and I won't have it. You were just tortured! That weasel will treat you with respect or I will kick him off the roof of this hospital." She glanced over at her mother expecting to be able to share a grin, but her mother looked as fierce as her dad.

"He's right Kelly. We haven't told you yet, but Alfred Hawley was killed during a botched kidnapping in England two months ago." Kelly's blood ran cold. She'd met Alfred when his family visited America ten years ago. His adoptive parents wanted to see if meeting another *found* child would help to jog his memories. It hadn't.

"Expect us to be protective of you."

"Mom, I'm twenty-five, I have my own life, you can't protect me twenty-four seven."

"Until those bastards are put behind bars, you're moving back in with us." The fear gripping after hearing about Alfred's death, eased. The idea of moving back with her parents for a little bit sounded wonderful.

She still couldn't stop the tears from falling. The wonderful gangly teenager she met was dead—he was so kind and funny. Alfred was three years older than her, and he was one of the youngest people to ever be elected to the House of Commons in England.

"Dad, they're going to find those motherfuckers and make them pay, right?"

"Oh yeah, little girl, oh yeah."

She couldn't keep her eyes open any longer, and slipped back into the comforting dreams she'd been having since arriving at the hospital. She dreamed of a place with a meadow and a kind woman she called Nana. Then there was Noah. Noah had been her imaginary friend all through her early childhood. If something broke, Noah did it. Who let the neighbor's dog into the house? Must have been Noah. She had a very clear picture of how Noah looked—beautiful milk chocolate brown eyes, short hair that still had some wave to it, not like the silky black curls of his childhood, and gorgeous light cinnamon skin.

In her dreams, she wasn't Kelly Wachowski, she was Kali, and they lived in a different world together. She'd never had these kinds of dreams before she'd been tortured. Kelly worried maybe the doctors were right, maybe she did have brain damage, but the dreams gave her such comfort she didn't really care.

Chapter Five

Five weeks later the doctors said she was healed, but she knew better, she knew she was the furthest thing. Trying to find some humor, her ability to laugh left the building yesterday. Things had gone to hell. If confusing dreams with memories were her only problem she could have dealt with it, but there was a lot more going on. Now she'd become a danger to the people she loved more than anyone else on Earth. It's why she had to go someplace safe. Somewhere she couldn't hurt the people she loved. She paced around the living room, looking at all of the mementos her parents collected over the years.

"What's this about Kelly, you're scaring me."

Kelly looked at the big blonde bull of a man standing in front of her. This man loved her like she was his own child.

"I've called Dr. Fredericks and he's recommended a neurosurgeon and psychiatrist.

I've met with the psychiatrist on a couple of occasions and she's…I think she can really help me." Watching her parents, her mother showed her normal compassion and patience but her dad looked like he was going to burst a blood vessel. "I'm hallucinating. They're not sure if this was brought on by the shock therapy they did on me while I was held captive, but bottom line, I'm seeing things, and hearing things that aren't real."

"So what?" Her dad came over and wrapped his huge arms around her. Kelly was short to begin with at five foot three and compared to her dad she felt like a doll, this time was no different.

"Dad, I have a real problem. I need to address it."

"So, you're suffering from Post-Traumatic Stress Disorder. I've served with men who've gone through a whole hell of a lot less than you did, and seen their struggle. I'm not trying to discount what you're going through, and I think it's great you're seeing someone. But you didn't bring your Mom and me in here to tell us that. You have something else planned and we're not going to like it, are we?"

"Dad, I'm hearing voices. Remember my imaginary friend from childhood? Noah?" She waited for him to nod. "I'm hearing his voice all the time. In my head. Not like he's talking to me, it's like I'm living his life or something. Like I'm tuned into the Noah radio station. He's some kind of soldier and he's giving orders, and he's…he's…well its bad." Kelly wiped the tears streaming down her face, thinking about the horror she experienced through Noah's eyes, and now again looking at the devastated expression on her father's face.

"The neurosurgeon never heard of anything like this ever happening before, even with the electroshock therapy I went through. He's the one who recommended I talk to Dr. Weston, the psychiatrist."

"Okay honey, what did the psychiatrist think?" her mom asked.

"Up until yesterday, she thought this was something we could work through with sessions. But then things changed." The tears came more quickly, and she could barely get those last words out.

"What changed?" her dad asked sharply.

Kelly shook her head wildly. She couldn't tell them, she just couldn't.

"Mike, don't push." Her mother pulled her into her arms, and made everything even worse.

"Mom, the shock treatments and whatever chems they gave me…they messed me up. Last week I ended up on the floor with my hands over my head trying to protect myself from a bomb. But yesterday…" The snot flowed from her nose and her mother, God bless her, pulled out a handkerchief.

"Mom, I waited behind the couch with Dad's gun for hours, it was trained on the door, waiting for somebody to come through it. I was waiting for the enemy to come inside so I could blow them away. I waited, and waited. I had my finger on the trigger. Then you came in with the groceries. I could have killed you."

Her mother hugged her close, but she looked over her mother's shoulder and she saw her dad's face. He was finally hearing what she was saying.

"I have to leave."

"Now that is complete and utter bullshit," her dad roared. "You're not leaving." Kelly's heart unclenched. She had been so sure he would hate her forever when she told him his adopted daughter had a gun trained on the wife he loved so dearly.

"So what's your solution?" Kelly asked as she gently pulled out of her mother's arms.

"We lock up the guns."

"The guns were locked up."

"I change the combinations."

"She's not going back to her apartment and that's final."

Kelly squeezed her mother's shoulder, feeling the steel beneath. Mike Waschowski came over and put his arms around both women.

"Of course she's not going back to her apartment, she's staying right here. We'll figure this out," he assured his wife.

"Dad, I talked to Dr. Weston, and we agreed I need someplace where I can be safe."

"Yes, right here."

"Someplace, where people can be safe from me. I need some time away from others."

"We. Are. Not. Locking. You. Up."

God she loved this man.

"She works with a great facility, and I'm going to go there for the next couple of weeks. I have to do this Dad. I'm not me anymore. I could have killed Mom." Looking at her father she saw her anguish reflected in his eyes. "I need to find out why I think I'm a soldier with a bad guy waiting behind every door. I need to get myself together, and Dr. Weston thinks she can help."

"How long does she think this will take honey?" her mom asked.

Kelly bit her lip.

"What aren't you telling us?" He had cops eyes.

"Dr. Weston has agreed if we don't make progress over time, low level shock treatments might undo what was done to me during my captivity."

"Over my dead body!"

"Honey, don't do this, give yourself time."

"I can take a leave of absence. I can be here twenty-four seven to watch over you. You won't be alone."

Kelly couldn't stop the choked sob as she threw herself into her father's arms. What had she ever done to deserve parents like these? She thanked the universe she'd woken up in Mike Wachowski's cop car all those years ago.

After a time she got herself under control. She

reached up and kissed her father's cheek, and gave her mother a hug.

"The cab's around the corner. I've got to go. I love you both so much. Dr. Weston said you could come and visit me this weekend." Kelly went to her bedroom and came back rolling her suitcase.

"Give me that little girl." Mike reached for the bag, and the three of them walked out the door. Kelly knew the next few weeks weren't going to be easy, but she was committed to this path. She refused to harm the people she loved. *And*, she wanted her life back, she wasn't going to let those bastards win.

Chapter Six

Sam barely suppressed a scream as he sat straight up in his bed, excruciating pain ripping through his head. He knew immediately it was Kelly. Oh God, had she been taken again? No, he would have been notified. He threw off the covers. Apparently, he was going to her apartment a lot earlier than he had anticipated.

He'd been stateside for less than twelve hours. Finally making it to Chicago a little after midnight and realized pounding on Kelly Wachowski's apartment at such a late hour wouldn't go over well, so he found a hotel to grab some shut eye. He'd been having trouble sleeping ever since he helped rescue Kelly a little over eight weeks ago. Flashbacks of a time before he'd woken up as a child with no memory on the island of Kauai invaded his dreams. Knowing they were what the media called *found* children, made him think these flashbacks were real memories.

He saw pictures in his head of a mother, father and brothers, and their memories gave him great joy. But by far, the strongest memory was of the little girl with wheat gold hair named Kalani, she had a giggle that could make the gruffest man smile. Those memories would have driven him crazy if he let them, but his adoptive grandfather, the man who raised him on Kauai taught him to believe in things that defied explanation, so he chose to believe.

Three hours later Sam stood in front of a man as big as himself, and that rarely happened. Mike Wachowski looked as tired as he felt. Both men stared at one another, assessing. Sam was sorry he hadn't thought to wear his dress whites, it would have gone a long way in winning over the Police Captain.

"I remember you. Kukailimoku, right?"

Sam was surprised the man remembered him, let alone pronounce his name correctly. When he said as much, Mike grinned.

"I'm Polish. I can't complain about people butchering our last name if I butcher other peoples."

Sam smiled, maybe this would go better than he had anticipated. "I'm here to see Kelly, Captain Wachowski." Sam watched the grin fade from the older man's face.

"I wish you could, but like I told you on the phone, when you couldn't find her at her apartment, she's not here, son."

"I don't mean to be disrespectful, but it's imperative I speak to her. I think she's in trouble. You know I was part of the rescue team, and you'll probably think I'm crazy, but I have this bad feeling."

"That makes two of us, but her mother and I visited her three days ago, and I can tell you she's is doing as well as can be expected."

Sam's blood ran cold at the phrase *as well as can be expected.* "Are you saying Kelly isn't fully recovered? It was my understanding the surgeries went fine, and there would be no permanent eye or brain damage. Was I misinformed?" He waited for Kelly's father to explain the situation to him.

"You weren't misinformed, and I don't want you worrying she isn't being watched over. The Chicago Police Department has her under watch, and while she is at this new facility she's being guarded twenty-four seven."

"What facility is she at, and why?"

"Look Sam, there was nothing physically wrong with Kelly, but she was having episodes. Hallucinations. She was convinced this was the right course of action. My daughter is smart as a whip. If she thinks this is what she needs, then I'm backing her. Even if it's killing me to see her drugged up. I just pray by the end of this it brings my little girl back to me."

"Pardon me Sir, but that hasn't told me

anything. I need to see her, I think she's being hurt." Sam endured Mike's hard look, waiting for him to make up his mind.

"I don't know how. Kelly voluntarily entered a psychiatric facility. Three days ago they started electro shock therapy. Kelly is convinced it was the only way to stop the hallucinations. Fight fire with fire, so to speak."

"Jesus, and you didn't stop her?" Sam asked incredulously.

"Son, you don't know how bad it was for her. She was having a hard time differentiating between reality and this life she had made up. Kelly was convinced she was a soldier named Noah, fighting in some jungle. Eleven days ago she got my gun from the lockbox and was hiding behind the couch for hours on end with it trained on the door waiting for her target to walk through. The only one who walked through was her mother with the groceries."

"Captain Wachowski…"

"Let me finish. She thought this commitment through in her normal thorough manner. As much as I don't want her to do the shock therapy, she assures me it will be medically supervised and nothing like what she went through before. She knows she's doing the right thing, and when she is convinced of something, well, there is no stopping her. She's sick son, and she's doing everything she can think of to get well."

Sam stood, trying to assimilate everything he just heard. It was unbelievable.

"Sir, my full name is Samson Noah Kukailimoku. I'm one of the *found* children. I have been in active combat almost every day since the day we completed the rescue of your daughter. I can't tell you what country, but it was the jungle. Eleven days ago I was in an empty building, where I waited for hours for a rebel to come through a door. I shot and killed him."

The older man sagged and had to grip the door frame. "Go on."

"For the last eight weeks, on and off, I've been tuning into your daughter's life, and it hasn't been making any sense. Then three days ago, I started having unbelievable pain. Now it makes sense, she started shock therapy then, right? It's like she's in a constant nightmare and can't wake up. It's why I asked for emergency leave and came stateside. This morning she was screaming in pain. It was worse than anything I felt before, it must have been because of the proximity. I felt it like it was my own."

"The shock treatment, you think you felt them giving her the shock therapy, don't you?" he asked aghast.

"I do, Sir. I don't think she has anything wrong with her. I think she has been tuning into my life the same way I've been tuning into hers. Can you take me to her?" Sam asked, trying to quell his panic.

"Come in, we need to talk to her mother." Mike ushered Sam inside.

Chapter Seven

She was flying in a sky of pink and gold. This time she was going to stay. No more pain. She was no longer going to bring pain to herself or the ones she loved. The woman in front of her was beautiful, and Kelly knew she was in the presence of goodness. She felt a deeper sense of homecoming than last time.

"Kalani, we love you, but now isn't your time."

"I've decided I want to stay this time."

"It's not your time."

Kelly tried to shake off the hands gripping her arms. Why was someone shaking her? She tried to go the other place—the beautiful one.

"Kelly honey, wake up. It's Dad, can you wake up?" Kelly stopped struggling.

"S'okay." She couldn't make her tongue work right. "Da." *What the fuck did they do to me?*

"What the fuck did they do to you?" Her dad's voice was outraged.

She swallowed and tried again. Her throat felt like it was filled with sand.

"I'm okay Dad. You can sto..." she paused. "You can stop with the shaking." Better. It still wasn't as firm and as clear as she'd like, but considering the shock therapy and the chemical cocktail, she thought she was doing pretty damn good. She grinned, and saw her dad's relieved smile.

"Glad to hear it little girl." She looked into her dad's blue eyes as he stroked her hair. She gave him the best smile she had.

"Is it visiting day again? Mom an' you and were just here, weren't you?" Kelly prayed she had it right. This morning's shock therapy had really thrown her for a loop. Maybe it hadn't been this morning. Was she was missing days like at the other place? God she hoped not. Dr. Weston promised it wouldn't be like that, but then again, she hadn't been expecting the pain to be so bad either. Today's was worse than the previous three days.

"Nope Kiddo, you're right as always, I'm early. I have a surprise visitor with me. I think maybe we have an answer to all of your symptoms. It's kind of *out there*, but it explains everything. I want you to come home, honey."

She was having a tough time comprehending what her father was saying. She couldn't tell if it was because they'd woken her out of a sound sleep, the medication, the shock therapy, or the fact she was fucking nuts and her dad's presence was a figment of her imagination.

"Talk to me Kelly. Are you okay? Dr. Weston told me you were fine, the shock therapy didn't harm you, even though it was painful. Please say something."

Kelly looked into the beseeching blue eyes and determined her dad was really in the room with her and she couldn't ignore him.

"I'm fine Dad. Just hard to understand what you're saying. What do you mean you can explain all my symptoms? I've been working on this with Dr. Weston and the aural and visual hallucinations are either mental illness or a side-effect of what was done to me by those motherfuckers." She winced and peeked up at her dad.

"Goddamn right, motherfuckers is the right word for them kiddo." He brushed the tip of her nose with his finger. "But honey, there is another explanation, would you let us tell you?"

"Who's us?"

"I want to invite Sam Kukailimoku into your room, okay, Little Girl?" Again her dad pleaded with his eyes.

Kelly had no idea what he was up to but she trusted him with her life. She nodded her head. That was a mistake, it hurt to move. He strode quickly to the door, and in walked Noah. Not the young Noah of her childhood, but a grown up Polynesian King, with the same wavy black hair, cinnamon skin and she bet if he smiled he'd have the same smile that lit up a room.

This couldn't be happening! Her hands tunneled

into her hair, gripping and pulling, seeing if pain would help her back into reality. She whimpered.

"Stop!" Noah rushed forward and gripped her forearms. "Kali stop it this instant!"

"Honey, you've to stop. It's okay, it's all going to be okay," Mike Wachowski's voice was soothing in comparison to Noah's commanding tone. "Don't yell at her Son," he admonished.

Noah didn't let go, he pulled Kelly's arms and stroked towards her wrists, looking at the angry scars. Softly brushing the tender flesh, one of his big hands grabbed both of hers, and Kelly automatically grabbed onto it. He pushed down, so her hands were pressed into her thighs, trapped under his heat. Then she looked into his beautiful brown eyes, and they glinted with strength. He cupped the side of her face, and for one wild moment she hoped he would kiss her.

"You know who I am, don't you?" She just stared. "Don't you," his voice was deeper, stronger.

She nodded.

"With words Kelly."

"Yes. But you're not real, you're a figment of my imagination." She watched as a corner of his mouth kicked up in amusement. Kelly tried to fight back the tears. She wanted to rant and rave. She hated how weak tears made her feel. Hell, anger was stronger, but it seemed like the waterworks were coming whether she liked it or not. How dare the universe send Noah to her?

"Honey, please don't cry."

Kelly looked at her dad, and saw the sheen of tears in his eyes. That's how it had always been, the few times she had cried, he'd cried right along with her. She loved this man. "Daddy, I'm so sick. This can't be real. He was my imaginary friend all through my childhood, and then I made him real in my head after those assholes took me. This is all a hallucination."

"I wouldn't do that to you, Little Girl. Please use your big brain, and open your mind and listen, okay?" You know I want what's best for you. If I can believe this, then you can believe. Please honey, just listen. This is Lieutenant Commander Samson Noah Kukailimoku of the United States Navy. He led your rescue team. He has an incredible story to tell you, and I need you to listen."

CHAPTER EIGHT

Noah loved seeing the interaction between father and daughter. It was obvious the man would do anything for Kali. As he looked at the woman whose face he held, he felt the same way. She was a unique combination of fragility and warrior and he was moved by both. He really wanted to take her in his arms and make it all better for her. But first he had to convince her she wasn't mentally ill.

Noah hadn't expected to talk to anyone but Kali when he woke up this morning. Now he was going to have to speak in front of her dad, and he decided to do some strategic editing. Having them both committed wasn't going to help the situation. He released his hold on her hands and cupped both her cheeks, looking deep into her beautiful navy blue eyes.

"Almost twenty years ago I woke up on a beach, naked, with no memory other than my name. Noah."

The sand was hot, the water warm, and the surf gently lapped at his ankles. He looked around and was pleased by his surroundings. No, actually he was very happy seeing the vibrant green vegetation in front of him, and the glowing blue ocean.

A sand crab scurried past him. Noah wandered down the pristine white beach, away from the sun, so he could see what was in front of him. He stopped when he saw the man, his concentration on the netting in front of him. Noah took in the worn sleeveless shirt showing thin arms with brown wrinkled skin. He waited, and the man finally looked up.

The old man put down the net he had been stitching and opened his arms to the naked boy on the beach.

"Aloha kakahiaka keki." The old man watched the boy tilt his head, as if replaying the words in his mind. Finally he responded.

"Aloha Pili Mua." Noah went to the man and looked at him as he sat on the white sand, arms still open wide. Finally he walked into the old man's embrace. Noah closed his eyes, he had felt puzzled and uneasy when he woke up with no memory, but the scent and feel of this man felt right—Kapu, his Hawaiian Grandfather. He had found his home.

As the years passed on Kauai, Noah was given his other names, Samson Noah Kukailimoku and every islander was his family. The man he'd met that morning was Kapu, an elder and became his grandfather, as he was to many of the children. There were not many people on the island, but he could speak the language of everyone he met. In the first two years he discovered he spoke Hawaiian, English, French and Spanish. Grandfather told him he was endowed with the gift of languages. When Sam and his friends looked at the old man, he finally said, "Languages are your superpower Grandson." Later Kapu explained to him how he developed his superpower for finding things.

"Since rescuing you, I have been having flashbacks of a time before waking up on the beach. In those flashbacks I had a little friend named Kalani. I called her Kali and we were inseparable."

"When I found a naked Kelly in my patrol car twenty years ago, she couldn't have been more than five years old. When I'd asked her what her name was, she said Kelly, but maybe she was saying Kali."

"I remember that day. I think you're right dad, I think I did say Kali. But I loved hearing your voice say my name in your accent." Mike grinned at his daughter, and they both turned to look at Sam or was he Noah?

"After your rescue, and I left you in the hospital, I had a mission in the jungle. I thought about you Kali. I had dreams of your life here in Chicago. I flashed to moments when you were still in the hospital, or in a house with your parents. I thought I might be losing my mind, or I was just obsessed with a really pretty girl." Noah flashed his most winning smile, and Kelly gave him a wan smile in return.

"Ten days ago, my fun little dreams started to get weird, and then three days ago they turned into nightmares. It was as if my dream girl was back in captivity, being drugged and I had to rescue her, so I took leave to find out what was wrong. This morning I felt a burning spike of pain in my head. Your dad told me you're getting electro-shock therapy, and I must have felt it." Sam knew he was wincing again at the memory, but he couldn't help it.

"It wasn't that bad. It wasn't like before," she assured him. This time her smile reached her eyes.

"It was worse before? No wonder you ripped your flesh to the bone. Do you realize what I'm saying? We're connected. I've been in the jungle fighting a warlord and his rebels. The reason you've been thinking you were a soldier named Noah, is because you've been experiencing flashes of my life."

She shook her head, dislodging his hands. "That's not possible."

"Kali, you're not going crazy. You're exhibiting the same psychic abilities I am. I think you and I knew one another before we woke up, me on the beach and you in your dad's patrol car. I think somehow we're connected on a psychic level."

He left off the part where he thought they might be from another world. He watched her assimilate his words, and turn to her dad.

"What do you make of this story, Dad?"

"Three things make me think it's real. Do you remember Owens and al Mussad, they're partners, and they come over to our house for barbecues all the time."

"Sure, I remember them."

"They've accidentally saved one another three times...each. Neither one of them should be alive, but somehow they just knew things, and were so in tune with one another it's crazy. They talked about these funny feelings and have gotten one another out alive."

"What else?"

"Two, I called Samson Noah Kukailimoku's grandfather and according to him, he was found the exact date you were found in my patrol car. I tried to get it verified with the Kauai Police Department, but the best they could do was narrow it down to the week. And three, well, I know you're not crazy. I understand about mental illness, I know how heartbreaking it is, and if I thought you needed help I'd be the first in line for you to get it, but Kiddo, you're not sick, so that's why I believe this."

Kelly reached for his hands, and Noah smiled in relief, and took her hands. "What was the name of the person who took care of me?"

"What?"

"If we have this connection from before, what was the name of the person who took care of me? Before we came here?"

Noah grinned. He untangled one of his hands, and reached out to stroke the wheat color hair away from her face, reveling in the fact she was going to be leaving with them. "You called your grandmother Nana." he whispered quietly. For just a moment he could almost feel the arms of the old woman as she held him close.

"Noah, it's real." He watched a smile bloom across Kali's beloved face and felt happier than he could ever remember.

"Yes, baby, it's real." He brought her hand to his lips and kissed her palm. They were together again. It had taken them twenty years to find one another, but they had done it.

"I was so happy in the meadow with you. No wonder I kept you with me as a friend even when I couldn't truly remember you." Kelly caressed the smooth skin of his cheek, basking in his presence. Finally she pulled her hand away, and looked at her father, breaking the intimate moment.

"Dad, can you go find Dr. Weston? I'm checking myself out. Is Mom here?" Sam was impressed with how fast she could go from fragile to take charge. Apparently nothing kept his Kali down for long.

"Your mom went to find Dr. Weston while Noah and I came in to talk to you. I wouldn't be surprised if she was working on getting your discharge paperwork completed. No moss grows under that stone." Kelly burst into laughter, delighting Noah. "As soon as Sam-Noah explained everything to us, your mom was positive you would be going home."

Kelly threw back her covers, and her Dad came over and shouldered Noah out of the way, pulling the covers back over her. "I think it's time for Noah to leave, and I'll help you get ready to go." After getting a look at Kali's legs, Sam was of two different minds. Part of him really wanted to stay and watch, but he knew right now she still needed time to recover. As he left the room, he couldn't stop thinking about her smile and those mouth-watering legs.

Chapter Nine

Kelly swung her legs over the side of the bed. When she tried to put weight onto her feet, she realized she wasn't steady enough to stand on her own. Her dad was there in an instant. She both appreciated and resented the consideration. God, she hated how prickly she was. Her dad gave her a look that told her he too could read her mind.

"Guess I needed to take it slower."

"Guess you did. What did you think of Noah?"

"Yes, what did you think of Noah?" her mother asked as she bustled into the room. "And tell me quick, I told him he could come back in as soon as I had you dressed."

"What did Dr. Weston say when you said you wanted to check me out?"

"She didn't have any choice. You voluntarily committed yourself, if you sign the papers to leave, you're free to go. Mike, get out of here we can discuss things after our daughter is dressed." As soon as the door was closed, Primrose Wachowski hugged her daughter. "Oh my baby girl…" She burst into tears.

"Mom, it's okay, I'm fine. I'm coming home."

"I've been so worried about you. I knew they were going to hurt you, and when that young man told us the pain you were in, I almost died." She looked up at the beautiful face of her mother, and hugged her close, sorry she'd ever caused her pain.

"I'm fine now."

"No you're not, you've lost even more weight, you're still not healed, and we still don't know where those motherfuckers who kidnapped you are." Kelly stared in shock at her mom, who still said horse pucky.

"Don't look surprised Kelly Rose Wachowski, it's the proper term for those people who tortured you."

"Mom, I'm going to be fine, you don't have…"

The knock on the door interrupted them. "Hold on," her mother called out.

"Let's get you dressed. I'd say we have two minutes max." She hurried to the dresser, pulled out underwear, jeans and a sweater. Her eyes welled up when she saw the jeans were at least two inches loose in the waist.

"Mom, it's going to be okay." Kelly hugged her mother with a trembling hand, and realized just how weak she was feeling. Who knew she was going to need time to recover from her recovery?

A louder knock sounded on the door. "Come

in," her mother called out. Her dad came in first, followed by Noah, they took up all the space in the small hospital room. How had she not noticed it before?

"How do you intend to make sure our daughter remains safe?" Kelly's mom asked.

"Mom, the school year is going to start soon. Now I know there isn't anything wrong with me I can move back to my condo." Kelly prayed she was telling the truth. She knew she had always healed fast the few times she got sick. A little rest and few good meals and she'd be fine, right?

"No way in hell, Kiddo."

Oh God, he wasn't yelling, he was using the smiling voice.

"You're coming home with your mother and me. Our house is easier to have watched than your apartment."

"I refuse to put you and Mom at risk. Find a way to make my condo easier to watch." Arguing with her dad felt good, normal, they always enjoyed their fights.

"There's the added benefit of a cop living with you, you'll be protected."

"You work, so it's a moot point."

"I've decided to take a leave of absence until these assholes are apprehended." She looked at him, he was serious.

"Dad, you can't do that."

"I can do whatever the hell I want."

"I'm going to live my life the way I want to live

it, and it includes moving back into my condo." There was no way she was going to let her dad put his life on hold for her.

"Listen here little girl…"

"I think I might have a solution. I'm going to stay with Kali." Kelly forced her eyes away from her father to see Noah grinning at her. Oh, she wasn't going to like this.

"Well, first you're going to have to tell me what I'm supposed to call you," Mike said.

"When I'm here with Kali, I'd like to be called Noah. It was my name when I knew her before." It worked, because Kelly couldn't see herself calling him any other name. He was her Noah, but still, she wasn't going to have another alpha male dictate to her, and she was positive it was about to happen.

"Noah, we don't want to hear any plan you might have. I really appreciate all you had to tell me…"

"You're wrong little girl, I'm *very* interested in what Noah has to say."

"Well I'm not. I'm not having some stranger stay with me!" She looked at him incredulously, he just raised his eyebrow, which raised her ire.

"Kali, we're not strangers. You and I have known each other all of our lives, we just didn't remember until now. I have months of leave saved, and I intend to stay here until all threats to you are gone."

Kelly narrowed her eyes as she saw the same

look of determination she remembered from another time, another place.

"This is my problem Lieutenant Kukailimoku. You can go spend your leave elsewhere. My dad is a captain for the Chicago Police Department, he'll have cops watching me. I'd say my safety is covered."

"Kali, I think you're forgetting the threat is also a threat to me. Didn't you say they kept asking you where you came from? Well they would want to get their hands on me too. I remember there being a crowd of children, not just the other *found* children besides you, Alfred and me. That means they would really want to get their hands on me."

"Oh my God Noah, I didn't even think. I'm so sorry, of course this impacts you. You shouldn't even be seen with me. Nobody knows you're one of the *found*. I forgot about Alfred being killed. You're in danger being seen with me. You have to leave now before they suspect something."

"It's too late now. We'll have to stick together."

She looked at her parents, and then back at Noah, all them were smiling at her. She knew the decision had been made. She didn't have much to pack, but her dad and Noah made quick work of cleaning out her closet and putting it into her suitcase. She was still having trouble keeping up with how fast her reality had changed. As fantastic as this story was, it made her much happier than the '*I'm crazy*' reality she'd been living with for the last few weeks.

When Noah bent to pick up her shoes all thoughts flew out of her head. She had never seen a more enticing ass in her life. She'd already been drooling over his body. She was in heaven. Kelly gave herself a mental shake. She shouldn't be having these kinds of thoughts about her super-hot imaginary friend, but he wasn't her imaginary friend, he was the delectable warrior who'd rescued her.

But no matter what her long denied libido wanted she had to focus on the fact this man was here to help. They had some weird-ass psychic connection, and he thought of her as some long lost childhood friend, nothing more. It didn't matter he had skin like melted caramel and she wanted to lick it to see how it would taste. *Damn it Wachowski, put a cork in it. For all you know he can read your mind!* Noah finished zipping the suitcase and picked it up, and gave her a slow smile.

Despite Kelly's mother completing a lot of the paperwork, there was still quite a lot for Kelly to read and sign. Dr. Weston seemed like a very nice lady, and she prescribed some pain medication for Kelly. She suggested Kelly take something now, but she declined, and that's when he'd enough.

He waited until the doctor and her parents were talking, and then pulled her aside. "Kali, take the medicine."

"What?" She looked at him with a dazed expression. He touched the spot right above her left eyebrow and started a soft circular motion and watched as she sighed in relief. She closed her eyes, and he wrapped his other hand around the back of her neck, gathering her close, continuing with the gentle massage. "Take the medicine Kali, I can feel your headache, it's a doozy." Her eyes shot open.

"I didn't think about you being in pain as well. I'm sorry, I'll take the meds." She broke away and went and talked to the doctor. Noah smiled, he'd hated seeing her in pain. The echo of her headache wasn't much more than an annoyance, nothing like the pain that jerked him awake that morning. Apparently taking care of herself wasn't something she thought was important. It was going to be one of Noah's missions while in Chicago. He watched as Kali's mom headed towards him.

"How did you manage to get her to take something for her headache?" she asked.

"Ma'am?"

"Well I know she didn't decide to do it on her own," she said as she sat down in the seat Kelly had vacated. "So, tell me how you convinced my stubborn daughter to actually take something for the pain.

"Mrs. Wachowski…"

"Call me Rose."

"Rose, I might have hinted I was feeling the pain as well," he admitted sheepishly.

"And were you?"

"A little bit, but it wasn't really painful, more of a dull ache."

"Oh, I like you." Rose patted his arm. "I could tell my girl was still hurting, but I couldn't get her to take any medication. I knew she didn't want to feel out of control, but she's safe right now, and we're taking her home where she can have a nap. When she gets up she can boss all of us around."

Noah chuckled.

"You know she isn't going to want to stay with you for much longer."

"She and her dad are going to have to fight it out. I think your plan to stay with her is stupendous. Of course, after they are done fighting, you'll have to pick up the gauntlet. With that in mind you're going to need to keep up your strength. You're invited to dinner tonight, we're having pot roast, mashed potatoes and homemade apple pie." As far as Noah was concerned everything was right in his world.

Kelly was angry, she didn't know what was getting to her more, the fact she had been ambushed by three people or everyone monitoring her food intake. She wasn't hungry. When did it become a punishable offense?

"If you are worried about where Noah is going to stay while he is in Chicago, let him stay in the spare bedroom here. He's not staying at my condo.

My spare bedroom couldn't fit him anyway, he's too big." Kelly smeared the crumbs of her dessert on her dish so it looked like she had eaten more, and glared at her father who glared back at her.

"Nonsense," her mother said. "Your father and I have stayed in your spare bedroom, and he's as big as Noah."

"Mom, you know I meant it metaphorically. Look, it's a week and a half before the school year starts. Everyone has been really patient with me considering the situation. The principal tore up my letter of resignation, and said I was welcome back whenever I could make it, so I'm going to call her tomorrow. I would have thought the school board wouldn't be thrilled to have someone with so much notoriety, but they backed me as well. I was really surprised. I do worry about what the parents of my students will say if they find out Noah is living with me. It won't go over well."

"Give me a break. I'm an old-fashioned Catholic, and even I know it's a load of horse pucky," Rose huffed.

Kelly blushed. It had been worth a try.

"Fine, if not Noah, then I'm arranging for off duty CPD officers to stay with you instead. Take your pick. Those men and women will have to leave their families because you can't handle having the man who volunteered to do this."

Kelly wilted under the guilt her father heaped on her.

"Fine, Noah can stay with me." She turned to

the man in question, where he was trying to look innocent as he plowed his way through a third helping of pie. "You're not going to be comfortable. I'm up at all hours. I have a hectic schedule. You're supposed to be on vacation, and I'm going to be working sixteen hour days for the first three weeks as I figure out lesson plans for two different subjects and set up meetings with each student's parent or guardian."

Noah looked at her. "Is anyone going to be shooting at me?"

"Maybe."

"Good thing I'm used to it. At least I don't have to deal with a jungle." Noah laughed. "You're a great cook," he said to her mother.

He was right, her mother was a great cook. Kelly wished she could eat like she used to. She wished she could have her old life back, where she didn't need a guard. She wished she wasn't worrying her mom and dad. She wished she didn't have the hots for Noah the way that she did.

It was going to suck needing a guard for the next few weeks. But the idea being an imposition on the hardworking men and women of the Chicago Police Department went against the grain. Unfortunately she both hated and liked the idea of having Noah on guard duty.

Chapter Ten

Staring as he carried the duffel bag into her home, the olive color was at odds with all the jewel tones in her apartment. She resented how comfortable he looked in her condo and she felt out of place. It just wasn't fair. Maybe it was her headache, after all she had only gotten out of a hospital bed this morning.

"You must be exhausted."

"Stop doing that."

"Doing what?"

"Rummaging around in my head."

He gave her a funny look, walked towards her and gave her a hug. She melted. Maybe it was okay if he could read her, if she got hugs. She hugged him back. He maneuvered her to the couch.

"I'm sorry Kali. I know this is a lot to take in." He sat beside her, and she rested her head against his chest.

She experienced a strong sense of déjà vu. She blinked hard, not wanting the waterworks start.

"Alfred's dead?"

"Yeah. They broke into his house, he fought back and ended up falling down the stairs and breaking his neck. At least it's what they think. His wife was at home, but she wasn't harmed."

"Thank God. I remember him, he had great parents. They were redheads like he was."

"Yeah, it's one of the things similar in all known cases. The *found* children were all matched up, in a sense, with people who were genetic matches."

"So there are six of us?"

"I don't think so. I remember a big group. I think there were many more who weren't publicized, like me."

"Yeah, I made the national news. Lots of people came out of the woodwork to adopt me, but Dad was the one who found me, and there was never a doubt in his mind he was going to adopt and raise me." It had been her favorite story growing up, her Dad finding her naked in the backseat of his locked patrol car. When he asked her how she had gotten there, she said she didn't know, but she asked for a blanket. Mike spilled his hot coffee all over himself, and began to swear in Polish. After two minutes, she repeated her request for a blanket only this time she asked for it in Polish.

"All of the *found* assimilated the different languages they were exposed to their first two years."

"How many do you know?" she asked.

"Seven."

Noah picked up her wrist and looked at the angry scar. "They don't hurt anymore," she rushed to assure him. He raised his eyebrow. "Well not much. You know I really don't like that you can feel what I'm feeling."

"Remember it works both ways. You were tapping into my life in the jungle."

Kelly shuddered, some of those memories were awful. "You hated what you were forced to do."

"Sometimes, yes. But it was the right thing. It needed to be done."

She felt his pain, it hadn't been physical pain, but it was pain nonetheless. "How are we connected? Were we always connected? I don't remember. I remember you as a little boy, but I remember us being together in a meadow. What do you remember?" He tipped her chin, and they looked into one another's eyes.

"It's *out there real Whoo Whoo stuff*. Kelly, maybe we should talk about this some other time."

"More *Whoo Whoo* than children waking up naked with amnesia all around the world on the same day? More *out there* than they all learned to speak multiple languages by just hearing them spoken once? We were lucky we weren't locked up and dissected."

"But that's part of it too, Kali. We were placed with the exact right people who protected us, who would never let that happen to us."

"So tell me what you remember, where did we come from, are we from another planet?"

"I think we came from an alternate universe. I remember somebody explaining we were coming here to make a difference. We were going to do things to help this world get back on the right track."

"Huh? Noah, that makes no sense, we were just children. I'm just a teacher. I teach ninth grade algebra and social studies, how in the hell am I making a difference," Kelly said using air quotes. "How could I be helping to put the world back on track? For that matter, what track does this world need to be on?"

"I don't know Kali. Think about me, I'm just a Lieutenant Commander in the Navy. It doesn't make sense to me either. At least Alfred was a member of the House of Commons. Look, it's only been since I met you, since your rescue, that bits and pieces of these memories have started to surface. They aren't making a whole hell of a lot of a sense to me either."

Kelly opened her mouth to ask another question, but yawned instead.

"Oh Kali, we need to get you into bed." Noah stood and he put out his hand. Kelly was so tired she took a moment, just looking at it, confused, to figure out he was going to help her off the couch. She put her hand in his and he pulled her up. As soon as she was standing he easily swung her into his arms.

"Noah, don't be an idiot, put me down, men don't really carry women." She yawned again, and he laughed. He walked across the living room towards the hallway.

"Men who don't carry women around are totally missing out. I take it your room is the one on the end?" Kelly snuggled against his chest and nodded. He must have understood because he opened the door and laid her on the burgundy comforter. Before she could even think twice, he had her shoes and socks off, and under the covers. He gave her a quick kiss on the lips and was out the door. Kelly blinked once and was asleep.

Noah called Rydell.

"Where the hell did you disappear to? Are you okay? Is the family okay?" It's the reason he was one of his best friends. No recriminations, just immediately worried about him.

"I'm fine. Remember the mission in Chicago?"

"Oh, you're with the girl."

"Fuck me, how'd you know, Dave?"

"There was something about her, and you were so protective. I could tell. You were out of sorts the entire time we were in the jungle."

"Shit man, it could have been because people were trying to kill us."

"People are always trying to kill us. Nope, you were distracted, not a detriment or anything, I would have told you, but I could tell she was on your mind."

"She was."

"Jesus, she wasn't taken again, was she?"

"No, it was something else, just a feeling I had." Noah let out a long breath, trying to figure out how to explain things to his friend.

"I'm never going to discount one of your feelings Sam, they've saved my ass too many damn times. Should I consider you off the rotation?"

"Yep."

"Permanently?"

Noah looked down the hallway to the closed door at the end. "Yeah, Dave, I'm not going to be going back into live action again. I'll be talking to the Admiral."

"I'm happy for you man."

"Thanks." They talked for a bit longer about the rest of the team. When Noah hung up, he realized he actually had a lingering headache and he went to check out the medicine cabinet and took some ibuprofen. Then he grabbed his duffel bag and went into the spare room.

"You didn't lie Kali, this room isn't big enough. I need to be in the master suite with you." Despite the long day, it took him a long time to finally get to sleep.

Chapter Eleven

Her condominium, which once felt too big, now felt like a matchbox. Every time she turned around she brushed against Noah. The man was always right beside her or behind her. She knew he was doing it on purpose.

It was the third day of school and she had gone to bed early knowing she would be up at an ungodly hour to start her lesson plans. She was rustling through the kitchen cabinets for some hot chocolate when she turned around and ran right into Noah.

"Dammit!" she said in a choked whisper. For some reason the darkness demanded a quiet tone, if not a vehement one. "You have to start making noise so I know you're behind me."

"Beautiful, I made enough noise to wake the dead." Noah plucked the container of cocoa from her hands and reached over her head for the tea kettle. It caused his chest to brush against her breasts that were only covered by the thin silk of her robe. Dammit. She didn't even have a nightgown on under her robe. As soon as he turned towards the sink to fill up the kettle she belted the robe tighter. She heard him chuckle.

"You've been here for two weeks, nothing has happened. At what point are we going to say this is silly and you go home?" She watched his shoulders bunch. His cinnamon color skin gleamed in the moonlight streaming through the kitchen window.

"I'm not leaving until the people behind your kidnapping are behind bars, or better yet, they're dead." He put the water on to boil, and then he reached around her again for two mugs. He took his time, and slid against her. She had a difficult time concentrating as he spooned the powder into the cups.

When the hot chocolate was made, he handed her a mug. "So, teach, why are we up so early?"

"I've got to get today's lesson plan figured out, and I went to bed too early last night."

"You've been burning the candle at both ends lately, Kali. Is it always like this?"

"Pretty much, at least at the start and the end of each semester. Especially when you're teaching two diverse subjects like social studies and algebra."

"I would have thought with your ability to speak different languages you would have been teaching a language course."

"That's what I requested, but because I don't

have as much tenure as other teachers, I didn't get it. Maybe in a few years." Kali sipped her hot chocolate and looked at the papers spread on the kitchen table.

"I bet you're a great teacher."

"What makes you say that?"

"The way you care. How much effort you put into this. Does every teacher e-mail all the parents and introduce themselves?"

"No. But doing that kind of thing makes this more of a partnership, and I've found it helps."

"Don't I see you e-mailing more than just the parents?"

"Yes, I talk to the parents, and sometimes they have me e-mail an aunt, or a grandparent, or an older sibling. Sometimes I have as many as five people on a mailing list for one child, it's kind of a safety net. In those cases, the child has a real high ratio of success. I've been doing it for the last two years. The principal is beginning to take interest."

"But it's one of the things taking up a lot of your time. It seems to make for long days."

"The kids are worth it." She kept her eyes on the math problems, because seeing the brown skin of Noah's arms against the white of her kitchen tabletop was just too mouth-watering.

"Is there anything I can do to help?"

Kelly thought about it. "Do you know anything about the Donner party?" When Noah nodded, she gave him part of the social studies project plan, and she focused on the algebra. They worked in companionable silence, and she did her best to keep her eyes on the paperwork. However, every time she looked up, Noah was looking at her.

Mai was kidnapped in Taiwan. They didn't have one fucking lead. Admiral Sakuro was furious, because Mai, Sarah and Niko had all been under close supervision by his team. Noah met the admiral nineteen years ago when he was in fifth grade. It was Nelson Sakuro, then Lieutenant Sakuro who introduced him to the Japanese language.

"It is impossible he did not know Japanese before today. This is some sort of trick." The imposing man was furious. Noah hadn't been afraid, he and his friends thought the man's anger had been funny. They were all aware of Noah's superpowers. He was like an X-Man. His teacher didn't seem as amused. She invited the Lieutenant to give a talk about the Navy, and she was not happy with the way he was talking to one of her students.

"Samson does not lie. He has an affinity for languages. He can learn them quickly."

"Nobody can learn a language that quickly."

"Samson can," Miss Leilani assured him.

"Prove it."

"How, he has already learned Japanese."

Noah and his friends watched wide-eyed as the Lieutenant and their petite Hawaiian teacher stood toe-

to-toe. Finally the gruff officer turned and looked at Noah.

"Can you do it again? Learn another language?"

"I think so." Noah had always been able to do so, he didn't see why he couldn't do it again.

"Do you know Portuguese?"

"I don't think so."

"Good. Tomorrow I'll bring a man who knows Portuguese, and we'll prove this was a trick."

"And when he learns the language, you will apologize for being rude."

Noah was amazed at Miss Leilani's bravery.

"If he can speak Portuguese by the end of the day tomorrow, I will apologize." He turned to Noah. "Sayonara."

The next day Nelson Sakuro brought in a man who could only speak Portuguese, and Noah had been able to converse with him within five minutes. From then on, Nelson had been an honorary Godfather to Noah, and he was let in on the secret Samson Noah Kukailimoku was one of the *found* children. As a result, he had made it a mission of the Navy to protect those children even as they grew into adulthood. He had all available resources working on finding Mai Zhang.

"I pulled Rydell out of the jungle. He's working on this now," the Admiral told Noah.

"He doesn't do investigations, he does recovery."

"Well we're going to damn well recover her," the Admiral said as he slammed down the phone.

Noah threw his cell phone on his bed, and pulled on his running gear. He needed to work up a sweat. He knew Kali was in the dining room grading papers, and he wasn't in the mood to play the flirting game.

"Noah, what's wrong?" She was waiting in front of the hallway when he got out of the bedroom. Dammit, he'd forgotten about their damn connection.

"Nothing. Nothing's wrong. I need to go for a run." He brushed past her. She grabbed his arm, and he jerked away causing her to lose her balance. She reached out and righted herself against the wall.

"Kali." Noah had her in his arms in an instant. "Kali, are you okay?"

"Don't be an idiot, I'm fine. It's you I'm worried about. What's wrong? And before you open your mouth to lie, remember who you're talking to." He looked into her beautiful blue eyes, and rested his forehead against hers.

"Mai's been taken."

Chapter Twelve

Kali didn't say anything, just gripped him hard around the waist and waited.

"We should have done a better job. We had eyes on her, but she didn't want full protection, and we let her. We shouldn't have listened."

"It was her choice to make." Kali's hands snaked around his neck pulling at his short hair. "Are you listening to me Noah? This is not your team's fault. This is not your fault. You're good men. You are one of the best men I know."

"I'll die before I'd let them take you again, Kali."

She yanked on his hair. "Don't you dare say that! You're doing everything in your power to keep me safe, but if they take me, they take me."

"I couldn't bear it if they took you from me. The only way they will ever get you is over my dead body." Looking at this woman in his arms, he realized it was the absolute truth. More than their connection from the past. It was the woman he had come to know.

"Noah, never say something like that again. I can't bear the idea of losing you now I've found you again." They stared at one another. Finally, Noah knew the time was right. This was not going to be some flirtation, some seduction, this was going to be the two of them making love. As his mind formed the thought, he saw the flare of acknowledgement and agreement in Kali's eyes.

"Will this ruin things? You were my first and best friend Noah. I couldn't stand it if this ruined things between us."

"Close your eyes Beautiful, tell me what your heart says." She continued to look at him. He gently brushed his hand over her eyelids. "Now, tell me what's in your heart. What is the right thing for Noah and Kali?" Her hands drifted slowly downwards until they were pressed against his chest, his heart.

"We were meant to be together. But I'm still scared Noah. I'm not good at this stuff. I'm afraid I'll screw up, somehow I'll mess up and destroy what we have."

Looking at someone who had their eyes closed was enlightening. It was as if their vulnerabilities all came to the surface, and Noah could clearly see and feel how Kali truly felt this step would somehow shatter their relationship. As if anything could ever come between them. He wouldn't allow it.

"Not going to happen, you can't do anything to ever mess this up." He wrapped himself around her, his head resting on top of the fine silk of her hair, drinking in her warmth and the scent that was Kali. "I know down to my bones this is the right next step. We belong together, Beautiful."

She pulled away and opened her eyes, looking deep into his. She nodded, and he swept in, his mouth soft, a gentle slide against her plump pink lips. Slowly he moved back and forth until she followed him and whimpered, then he swiped his tongue against her bottom lip, asking for entrance. She opened eagerly, and he went from soft to carnal, unable to stop his need to conquer. Kali's answering moan, and the way she pressed tightly against him was a balm to his senses. Suddenly he was scared, and it broke through his haze because it was Kali, not him.

"Beautiful, what is it?"

"I need you so bad. It's going to hurt when you leave. I mean when your leave is up." She shook her head, white gold hair flying around her face.

"I'm not leaving Kali." She looked at him for long moments and then grabbed him around his neck. He gripped her ass and hoisted her up, heading for her bedroom. He laid her on the bed and followed her, relishing the feel of her beneath him. She was petite, and because of all she had been through, she was even more delicate now. He needed her so badly, but he needed to take care with her. He lifted up, so as not to crush her.

"No, I like you where you are." Kali pulled him back down, but there was no way her feminine muscles were a match to his masculine ones.

"Careful. We're going to be careful. I don't want to hurt you."

She pulled at his hair, giving up on trying to pull him down. "You can't possibly hurt me. I want to feel you. You feel so good on top of me. Please Noah," she breathed hotly into his ear as she nipped at his lobe, sending shivers down his spine. God she would be the death of him. He arched up and away, and she wailed his name, until she saw him rip his shirt over his head, then she stopped mid-wail.

"Clothes. Undress, Beautiful," he prodded.

Kali clambered onto her knees and started stripping. Noah stopped unlacing his running shoes, watching helplessly when she was down to her bra and panties. Suddenly Kali stopped, hesitant.

"What? Please don't stop now, I'm begging."

"I've never been with anyone like you before," Kali motioned to his chest. Noah looked at himself in confusion. Then he looked up, his eyes sparkling.

"You've only been with girls? That's hot."

"No, you big goof. I've never been with someone who looked like a damn underwear model. I know I'm pretty, but for God's sake, I'm nowhere close to your league. I just can't do this. Why don't we try this after I'm back to my fighting weight?" Kali reached for her shirt, but before she could, he grabbed it and threw it across the room. Noah had her flat on her back, with one of his big hands under her cupping her ass, in less time then it took to blink.

"Are you kidding? I think you're beautiful."

"I know I have a pretty face, but seriously Noah, have you not looked at me? Right now I look like a boy, not a woman. I've never been on the voluptuous side, but now I barely have hips and my ass is nonexistent!" she wailed.

"Not pretty, beautiful. Everything about you, including this slender body is beautiful, and I've been imagining every inch of it pressed against me since I've moved in here. Don't you understand my life? I live everyday where it's hard and dangerous."

He looked at her reverently. "The idea of someone as soft and warm as you," he said brushing a kiss against her temple. "Makes my heart melt."

"Looking at your tender curves," he said breathing a caress down her cheek, towards her mouth. "Makes me hard as stone."

"Having a woman as kind and beautiful as you in my arms," he said tasting the softness of her lips. "Makes me believe dreams really can come true."

His lips sought hers, and she welcomed him, seduced by his words and the emotions conveyed. She didn't even notice as he began teasing the silk and lace off her body. It wasn't until his lips started drifting downwards, and he took a slow long lick across her right nipple she realized she was naked.

She raised her startled gaze to his satisfied eyes. "Kali, let me show you, please." Noah waited a beat, and finally she nodded. He bent to his task, lapping at her sensitive nipple, delighting in how the blood flowed to it, and it puckered and engorged at his ministrations. When Noah brought his hand to play with her other breast he was amazed at how it covered half of her chest. He hadn't been lying, there was no part of her he didn't desire, no part of her that didn't set him on fire, but her body's fragility did concern him, and he was determined to make sure she regained her health.

Lightly brushing his calloused thumb around her areola, he continued tasting the sweetness of her skin, drinking in the scent of her, and enjoying her sighs of pleasure. When she was shuddering and arching up, he took her into his mouth and suckled her, but winced from her nails in his scalp.

"Oh my God, you're good at this. Stop, let me roll over, please." Noah kept her where he wanted her, and switched sides, releasing her breast with an audible pop. Before focusing on the left side, he took a moment to see Kali's pale skin flushed, her eyes at half mast, glittering at him, promising retribution. Noah bent down to the tantalizing swollen pink bud of her nipple, taking it between his lips and laving it with his tongue. Never had a more responsive woman been in his arms, it was intoxicating. It was also tough on his self-control. He couldn't roll over and let Kali have her way with him, because he had a damn short fuse where she was concerned. He had a plan, he was going to make Kali come a half dozen times and then she could play.

He left her breasts and headed south towards her pussy, but as soon as he lowered his head he felt her begin to tense. He looked up and he could read her like a book. Instead of seeing the cute little inny belly button, he saw what she did—a concave stomach and her hipbones sticking out. This thinking needed to stop. He wanted the woman she could be, and it was up to him as her lover, to reassure her she was *everything* he wanted.

Noah shot off of the bed. "I'll be right back. I expect you to be right where I left you, if you move an inch, there'll be hell to pay."

Chapter Thirteen

Kali watched him leave the room. The man was certifiable. What the hell? They were just getting to the really good part. Granted, she was a little tense because he was up close and personal with a stick figure, but she was handling it. Maybe he was sick of her insecurities and had decided to go back to the guestroom? But then why did he tell her to stay the way she was? Why should she listen to him anyway? Maybe now was a good time to say this experiment wasn't working and to get back into her clothes. Kali looked around for her underwear, and it's where Noah found her when he returned, maneuvering the big decorative mirror that had rested against the wall in the living room.

"What are you doing?"

This did not bode well.

Noah leaned it upright against her dresser and turned back to her. "The better question is what you are doing holding your clothes?" He tipped his chin towards the bra and panties in her hand. "I specifically told you not to move." His voice lowered an octave and it did funny things to her nervous system.

"You were taking too long, I thought you'd changed your mind."

Noah nodded his head as if he had made a decision. He walked over to the bed and took the underwear from her hands and calmly tore the panties and bra and dropped them to the floor.

"I..." Kali gulped. "I really liked that lingerie."

"Then maybe next time you'll listen to me."

She couldn't read him to save her life. He didn't look mad, he looked calm. He looked determined, even satisfied.

"I like you naked. You're beautiful. Every part of you, inside and out, is beautiful Kali. You're a teacher right?"

"Yes, but you know that." It was tough getting words out when he was looking at her like that.

"This afternoon's class is, Kali is Beautiful 101. You're not leaving this room until you get an A+."

Suddenly Kali was very scared of the mirror, and Noah must have seen or picked up on her fear.

"Love. How can you even doubt yourself the slightest bit, when you have men dropping to their knees in your wake?"

Kali couldn't stop the snort of laughter.

Noah gently wrapped his hands around her rib cage, right under the slope of her breasts and easily lifted her to stand on the bed. Suddenly she was towering an inch or two above Noah's six foot three frame. She liked this new view on life, until she realized how much easier he could see her body. Noah's hands slowly drifted downwards, caressing her belly, her hips, and squeezing her butt before sliding down to her thighs.

Kali couldn't stop the tremble. She looked at Noah's face, wanting to see his expression, wanting to see just how beautiful he was finding her now he could see and feel how she really looked. But what she saw on his face took her by surprise. He looked like a starving man who just found food.

His hands continued their descent to her calves and then to her feet. She watched as he bent down and swirled his tongue in her belly button. He looked at her and smiled. It reminded her of when they were children and they shared treats from Nana's kitchen. He always had that expression, because he was always snitching an extra cookie from Nana's cookie jar.

"This is what started the problem. I wanted to play with your belly button and you tensed up. Will you lie down for a little while and let me play? Please love? I promise not to be good. I really want to play, and you are the best playground I have ever seen in my life."

Kali couldn't stop giggling. She still wasn't convinced of a damn thing, but obviously he was willing to have sex with her, and God knew she wanted to make love with him, so what the hell right?

"Make love."

"What?

"I want to make love with you." She smiled up at him. *Whatever*.

Noah eased her down onto the bed, but he was frowning. Kali got the feeling he once again figured out she didn't totally believe the beautiful thing. Or the making love thing. Well he was going to have to cope. He was getting sex out of the deal, it was going to have to be enough.

"You don't believe me, do you? Let's see about that." He flipped her over onto her stomach as if she weighed nothing—to him, she probably didn't. He brought her to her knees, her butt resting on her calves. His big body enveloped hers, resting over her, and she felt his cock nudging against her bottom through his sweat pants. He was huge everywhere.

"That's it Kali, feel what you do to me. I'm seconds from coming, just from feeling you against me." His hands cupped her breasts, then skimmed down to her stomach, his fingers barely brushing the sensitive skin, making her tingle. Her tummy trembled at his touch.

"That's my girl," he said, kneading the fragile flesh, grinding his hips into her ass. "God is every part of your body soft and tender?" In a flash he had her on her back again, her hip cupped in his big hand, his mouth open and sucking on her belly. She felt his tongue licking and she couldn't help but arch into his caress. She never realized how sensitive she was there, how the slightest sensation lit up all her senses and shot right to her sex. He moved to the bottom of her breast, and suckled some of the flesh, bordering on pain.

"More. Harder." Noah complied, increasing the pressure and Kali realized he was going to leave a mark and she didn't care. Sparks were shooting from that spot up to her nipples, down to her clit. Oh, God. Her legs were wide open around his chest, she couldn't push like she wanted. He was too broad. She rubbed side to side, trying to get the friction her clit she desperately needed. Her juices were leaving a trail of wetness on his chest, but she was too worked up to be embarrassed. He had to help her. Finally he released her flesh, but then he trailed tiny bites downward, until his tongue was swirling in and out of her belly button, almost as if it was his cock working its way into her pussy.

"Noah, it's too much," she whined.

"No love, it's not enough." Then his head went back down. His big hands barely touched the skin of her stomach, causing her to shiver in delight. It had become one big erogenous zone.

He reached around her, his hands finding her butt and squeezing, which only made her push harder against him.

"Kali you feel so good. If I hear you say one more disparaging remark about this gorgeous pert ass, I'm going to paddle it, are we clear?"

His words cleared the haze, and she looked at Noah, really seeing him past the fog of lust. He wasn't teasing, he was looking at her with a serious expression. She stopped moving, but his hands continued to worship the slight curve of her butt, his hard cock pressed against her thighs.

"Yes beautiful. You're beginning to understand. I'm serious, and you would love every minute of it."

Noah moved, his lips meeting hers, his taste warm and comforting as his tongue slid sensuously against hers. This wasn't just a kiss of passion, it was gift, a feeling of safety, of love, of acceptance and homecoming. Finally when she had no breath left, he lifted his body, pulling her with him. Pulling her off the bed, he stood her in front of the mirror. He towered behind her, his body dwarfing hers.

Lifting her arms and he had her clasp her hands behind his neck, her breasts thrust out, unable to hide. He traced his fingers down her arms to the ladder of her rib cage, coming around to gently cup her breasts, thumbs teasing her nipples making her gasp. She closed her eyes, content to focus on the sensation and close out the picture her body made.

"Open your eyes, love. See what I'm seeing. Look at the woman I see. Look at her sliding against me, so sensuous, so God damn hot I can't take off my pants or I'd be buried deep inside her. The dainty figure that fires up every man who sees it. You make every man think of nothing but sex. Looking at those lean thighs makes think how they'll grip me when I sink inside of you."

Kali looked at every part as he described them. What's more, she could feel his sincerity, his passion, his need. Then she looked at his expression, and his hunger took the strength from her legs. Only his arm around her waist kept her from falling. She pressed backwards, grinding her ass in circles against his erection, and watched in amazement as he struggled to take a breath.

Kali smiled at the satisfied woman in front of her, and realized she really had been looking at her body through a skewed mirror. She liked Noah's mirror. She liked the mirror in front of her, the one showing a body causing the gorgeous man behind her to have trouble breathing.

"I get it." She turned around, wrapping her arms around Noah's waist, surprised to hear him groan.

"What is it?"

She saw his gaze glued to the mirror behind her, and she looked over her shoulder and she saw what she normally would have considered her barely there butt. She watched as his big hands kneaded the pale round globes.

"You kill me Kali. The things I want to do to you." He bent down and nuzzled her neck, setting his teeth against the tendon, bit down, making her arch into his hold even more.

"I want you naked." She pulled at the drawstring of his sweat pants, and he quickly grabbed her hands in one of his.

"You can't, once I'm out of my pants, play time is over. I'll be in you. I want this to last."

He spun her around and laid her flat on the bed. "Now where was I?" He smiled at her and Kali shivered in anticipation, not an ounce of insecurity ruining the moment. He trapped her hands in one of his while his other large hand skimmed her body and she caught fire. At the same time she relaxed knowing this man desired her, wanted her, and when he called her beautiful it was more than an endearment, it was how he saw her.

As his finger traced the circle of her belly button he looked at her, his eyes intent. "Are you with me Kali?"

"Oh yes," she sighed, tugging at her hands.

"None of that, this is my playtime." His fingers drifted low, pausing at her navel, and she mewed in protest. He chuckled as he moved lower, finally tracing the outer lips of her sex and she cried out. It was as if an electric current shot through every part of her body. She gripped his hair, loving the silky texture, and pulled. "No," his voice was the low tone and made her clench even tighter.

"This first time you're going to let me."

Kali looked into those deep dark eyes and saw both a command and a plea. This meant something to him, she didn't understand it, but for some reason Noah wanted to gift her with his love and care, it was clear in his gaze.

He nodded. "Yes, love, my way this time. Next time we can play together, but this time I need to show you how I feel." He cupped her sex and Kali arched into his touch.

She thought about what he said through her haze of passion. The silly man had been making her feel important and cherished for the last two weeks, and in the last half hour he had managed to undo years of insecurity. How he thought he needed to do more to show her how he felt was beyond her. But as Kali looked into those glittering brown eyes, she could no more deny him than she could deny her lungs their next breath. She released her hold on him.

"Okay, I won't touch. At least not this time," she assured him. She watched as he relaxed infinitesimally.

"I almost lost you before we even had this chance. I need this." His big hands drew her thighs apart. She should breathe in, but it was beyond her. He spread her knees outward, and lifted her feet so they were resting on his shoulders.

"Beautiful." He smiled as his head dipped towards her mound. "You're so wet for me, I love that," he murmured before his tongue licked the valley of her sex.

Kali tried to keep her eyes open, seeing Noah's enraptured expression was intoxicating, but as he slowly thrust two fingers inside of her, her lids drifted shut. He brushed his tongue around his fingers as they pushed in and out of her core. She spiraled upwards. If only he would touch her clit. He chuckled.

"I want my honey." As if those words were magic she pulsed in excitement and more silky cream flowed, he hummed his satisfaction.

"Please, Noah, I need…" Kali's eyes opened just a fraction and saw his arousal, his pleasure, and it spiked her own. "Please…" the last came out as a gasp because he twisted and spread his fingers finding a spot sending sparks through her, keeping her on the knife's edge.

"Noah! Now!"

He took her swollen clit between his lips and sucked hard, and she shot off into oblivion. Even as she howled his name in pleasure she felt his rush of satisfaction and pride through their connection. It anchored her.

"Noah, enough, I need you with me, I need you."

"Oh love, I need you too."

He'd bought condoms three days ago and felt like a heel. But he had hoped, wanted, and needed. He looked at Kali, seeing her satisfied and greedy made him harder. He sheathed himself and shuddered as she looked at him with avarice.

"I was wrong, you shouldn't be an underwear model. You should definitely be a nude model." He barked out a laugh, and she grinned at him.

Kneeling on the bed, he parted her thighs to open her wider, and placed his cock at her entrance. God, he would never forget this moment, how it looked when his flesh began to part her soft pink folds. She was so hot and tight, he made small thrusts forward, watching her face, ensuring he wasn't hurting her.

"Too slow," she panted.

"My way."

"Faster, I need all of you."

"You'll get me." He pressed further amazed by her heat. Her channel was a warm velvet fist, and he was breaking into a sweat.

Wrapping her legs around his waist, she gripped his ass, her nails biting into his flesh. He surged in to the hilt, and she shouted his name, a smile on her face.

"Again Noah, do it again."

He did it again, and again, and again. He felt her pleasure and she felt his, an endless loop taking them higher and higher until finally they exploded into the stars, to another universe.

Chapter Fourteen

Why did she have to get more argumentative after becoming his lover? Then again, who the hell really cared when he got to share the heaven of her body for the last ten days?

"So while cops are watching me at the school, what are you doing? Is it dangerous?" Damn, and here he thought smart women were attractive.

Kali had dressed to the nines, and they were at her favorite Chinese restaurant. She wanted a night out, a real date. She took him to one of her favorite places, a restaurant where she'd known the owners since she was a child. As a matter of fact, they were the ones who taught her Mandarin.

"No it's not dangerous, it's really pretty boring. It's just reconnaissance."

"Shouldn't the CPD be following up on leads not the Navy?"

God watching her eat with chopsticks was

arousing. There was something about red lipstick, and noodles that was totally doing it for him.

"The Chicago Police Department is looking into things, but there is a dedicated unit the admiral put together two years ago when an attempt was made on Niko Evanoff. Since then, we have a pretty good network set up to track some of these groups." *Fuck!*

Kali put down her utensils and patted the side of her mouth with her napkin and then slowly took a sip of her wine. "Groups?"

Fuck!

Noah was silent. He'd never wanted to share this, nobody needed to know they were a target, let alone a target for no good reason. Telling Kali's father had been hell. Still. "There have been three groups identified who want to interrogate, capture and or kill the *found*."

"Noah, I lived it. Last night you help me through a nightmare. I know the level of hate. Why did you keep this from me?"

"Because you didn't need to know there was more than one crazy group of assholes," he hissed. "Fuck Kali, *I* didn't want to know there were groups of people who wanted to capture me, who wanted to *kill* me. I sure as hell didn't want *you* to have to know!"

Her eyes went liquid, and she reached across the table grabbing his hand, and turning it over so their fingers tangled. "I don't want *you* to know either, Noah. But I thought we were in this together, aren't we?"

"Oh yeah, definitely."

"Then you can't keep things from me. I need to know these things." He reached across the table, and tucked a strand of hair behind her ear.

"Okay, I promise."

"So, tell me what you've learned." He told her. They had actually taken down one of the hate groups operating out of Idaho.

"Why are you calling them a hate group?"

"They were a break-off faction of a white supremacist group operating in Idaho in early 2000. They were convinced the *found* were here to take over America."

"That's preposterous. Only Sarah and I were found in the United States, how could just the two of us been looking to take over America?"

"It wasn't the fact you were *found*, Sarah is black, Mai is Taiwanese, and Niko's Russian."

"So the fact Alfred and I are the poster children for Anglo-Saxon doesn't matter?"

"Ah baby, you know you can't use logic to try to understand them. They weren't logical when they were hating Jews, they weren't logical when they were hating blacks, and they're not logical when they're hating the *found*. When Marty and his team took them down last week they were armed to the teeth. They intended to blow up the hospital where Sarah practices."

"Oh God, Noah." Kali pushed the half-eaten meal away. He pushed it back in front of her.

"I can't eat."

"All of your clothes are falling off of you. You were kept for over six weeks. You need to eat." He looked at her and saw her wince and kicked himself for bringing up her captivity. He suddenly felt echoes of her pain in her wrists, ankles and head, as she felt residual pain.

"Does it really matter to you? How I look, I mean?"

She was kidding right? He got up and walked around to her side of the booth, and wrapped an arm around her. She laid her head on his shoulder, it seemed his Kali liked sitting side by side.

"I'm sorry I brought up everything, now please, let's finish our meal, this food is fabulous, just like you promised."

"Really I can't eat."

Noah closed his eyes and as he concentrated his stomach tied up in knots. He had an idea because he was still pretty damn hungry.

"Kali, put your hand on my stomach." She looked at him in confusion. He drew her hand to his stomach, and placed his over it. "Close your eyes, and feel what I'm feeling." Taking a deep breath, he inhaled the aroma of the ginger, beef and noodles in front of him. Her eyes popped open.

"You're hungry. Really hungry."

"Yeah, but now how are you feeling? Is your tummy still tied up in knots?"

"No," she looked at him in wonder, and he couldn't help himself. He dipped in for a slow kiss.

He wasn't just hungry for food. He pulled away and she giggled.

"What?"

"You look cute wearing lipstick." In for a penny, in for a pound, he leaned in again, his hand cupping the back of her neck, angling her head just so. He tasted the flavor of the food, but it was overpowered by the sweetness of Kali. He could die a happy man, immersed in the arms of this woman. Their stomachs growled in unison and they broke away laughing.

"I guess this empathic thing works both ways," Kali said as she dabbed the lipstick off his lips.

"It does work both ways. Haven't you noticed how in tune you are to my emotions?" She didn't think she could feel him the way he felt her?

"Yeah, but it's just your emotions, I didn't think I could feel you physically, like you feel my headaches and things."

"Beautiful, what about in bed? Haven't you noticed how we have this feedback loop that spirals higher and higher?"

She bowed her head and mumbled. "I thought it was normal."

"You mean that's how it always is for you?" Noah's voice rose and he couldn't stop the feeling of indignation coloring his voice.

"Lower your voice. No. It's never happened before. But I've never experienced, well you know. With a man. I mean, of course I've had. But never with a man. You mean that's not how it always is?"

She looked up at him in wonder. "Because every time we make love it's better than the last time, and the first time was the most beautiful experience of my life. I was dying thinking you feel it every time you're with another woman."

"Oh Kali, it's never happened for me either." His fingers massaged her scalp, luxuriating in the warm feel of her satiny hair. "It's you. It's us."

She dropped her head to his chest. "Oh."

"Now we cleared that up, eat your food." The rest of the meal was torture. Even though her lips were now devoid of paint, the slick pink color still had him thinking of her engulfing his cock. Thank God he was wearing jeans and not slacks. But maybe not, the zipper was biting so deeply into his engorged flesh he might end up with a permanent scar.

Making love with Noah might be the most spiritual thing ever, but living with him twenty-four seven was beginning to get on her last nerve. "Don't you have to go out on a run?" It was three weeks after they became lovers and Kali found out they had two Navy men watching her, as well as CPD officers.

"Is the honeymoon over?"

"I think I'm going to go out with my friends tonight." It was Friday and she hadn't seen Michelle and Lexi since she had been released from the hospital.

"Great, I would love to meet your friends."

"Nope, you're not invited." She watched as Noah grinned, and realized he was yanking her chain. "Aren't you getting sick of spending all this time with me?" She saw a quick flash crossed his face, and then it was gone. She couldn't place it, so she centered herself, reached out, and felt his hurt.

"It's no problem, Beautiful, we both need our space."

"Noah." She got up from the table and wrapped her arms around him, barely able to get her hands to meet. "I'm sorry, I forget how closely we're connected. You need to come clean if something's bothering you. I'll also try to figure out what the hell is going on in my mind when something is bothering me, so I can express it better. Let me be clear. I love having you with me. You give me peace. You're my best friend, and…" It was too soon to talk about love, but she was going to explain what else was going on.

"It's not you. It's having you here, in my apartment. It doesn't allow me to pretend someone isn't still after me. For just a few hours I want to go out and act like a normal person again, someone who isn't the target of an international conspiracy. Having people watching me from a distance where I can't see them is fine. Ya know?" She felt him relax, and she relaxed.

"I get it and it makes perfect sense. I should have thought of it sooner."

"Hey, no beating yourself up." He smiled at her, putting her world back in balance.

"So when will you be leaving?"

"We'll probably meet up for margaritas and dinner at our favorite cantina, but not for a few hours. Why? Do you have an idea of how we might spend our time?" God, she hoped so. She'd become a sex addict where this man was concerned.

"I think I can figure out a way for us to while away a few hours until you have to meet the girls. Why don't you give them a call to set things up, and I'll check my e-mail." She almost reconsidered calling her friends as she watched his ass walking down the hall towards the guest bedroom. She shook her head to clear it. She made the calls, and was happy to find out even Lynne, Michelle's sister, could join them. It was going to be a real party.

Lexi grabbed her hand and shoved up the sleeve of her blouse staring at the scars on Kali's wrist.

"Jesus Kelly, I knew it was bad, but I didn't realize." Kali looked in horror as her friend burst into tears. Lynne picked up a wad of paper napkins and handed them to Lexi.

"It's over. I'm back and I'm safe."

"She's safe and banging the superhot bodyguard. Tell us more, we want to hear more stories about Lieutenant Noah, Mommy, please."

Kali laughed at Lynne's antics, watching as Lexi gave a watery smile.

"He's wonderful. He helps me grade papers, he listens to me, and he now knows all the names of the kids in my classes."

"To hell with that, what's he like in bed?" Michelle asked.

Kali tucked her head down and concentrated on her enchiladas.

"She's blushing, you've got to love those Scandinavian genes."

"I've never seen her blush like that before," Lexi said, joining in the fun.

"Because she never had anything worth blushing about. Her one and only boyfriend was worthless. What was his name? Wally? Willy? Limpy?"

Kali almost spit out the food she was chewing.

"His name was Walter. He was a nice man."

"He treated you like shit, and from everything we *didn't* hear, he was useless between the sheets," Michelle bantered.

"Remember how he told her he would have handled it when one of her kids didn't turn in their homework? Then he had an opinion about how her dad should be supervising the men in his unit." Lexi rolled her eyes.

"I thought the best was when he actually told Mrs. Wachowski how she might make better Swedish meatballs if she used maple syrup instead of honey," Michelle laughed.

Kali winced and took a long sip of her margarita, trying to block out the memory of that family dinner.

"Noah gets along famously with Mom and Dad. The only real problem we've had at dinner is when he ganged up on me with my parents." All three women beamed. The only man who treated her as well as Noah was her dad.

The conversations flipped around the table, going to one another's jobs, boyfriends and families. When it came to Kali's job, all three women were fascinated by the e-mail system she set up, and how the principal wanted to set it up for the whole school.

"What are you talking about, it's no big deal."

"What's your success rate for drop outs, compared to other teacher's students?"

"It can't be measured because the students all have multiple teachers. It's not like they have one teacher."

"Yeah, but you teach social studies and algebra. Of the ones taking both of your classes, how many dropped out last year?"

"Zero."

"What's the drop out percentage for ninth graders in your school?"

"Eight percent."

"Fantastic. You have 180 kids going through your classes on average?"

"More like 120 individual students."

"That's ten kids you saved from dropping out of

high school. Do you know how much of a difference you made? If it wasn't the e-mail thing, it was you. You did it Kelly."

Once more Kali found herself looking down at her plate of food.

"You're still planning on going into school administration, right?" Michelle asked.

"It's the plan. I love teaching don't get me wrong. But I think I can make more of a difference at a higher level."

"I agree," Lynne said, as she waved at the waiter for another round of drinks.

"This has to be the last round for me. I've got to get home to Chris and Jeffrey."

"How is Chris doing? Does she like being pregnant again?"

"She loves it," Lexi said talking about her partner. "I'm just lucky I have a partner who wanted to give birth. I wanted kids, but I gotta tell you, the idea of spending nine months pregnant and then giving birth never really held much appeal." They all laughed. "So I'm going to go home, put our son to bed, and pamper my best girl."

"Sounds like a plan."

Chapter Fifteen

"Get out! Get out now!"

"What are you talking about?" Noah slammed his beer on the coffee table and ran to the guest bedroom to grab his duffel. He pressed the speaker on his phone and threw it on the bed as he started unplugging his laptop.

"Mai. Her kidnapping was an inside job. One of Sakuro's men was in on it. I just got done interrogating him," Rydell said.

"Fuck." Noah made sure his passport, gun and knife were stashed, and then picked up his bag and phone and ran into Kali's room, and riflled through her lingerie drawer. "Keep talking Dave. Who can I trust?"

"Sakuro and our team, but they're all still deployed. That's it. You're going to have to get Sarah. Sakuro said he'd find someone to take care of Niko."

Noah closed his eyes. He didn't care about

Sarah, he only cared about Kali. There was no fucking way he was going to allow somebody to torture her ever again.

"What else did the man you interrogated say?"

"It was bad Sam. They think that the *found* are a race of superior beings. They intend to interbreed them with the highest bidders."

Noah thought he was going to throw up. "Is this the same group that kidnapped Kali?"

"It was just like we thought, he didn't know what I was talking about."

"Just how many of these fucking groups are there?" Finally! Noah grabbed her passport and went to the dining room table and picked up Kali's laptop.

"Jesus Sam, I just don't know." Dave Rydell sounded exhausted.

"When was the last time you slept?"

"It doesn't matter."

"Yes it does, you know it does. You're of no use to Mai if you can't think." Noah was out the door and in his truck. "I've got to go. I'll call you back."

Tires screeched as he left the quiet complex. He voice dialed and kept the phone in his lap. "Rose, I need to talk to Mike."

"Okay, he's in the garage. I'll get him." God love a cop's wife. No questions, just an immediate response.

"What do you need, Son?" Mike's reassuring voice answered.

"Tell the two cops on Kali to get up and

personal. I'm going to be there in less than fifteen, and then we're going off the grid."

"Oh shit, you've been infiltrated."

"Yeah. I'm *so* sorry Mike." He hated it was his people who might have been responsible for Kali's kidnapping.

"Not your fault Son, you can't be responsible for other people's actions, only your own. I'm going to get a burner cell and call you. How secure is yours?"

"Nothing is secure anymore. Absolutely fucking nothing. You get your phone, but I'll get ahold of you through your precinct somehow not through a direct line."

"You take care of my daughter." It wasn't a request, it was a demand. Mike Wachowski hung up.

It was the longest twelve minutes of Noah's life.

There were four ambulances outside the restaurant when Noah pulled up. He never met Kali's friends, but it was easy to assume they were the three other women beside Kali who were on stretchers. Kali was being put into one of the rigs, and two men were arguing with the EMT. As he got closer he recognized one of the men as Chief Petty Officer Riggs, the other he had to assume was one of the CPD officers Mike assigned to Kali. Since the EMT was just waiting, he had to assume Kali wasn't in life-threatening danger.

"Gentlemen, do we have a problem here? What is delaying Miss Wachowski from being taken to the hospital?" He kept his voice calm, not singling out Riggs.

"Hey Noah, I knew since you weren't here, you'd want me to go with Kali," Riggs said smoothly.

The cop gave him a hard look and didn't say anything. Noah didn't know his name, so he decided to wing it. "Bob, I figure you were thinking the same thing?"

"Yep."

Noah looked over to the EMT. "Well this is easy enough, since I'm here, I'm going to the hospital with Kali."

"As I told your two friends, everybody needs to follow. Them's the rules." The EMT finished loading her into the rig, and Noah grabbed his arm. "What's wrong with her?"

"All of the women were given an overdose of GHP. Look, this is serious man, we have to get them to the hospital, now." Jesus. He turned to the two idiots, and realized Riggs was gone. Fuck!

"Did you see which way he went?"

"It's okay, he and his partner came in one car and we have back-up on them. They're not getting out of our sight." But it still left whoever slipped the women the drugs. He had to get to the hospital. He looked up the street and saw the ambulance take a left instead of the right towards the hospital.

"The ambulance. It's going the wrong way." He

ran towards his truck. The cop followed him. They got in, and the cop called in the ambulance's coordinates and description.

"It'll be easy enough to spot, it has a blue truck tailgating it," the cop yelled into his radio.

Noah concentrated on his driving, navigating the streets of Chicago, avoiding pedestrians, and following the ambulance with its lights and sirens going. It took a corner at breakneck speed.

God, the damn transport almost tipped over, and Kali would roll around like a pinball. "What is he trying to do? I have to back off or he'll wreck." Noah slammed his hand on his steering wheel.

"They're setting up a roadblock about a mile up ahead," the cop explained.

"What makes you think he'll be at the roadblock?" Noah yelled.

"This is a one way street, it's the main thoroughfare to the freeway." Okay, it sounded promising.

Noah eased off the gas even more not wanting the ambulance to speed any more than it was already. Now he was sweating bullets about the drug coursing through Kali's system, but he realized they wanted her alive, so they couldn't have given her too much, unless someone fucked up. God knew it happened often enough. Look at the stupid asshole who was driving the ambulance.

"They've got a doctor waiting at the roadblock, Sir. They'll take care of Mike's daughter." Noah could hear the respect in the man's voice. He could see where Mike Wachowski would garner that from the men he worked with.

Noah watched as the driver came up to the roadblock and slowed down before stopping. He got out of the driver's door and got on his knees with his hands behind his head. "Don't shoot." Either he watched a lot of cop shows or he had been in this type of situation before. Cops immediately swarmed him. Noah and the cop, who had ridden with him, were opening the EMT doors.

"I'm a doctor, let me through."

Noah heard the man behind him, but he didn't wait, he saw Kali propped up on her elbows on the gurney and he climbed into the ambulance.

"Noah, I think I'm going to be sick." Then she leaned over and threw up all over the floor.

A man elbowed his way past Noah and held Kali's head, while Noah grabbed her hand. The man grinned at Noah. "Best thing for her. It'll clean the garbage right out of her system."

They didn't take Kali to the hospital, instead there was a free clinic nearby, where the doctor worked. They kept her there until four in the morning. Mike snuck in and gave his baby girl a hug good-bye, and dropped off the suitcase Rose had packed. He also explained the other three women were doing well, before handing Noah a set of car keys.

"The car's clean, I just bought it for cash."

"Where in the hell can you buy a car for cash at three in the morning?" Noah asked.

"If a cop doesn't know the best places to buy cars at three a.m., then he hasn't been paying attention to his city," Mike chuckled.

Noah had to agree.

"I'm sorry, I don't have any cash to give you. Rose and I used everything we had, and we went to her sister, and my brothers to get the cash for the car."

"Don't worry, I have some, and Admiral Sakuro has this project funded. There are lockers and safety deposit boxes loaded with cash across the world for us. He knew this could get bad."

"I don't get it, why is the Navy so invested in the *found*?"

"Sakuro convinced them as soon as he became an admiral seven years ago and the first terrorist group popped up. Niko had already graduated from college and was on his way to a masters in engineering, and Nelson knew about me. There are six others that different countries have quietly admitted to, and everyone, besides me, is moving up in their chosen fields." Mike gave a grunt of laughter.

"What?"

"I've looked you up Lieutenant Commander. I'm sure they give out bronze stars and silver stars to just anyone." Heat creeped up Noah's neck, he hated talking about his medals.

"It's me not doing anything to contribute. I'm

the square peg in the round hole." Both men turned around to see Kali, looking paler than her hair if even possible. This time both Noah and Mike laughed.

"Sure go ahead and laugh at the sick girl."

"Little girl, you don't listen to those administrators at all, do you?" Noah saw her genuinely perplexed look and he couldn't understand how she was unable to see herself. Her father continued, "You have only been teaching for four years since you got your masters, and the school board stepped in to make sure you got hired back even though you were so late in applying."

"They probably thought all the publicity surrounding my name would somehow get them more funding."

"They wanted you because of the ideas you've been implementing. You're being fast-tracked up the ranks. Your contribution is going to be education." She still didn't look convinced.

"The two of you are a great match. I wonder if this is a side effect of all of the *found*. You don't think you're doing anything special," Mike speculated. "Oh well, you better get moving. I talked to Chang at the front desk. If you call in, just ask for Firearms Regulations Department, he'll call me over to the main phone line."

"Got it. Come on, Beautiful, time for us to go." Noah watched as Kali looked down at herself and grimaced. Mike grabbed her in a big hug.

"You look wonderful, little girl. Take care of Navy boy."

She laughed.

Mike patted him on the back and gave him a meaningful look, Noah understood it. He was to take care of his daughter and he intended to.

He reached for Kali's hand, and she took it like it was the most natural thing in the world. He had a flashback to another time, another world, and smiled. She looked up, startled, and then gave him a blinding smile. They were on their way, just like they had been all those years ago.

Chapter Sixteen

Kali laughed at the bagful of junk food Noah managed to acquire at the 7-11 the first time they stopped for gas.

"Really? Are you planning for the Zombie Apocalypse? Are we having a slumber party for fourteen year olds? Maybe we're going to ComiCon? Noah, do you really eat like this?" She pulled out three Hostess products, four candy bars, Nutter Butters, beef jerky, toffee peanuts, toffee cashews, pretzels, yogurt covered pretzels and the two cans of diet soda.

"Hey, that's my bag. Your bag is here." Snatching his bag back, he handed hers over. It was supposed to contain an orange juice and a breakfast sandwich. Instead she found three of each.

"Hungry much?"

"Give me my breakfast woman." He opened the console between them, and dumped the contents of the plastic sack, then held out his hand. "Gimme."

She giggled. She had found herself doing it a lot since he came into her life. She unwrapped his sandwich and handed it to him, then uncapped the juice and held onto it until he handed the sandwich back to her. Never once did his eyes leave the road. His training was obvious.

"So where are we going?"

"Georgia."

"Sarah?"

"Yep."

"Do you think the men guarding her are compromised?"

"I've got to assume so."

"If they are, they're not going to want you to take Sarah away. If they're good guys, they won't want to let her go. You're screwed either way."

"Looks like."

Okay, now she wasn't giggling.

"Do you have a plan?"

"Not really. I'm going to wing it."

"Since my mom's not here, I'm calling bullshit." She looked at his profile and prayed she was right. He looked so serious driving. Resolute. Her dad always looked like that too. Her mom said it came from having been called on too many traffic accidents. Kali didn't know what Noah's excuse was.

"I might have an ace up my sleeve."

"Huh?" She'd lost her train of thought.

"I called in some reinforcements. I don't know if

they are going to be there in time, if they aren't we'll punt."

"I thought you said we can't trust anyone."

"These guys aren't just anyone. These are men I trust with my life. More importantly, I trust them with *your* life." He gave her a quick reassuring smile.

"You called your team in from the jungle, didn't you? How could you? Did the admiral transfer them stateside? No, it would have looked too suspicious. What did you do?"

"Did I ever tell you how attractive intelligent women are?"

"So what did you do?"

"There's one hardship leave, one emergency medical leave, and two regular leaves."

"Well, *that's* not suspicious."

"It's been done before, and their temporary commander approved them all. It won't raise any flags to the people we're worried about, that's the main thing. Nate will be here first. He should already be in Atlanta by the time we get there. Now the knot in your stomach has relaxed, can you finally eat the breakfast sandwich?"

Boy could she.

"Miss Kelly, it is good to see you looking so well." Here she thought Noah and her dad were big men. Nate made both of them look puny. He had to be six feet six, and his muscles had muscles. Despite the fact he was huge, he wouldn't allow her to get into the backseat of the car. They all admired the view from the parking garage looking over the Atlanta airport.

"Defensive Tackle?"

"You got it in one." He smiled at her.

"Don't be flirting with my woman, Nate. I happen to know the bigger they are the harder they fall."

Nate gave Noah a smile as well. "We missed you man. How can we help?"

Noah opened up the console and passed Nate the stash of goodies he had purchased.

"Oh man, I was going to help you no matter what, but now, you get my first born." Kali looked on in awe as he opened up the beef jerky and a cherry pie at the same time and took alternate bites.

"First, we have to hide Kali, then we have to pull Sarah Johnson out from under Navy supervision."

"Yeah, I talked to Dave Rydell. I can't fucking believe this shit," Nate said between bites. "Do you have anything to drink?" Noah handed over a warm soda. "Thanks."

He finished the food, drank half the soda and proceeded to plop some of the peanuts into the half empty cola, and continued to drink until he was at the end and then he chewed. It was fascinating.

"So Sam, can you two tell me more about being *found*?" he asked as he opened up one of the candy bars and took a bite encompassing half the bar. It took Kali a moment to remember Noah was actually Samson Noah Kukailimoku, Sam to his friends.

"Yeah, my adoptive parents kept it quiet, and the Islanders are notoriously closed mouthed about their people."

"That's freaky. So do you know where you came from?"

"Bits and pieces are coming back. Kali and I basically had amnesia for the past twenty years until we met again. We mostly remember one another in another place."

"Do you know why you came here?"

Kali liked this man, he was filled with open, honest curiosity.

"I remember we were in a stadium, and someone, another child got up to speak. She said we were coming here to help, to make a small difference for good. Something about a tipping point. I didn't understand it then, and it still doesn't make a damn bit of sense to me. Nate, she couldn't have been more than four years old, and an entire stadium filled with people gave her a standing ovation."

As Noah described it, Kali remembered a little girl with brown hair, blue eyes and a smattering of freckles across her cheeks. She remembered thinking the girl was even smaller than she was, and how scared she would have been on a stepstool talking in front of so many people. Even standing in the center of the stadium holding Noah's hand, and surrounded by other children, had been scary.

"So if the *veil was lifted,* so to speak, after meeting Kelly, do you think you were meant to be together?" Nate asked as he ripped open the package of ding dongs.

"Absolutely." Noah reached over the console and pulled Kali's hand into his. "We were absolutely meant to find one another and be together." Kali could only look at Noah in stunned silence.

"Breathe Kali," he murmured.

She let out a big gust of air and glared at him. It was so disconcerting being around someone who could feel what she was feeling. He laced his fingers with hers, and then slowly brushed his thumb against the pad of flesh on her palm. She no longer cared he could feel what she was feeling.

He gave her a tender smile, and then turned back to look at Nate. "Okay, so I figure you've been talking to the team?"

"You know it. Mathers will be here tomorrow. In the meantime, we have someone to meet so Kelly can get a new identity. As for you, Riley is flying into DC to pick up cash and papers from one of the safety deposit boxes. He should be here by Wednesday. He had some problems getting his paperwork approved for leave, otherwise he'd be here sooner.

"You seem familiar." The words came out of her

mouth before she had a chance to think them through.

"He was one of the men who helped rescue you, Beautiful. Everyone you are going to meet, were part of the rescue mission to get you out of that hellhole."

Kali shuddered, the thought of people, besides Noah, seeing her when she was destroyed made her ill. He pulled her over the console and gave her a hug. "He's family, Kali. They all are." He ran his fingers down her back, and the panic slid away with the stroke of his hand.

Noah settled her back into her seat, she relaxed and turned to meet warm hazel eyes.

"We were really worried about you Kelly, but not as much as we were about Sam here. I thought he was going to pass out when he saw how bad your wrists were torn up when we got inside the chopper." His cheek creased, Kelly realized he must have had quite a following while he had been playing football.

"So Noah was woozy at the sight of blood?"

"Noah, huh? It works I guess. Well, Noah, was sure as hell worked up at the sight of *your* blood, for damn sure."

Kali imagined Noah broken and bloody like she had been and realized she couldn't have kept it together. She felt a wave of panic, and realized it came from Noah, he had a flashback to the night of the rescue. It was time for a change of topic.

"So Nate, I gotta tell you, I'm not really liking

the whole, stash Kali away, part of the plan." Nate's grin got even broader. Now she felt a definite sense of annoyance coming from Noah, but this she chose to ignore. "Sarah's not going to be willing to go with you guys because you ask her to. You're going to need someone like me to convince her it's in her best interest to go with you."

"She's smart too, Noah. You know we all appreciate beautiful and smart in our women." Nate seemed to be laughing at Noah.

"Back off Goodman," Noah growled. Kali gaped at him, he had literally growled at his friend. Nate could not possibly be chuckling. For God's sake, couldn't they see her?

"For God's sake, can't you see yourself?"

"Did you just read my mind?"

"No. Of course not."

Kali stared at him, she could feel the sincerity and shock coming from him in waves.

"Whoa. I knew you two were connected. We all did. But you can read each other's minds?"

Kali ran a trembling hand through her hair and gave a weak smile to Nate.

"It's more we can feel what one another is feeling."

"You're not going with us. We do rescue and recovery missions all the time."

"She doesn't think she needs to be rescued or recovered, she's going to think you're kidnapping her. How are you going to keep her from hurting herself? From hurting you?" Their laughter pissed her off.

"Kelly, just how is Sarah Johnson going to hurt us?" Nate asked between chuckles.

Her ears were about to start bleeding. These men were going to end up getting killed. Of course Kali knew everything there was to know about Sarah Johnson. She was another *found*. Unlike Kali, she was brilliant. She was currently an intern in the busiest ER in Atlanta, and also put in hours at a free clinic in the inner city. She was amazing. She also grew up with six, count them, six older brothers.

Sarah Johnson might have made the grades in high school and gotten a scholarship, but the girl was tough. That, along with smart, and she would give anyone a run for their money. It could end up getting Noah hurt, which was unacceptable in Kali's book.

"I'm not going along with your plan."

"It's unacceptable."

"Funny you should use that word Noah, I was just thinking it was unacceptable you be hurt or killed because you didn't do the smart thing and use me to help. I'm going with you when you go to get Sarah. She knows me."

"What do you mean she knows you?"

"I mean she's studied me, she knows exactly who I am."

"Oh, makes sense. You've studied her, too." Noah said slowly. "Mathers downloaded a file, it's really comprehensive."

"Did it tell you she actually got into a knife fight with a gang member and beat him, when she was ten and he was fourteen?"

"No shit." Nate whistled as he scrolled through his phone. "Nope, not on here. I can't believe Mathers missed it. How'd you know about it?"

"It was in her school newspaper. I downloaded it, when I was in grade school. I made up stories in my head about how mad her brothers must have been."

"I'm betting the punk who pulled the knife didn't have a happy life afterwards," Nate muttered. "I vote for taking Kelly with us."

"Her name is Kali, and I vote against it."

"It's two against one. You're outvoted."

"This is the military, the lieutenant makes the rules, and I say you're not going."

"Noah, you know this is the right thing to do. Sarah will listen to me. This will work a hell of a lot easier. You know that."

"Here's what you're not getting. You're a target too. The two of you together will be like a Thanksgiving feast for these guys. I am not putting you in the same spot at the same time. Are we clear?" He was every inch the leader.

"Okay, you're both right, we do need Kali to convince Sarah to come with us. So now all we need is a plan."

Kali knew she wasn't going to get her way, but Noah was so hot when he was the commander, it didn't matter.

CHAPTER SEVENTEEN

Noah loved seeing his team together in the little hotel room. It would have been better if Riley and Dave were there, but it would have put Kali in to shock, too much testosterone in one small area. Thank God for Mathers.

Sierra Mathers was one of those beautiful redheads, with honey gold skin and no freckles. Noah and the other men on the team wondered if having her in the unit would end up being a problem, but within three days of her working on their electronics, nobody cared. She was a magician, and it was all that mattered.

Sierra had been working on finding a way to get to Sarah Johnson since the second he had called her. Now she and Kali were comparing notes. "How in the hell did I miss that? Even if the school newspapers were deleted, my searches should have pulled them up."

Kali was practically on Sierra's lap at the desk in

the little corner of the hotel room. Why was there something erotic about seeing two beautiful women cuddled so close together? He turned to where Nate was on the phone talking to Kota and saw he was watching the two women with interest. They grinned at one another. Yep, their penises were just hard-wired that way.

Nate hung up. "There are four total. Two on. Two off. They break it up into eight hour shifts, the next trade-off is five and a half hours from now."

"Kota's sure if the relief doesn't come the ones on duty will make a play for Sarah?"

"Yep."

"Why?"

"It's me, Lieutenant," Sierra piped up from the desk. "I've got their room under surveillance."

"How the fuck did you manage that? And when?"

"I did it before reporting in to you. They have adjoining bedrooms over at the Marriott and I went in as housekeeping and planted some transmitters. They only record when somebody's talking, and then they translate into text, and feed them to me." She held up her phone. It boggled his mind.

"Their protocol is very specific. If anyone is a no show, grab the girl. Otherwise they're waiting for their orders. If they do grab her, they have a location they're supposed to take her, but they haven't said where it is."

"We need to find out where they planned to take her, and back track these fuckers. Wasn't Kota supposed to be here already?" They turned at the knock on the door. Nate went to answer it.

Kota came straight over to Kali. He wasn't quite as big as Noah, but his presence was imposing. Kota's Native American ancestry was immediately apparent.

"Hello Kelly, I'm Dakota Blackthorne. I've owed you an apology for a good long time." His voice held the fresh twang of the west.

"I don't understand."

"I caused you unnecessary pain when you came aboard the helicopter. I grabbed you by the wrist."

She could see just how sincere he was, and how upset at the thought of having caused her pain, it was clear on his face. She tried a quick experiment, she took a deep breath and released it, centering herself. She reached out and felt regret that wasn't her own. Looking into his eyes she didn't see any of the recognition she did when Noah felt her *sensing* his emotions. But there was not a doubt in her mind. Kali was feeling some of what Kota Blackthorne was feeling.

"I know Noah and his team, none of you would hurt me on purpose. There must have been a reason."

"Noah?"

"Yep. We're calling Sam by his middle name now," Nate called from the bed where he was pawing through the contents of the suitcase Kota brought. It contained a small arsenal.

"Well Kelly, Noah is right, we would never intentionally harm you, but it doesn't excuse the fact I *did* harm you, and I'm deeply sorry."

Kali couldn't stand it another minute. She wrapped her arms around him in a fierce hug. His relief came through clear as a bell. Then she felt some distinct irritation. She let Kota go and turned around and sought out Noah. He was looking over Sierra's shoulder, but briefly caught her eyes and gave her a rueful grin. She laughed.

Noah royally pissed off Sierra, but he really didn't give a shit. The unit had taken their argument into the adjoining room, and Noah had to have a balls-out conversation with Sierra. One he never thought would be necessary.

"Do you really think you being a woman plays into whether I think you're capable in the field, Chief?"

"I didn't until today." Sierra bristled with indignation. Nate and Kota were stone-faced, waiting to see how Noah would handle the situation.

"Sierra, I have only ever cared how I could best use my people. I haven't fucking liked it, but have we not used your feminine attributes from time to time to lure guards away from their posts?" Noah watched as the light dawned.

"Yes Lieutenant." Good, her head was out of her

ass. "You're using me to work with the women, because I'll be the best to work with them."

"If you question me in front of civilians again we're going to have a hell of a problem, do I make myself clear?"

Sierra squared her shoulders and looked him straight in the eye. "Yes Sir."

"Good. Now go babysit the civilian, and make sure she lures in the second one." They all laughed.

"Be careful. I'll have all the communications here, if any of you run into problems, you can link in, and I'll be able to coordinate."

Noah watched Sierra go into Kali's room. He turned to Kota and Nate. "Nate, you sure you've got the guys in the room? We could go get them first, and then go get the two on duty."

"You know they might ping the ones in the room, so it's better to hit at the same time. Of course I can take them out." Noah looked at the man, and realized the two stateside Navy men wouldn't know what hit them. Each group planned to take one person alive, so if it turned from sugar to shit, they would have a back-up person to interrogate.

"Kota, you're the one who scoped out this scene today. What do you think of our two targets?"

"I think they're amateurs. I went into the ER, even if I hadn't known she was being watched, I would have thought she had an ex-husband who hired private investigators to keep an eye on her."

"Navy guys couldn't be that bad," Nate protested.

"Oh yeah," Kota confirmed. "Right down to windbreakers."

Noah groaned. Taking out such obvious targets was going to make it harder for them. "So what's your plan?"

"Since Sarah is an intern, we see her from the lobby. She's one of the first people working on incoming cases. You see these guys popping up like prairie dogs every time an ambulance pulls up to the bay. We're going to pull the fire alarm right before their shift break. It'll have everybody scrambling, and have them popping up. We can casually take them out on gurneys." Kota held up two syringes and Nate laughed. Noah swallowed, feeling slightly ill. It was too much like Kali having been drugged the other night.

"Good planning, Kota. Let's get moving. I want Sarah in our hands in the next three hours gentlemen, and I want to know who in the hell is behind this little venture."

"He told me you would be contacting me. I know you're speaking under duress." Kali wanted to hit her head on the desk. She glanced at Sierra, who looked as frustrated. They had been on this Skype conversation with Sarah for twenty minutes, and it was an endless loop. She believed she was Kelly

Wachowski, and she was a *found* child. Kali had been right, she had been following her movements over the years the same way Kali had been following hers.

"Who is telling you I'm speaking to you under duress?"

"I can't tell you, it's classified."

"Sarah, we might not have ever met, but you *know* me. Do you really think I would bullshit you, or put you in harm's way?"

"I think if someone is threatening people you love you would do anything to save them, just like I would, Kelly. Dan and the government is doing everything they can to help you and your family. You just need to hang on a little while longer. Help is on the way."

"Sarah, this is important, is he there with you right now?"

"Kelly, I can't talk about that. Hang in there girl. We're going to get you back."

"I'm not being held captive. My family isn't in trouble."

"Just hold on another day or two Kelly."

Sarah disconnected. Kali dropped her forehead onto the desk.

"Kali, focus. She's still at the hospital, I have her cell phone pinpointed. We have to get to her."

Sierra was right. "How?"

"They don't know me, I can be seen. You have to be disguised. You're the patient, I'm the relative. Your disguise is you're covered in blood. It should get you seen in the ER, and passed whoever is watching."

Kali grinned.

"Couldn't we have used ketchup?"

"Blood, we needed blood."

Kali was still gagging as she remembered Sierra cutting her own thigh to get blood to cover the bandages adorning Kali's head.

"I've cut myself worse shaving my legs, now buck up. Remember to lean on me and let me do all the talking.

Despite Sierra's sob story, and Kali's pathetic appearance as they showed up at the nurse's station, they were going to have to wait to see a doctor.

"Fill out this insurance form in the meantime," the nurse said, handing them a clipboard. Kali closed her eyes and fell to the floor.

Orderlies immediately rushed over to Kali, and lifted her up onto a stretcher, to take her back to the back.

"Wait here Lady, only patients beyond this point"

Somehow Sierra had managed to force her way behind the ER doors. Kali heard them telling her she wasn't allowed back there on numerous occasions, but she felt her hand holding hers as she was laid on a table and a curtain was drawn around a bed.

"No. She's afraid of men. It has to be a female doctor." God, Sierra was good.

"I'm here. Let me take a look at her. What's her name?"

"Kelly, her name is Kelly, Dr. Johnson."

"Kelly, can you open your eyes for me." Kali lifted the bandage out of her face and looked up at Sarah Johnson, who gaped at her in surprise. Then she looked from Kali to Sierra and back to Kali again.

"So you weren't bullshitting me."

"Nope. But you can't trust the Dan guy." Kali watched the emotions play over Sarah's face, and then felt her outrage as if it were her own.

"I'm going to sic my brothers on that asshole."

"No time. You're a target. You and I both are. The good guys are taking care of most of Dan's team, but they didn't know about Dan. We've got to tell them, but first we have to get you out of here and safe. Where's Dan?"

"He's going to contact me tonight so we can meet. He told me it's not safe for me. I'd end up a target like you, and I might need to be put into protective custody."

"I'm sure he did," Sierra muttered. "Look, the one thing he said that's right is it's not safe for you. You heard what happened to Kali, right?" Sarah nodded.

Kali grabbed Sarah's hand. "And Alfred right?" Sarah's eyes welled with tears. She nodded. "Mai Zhang's been kidnapped. They're keeping it quiet, but Sarah we're in trouble."

"My family will keep me safe."

"My dad is a chief in the Chicago Police Department and even he wanted me to go with Noah. This is the right thing to do." Sarah gripped Kali's hand tighter and looked her in the eye.

"You trust these people?"

"With my life. With my family's lives."

"Okay, let's go."

Chapter Eighteen

The mission was a success, it had gone like clockwork. Then Noah got back to the room, and found Sarah with Sierra and Kali. Kali still had some blood in her hair, and even though the women explained what happened he lost his mind. Literally lost his mind.

Noah didn't care what the others thought as he dragged Kali out of the room down the hall to a private room he had booked.

"Take off your clothes."

"Noah?"

"Now." His boots hit the floor, then the knife, gun, and jacket. She stood there, her blonde hair still in disarray, some strands still showing red. When he was down to his jeans he grabbed her around the waist and yanked her against him.

"Don't you *ever* put yourself in harm's way again. Ever. I would die if something were to happen to you!" Noah jerked the T-shirt over her head and had the bra off her before she had time to react.

"Noah, Sierra was with me. We were in a public place. We were perfectly fine..." His tongue thrust into her mouth and the sense of panic began to slowly dissipate. God, the taste of her, the heat of her. Just her, just Kali, how could he have gone through the last twenty years not remembering her? He tipped them onto the bed, frantically pulling at her khakis. Thank God all of her clothes were loose, so he could easily remove them. He skipped trying to unbutton or unzip anything, and pulled them off her. He saw the plain white cotton panties she was wearing and smiled. Only Kali could make those look good.

"Quit ogling my sexy lingerie and strip Kukailimoku. I want to see the goods."

He ignored her, and slowly pulled down her panties. Kali's light blonde curls were already damp. He watched in fascination as the lean muscles of her thighs tightened as she went to clamp them together, but he was having none of that.

"Open Kali. Spread your legs for me." He looked into those blue depths and saw her hesitation, but he also felt her curiosity, and he could definitely see and smell her desire. They hadn't played these games in the bedroom, and now they were at a point where it wasn't a game. She had put herself in harm's way, and Noah had a deep seated need to exert his dominance over his woman. He didn't want to, nor would he ever hurt or humiliate Kali, but this?

"Kali, part your legs." He watched as the plump white lips of her pussy slowly opened, showing him the slick essence of her arousal. She trembled and he stroked the glistening pink folds. "Wider." He watched her with steady eyes, as she struggled with his command, but her knees drifted outwards, allowing him to push and twist two fingers into her hot, tight channel. Her whimper was music to his ears.

"Noah?"

"You are mine. This body is mine. You are mine to care for. You will not take risks with what is mine."

Her eyes turned a deep navy, their wills clashing as her hips arched into his caress. "I knew what...hmmm"

He rubbed circles on a spot inside her, his thumb teasing her engorged clit, and was rewarded with a burst of honey.

"Noah, more." She pressed into his hand.

"No. Not until you agree that when it comes to your safety I am in charge." Her eyes were at half-mast. He felt her confusion, her anger, but underneath it all, he felt her understanding. He wasn't above using that.

"Please baby, I need this," he said as he continued stroking in and out, his eyes leaving her face to see the beauty of her sex splayed before him. "I need to know you're protected."

"But…"

He delved deeper, and Kali arched higher, so close he felt the burn.

"If I feel you're in danger, I'm not focused, and I might make mistakes." Her hips dropped onto the bed with a thud.

"Oh no." He was right. "Noah, I wasn't thinking. I forgot how connected we are."

"We still are Kali." He licked along the folds of her sex, around his fingers, tasting all of the honey he had been dying to sample.

"Noah!"

He felt her explode, and it was amazing. He actually experienced her orgasm, and had to exert all of his control not to come. There was no way he was going to deny himself the pleasure of coming inside this woman's body. Stripping out of his jeans, it took him moments longer to put on the condom than it should have.

Looking at Kali lying in front of him, he realized he had everything he could ever want. Somehow his life had come into complete focus. He was blessed, and he was going to die if he didn't get inside her.

Kali realized Noah had used sex to manipulate her into agreeing. She resented it, but she couldn't blame him when she had felt his anguish. She reached out and grabbed hold of him, he was her everything, and she needed him inside her. He started slow, he always did, like she was some kind of delicate thing. This time she was having none of his nonsense. She wrapped her legs around his hips and took him inside her in one fast plunge, rejoicing in the feel of him.

"Kali!" He looked at her, his eyes filled with concern and censure. She smiled beaming with contentment.

"You feel so good, and I needed you. Now move. Fuck me, Noah." He hesitated for all of a second and then pulled out and thrust deep and hard. God it felt good. "Again, and again, and again." They grinned in perfect accord. Kali looked into his eyes, as they turned from brown to black and filled her vision, filled her world. She saw her blue eyes through his, for just a moment, and they glowed like sapphires. Then both colors splintered into the night sky, and she flew with Noah.

They spent the night in the room, making love and talking. She was remembering the times with her Nana, and he had vague recollections of his parents in the other place. He told stories of his time on Kauai, of meeting Kapu, which meant Grandfather in Hawaiian. He explained his grandfather was literally the grandfather to many on the island, and figuratively Grandfather to the rest.

"I had an affinity for languages early on. Then during a game of hide and seek with some of the other kids, I found Conner in his secret place. There is no way I should have found him up the tree, but I knew where he was. He and I went to talk to Kapu, and he said I had developed another superpower. He didn't make a big deal about it. It was his way. All of the children of the Island were made to feel special, and none made to feel odd or peculiar. I remember Anna had a stutter, and Kapu said she was practicing so she could eventually speak better than everybody else, and he was right she did. She became the president of our drama department."

"He sounds wonderful. It must have been hard when he passed."

"Oh, he's still alive and kicking. He goes out and fishes at least twice a week. I talk to my parents, and he is mentoring all of the young children of the Island to this day."

"Is it how you were able to find me, because of this ability to find things like you found Conner?"

"Partly. We finally had the intel you were being held in the abandoned business complex, but yeah, when we got there, I was able to tell which building you were in."

"I don't understand."

"This time was so much stronger. I would have been able to tell what building a target was in. But because it was you, I could feel your pain. I knew what building you were in, sure. But Kali, I felt you. I knew *exactly* where you were in the building, and I knew we had to get to you fast or you weren't going to make it.

"I wonder why Sarah and I don't have any special abilities."

"You do Kali, you have a way with children. That's why they want you to teach, and why they need you in the school system. I suspect Sarah has some affinity for healing. They probably aren't really major abilities, but just enough to make a small difference. Hell, everybody has something, not just *found* people. You know that. Look at your dad."

"He is a born protector."

"My point exactly. I think we're just more in tune to what our purpose is."

"Maybe." She still wasn't convinced. But then again, there had to be a reason they were here, didn't there? "Noah, I don't remember as much as to why we came here, I was so young. I remember you made the decision to come, and I made the decision to follow you. Why did you come here?"

"It's still kind of fuzzy. I still remember somebody saying something about a tipping point. I remember it being really important. That's about it." Kali felt his frustration, and ran her hand down his chest, smiling at him as she reached his penis.

"It's okay, Noah. Don't stress about it. You've remembered a lot. Why don't you try to relax? I think I can help." Kali slid down his body, smiling. She soon had him tensing up again, but eventually he was totally relaxed.

Chapter Nineteen

"Sakuro took them all into custody, and we found Sarah's Dan," Nate said as soon as they entered the shared rooms. Noah smiled. He loved his team. Riley was there waiting for him.

"Hear your name is Noah these days," he said with a grin as he waved from behind Sierra at the computer. She had an even a bigger set-up then when they left the room yesterday. Yep, it was definitely turning into a command post.

"You guys are an acceptable team."

"That's what we strive for, *acceptable*," Nate said with a grin. "So we have an idea of where the leadership is to this fucking organization. They are outside of Dallas. Since its Riley's stomping grounds, he and Kota have tickets out in four hours."

"How tight is the location?"

"Pretty good. They're operating out of a business in Denton. They're trying to blend in with the University there. It's not a bad cover."

"Actually, it's just one little subsidiary of a huge organization called Rixitron. Rixitron is a multinational with its grubby little tentacles in everything. This subsidiary houses their Senior VP in charge of, get this, Undeveloped Acquisitions." Sierra's disgust was clear.

"Who is this Senior VP?"

"Some slime bucket who actually worked a Ponzi scheme back in the day."

"So we know exactly who they are and where they're located, that's good." Noah gave them a steely look. He knew when he was being handed a line of bullshit.

"We don't know exactly who the people are within the business. Two of the people are this Dan guy's contacts."

"So you need me."

"Nope. Riley and I have this covered," Kota said with absolute conviction.

"You know I'll find them."

"You're not going Lieutenant and that's final."

Noah looked over at Kali, she was amused. She knew his team was trying to protect him, and not being insubordinate.

"Sierra, book me on the plane to Dallas. Riley, I'm going with you. Kota, you're staying here." There was no more discussion. He could practically hear Nate's teeth grinding, but his unit knew this was the best decision.

"Why isn't someone in the room with Sarah next door?"

"I have eyes and ears on her, Lieutenant." Sierra indicated one of the three computer screens in front of her. She was amazing.

"Is she asleep or awake?" Kali asked.

"She woke up about a half hour ago."

"I'm going in to see her." Kali let go of his hand and knocked on the adjoining bedroom door, waiting to be called in.

"So what didn't you tell me?" he asked turning to his team.

"They have their sights on another target. He was never reported. He was raised on an Indian Reservation in New Mexico. Dan thinks he's already been taken, but because it was handled by another team, he's not sure."

"Fuck."

"Do we know if these are the same fuckers who took Kali?"

"Nope, we weren't able to determine that either," Nate said delivering the bad news.

"This just keeps getting better and better."

"Noah?" He hadn't heard her come back through the door. "Are you okay?" He went over to her, and kissed her forehead.

"Just ironing out some of the logistics of the plan, and realized we still needed a little more intel. Nothing to worry about."

She gave him an appraising look, and nodded her head. He understood what she was telling him, she would let him get away with the lie at the moment, but she would be questioning him further later. He intended to be gone before she had a chance to ask those questions. She stepped back into the other room.

"Okay, how in the hell is Sakuro dealing with the fact he is now holding rogue Navy men?"

"He has them held by people he trusts on Kauai. He said you'd know who he's talking about." Noah grinned. Well it was one positive, at least the admiral was using his head. Those retired swabbies would bury those assholes so deep they would only come up for air when Sakuro wanted them to.

"Hey, I was just able to get you seats on an earlier flight to Dallas," Sierra chimed in.

"Great. Riley, do you have contacts to get us armored up once we land?"

"Already taken care of Lieutenant." He loved his team, even if they were only acceptable. When he said as much, Nate threw his empty candy wrappers at him. There were a lot of them.

"Riley and I will be back tomorrow night at the latest. If everything goes to plan, Sarah should be able to come out of hiding."

"I notice you didn't say I could come out of hiding." They were back in the private room where they had made love. They were lying on the bed fully clothed, knowing they didn't have much time together.

"We still haven't determined this is the same

group of fanatics that kidnapped you. Unfortunately the *found* have been targeted by more than one group of crazies. This doesn't sound like the same group from what we learned from Dave Rydell's interrogation of Mai's kidnapper." Kali wrapped her arms around Noah. It was obvious he wanted to fix everything for her, but sometimes he couldn't.

"I know you, and now I know your team. You'll figure this all out, and soon I will be able to go home."

"Yes you will," he promised. Kali felt their desire rise, she loved that she could feel his as well as hers. His was fiercer, more urgent.

"Yours is softer, it comes in pulses and waves."

"So you can read my mind," she rubbed her cheek against his shirt.

"Close your eyes, Kali. Just relax, let's try an experiment."

"You're thinking about my breasts. You always think about my breasts."

He snorted.

"I told you to concentrate, look deeper. Yes, I was thinking about your breasts, specifically your nipples, but there was something else too."

Kali took a deep breath, she loved how he smelled, his heart beat under her cheek. He held her even closer. He loved her. He didn't want to leave without her when they were children. He'd loved her then as a child, but now he loved her as a man.

"You want us to have children together."

"And grandchildren. I want the whole nine yards, Kali. I know I don't have the ring, but will you marry me?"

She looked at this man, the most beautiful man in the world, inside and out, and couldn't imagine growing old without him.

"Of course I'll marry you." Kali reached to kiss him, and stopped. "I read your mind. I actually freaking did it. Oh my freaking God!"

Noah cupped her cheeks, and kissed her. She got lost in his taste, and color and feel. She pushed against him, relieved to feel his erection swelling against her tummy. He pulled away.

"Beautiful, we don't have time. I have to leave."

"This better not be the start of a trend."

"Trust me, it's not. Expect to be ravished when I return."

"I do." God she loved the sound of that phrase.

Chapter Twenty

"The first thing I remember is being squirted with water by DelRoy. It was the summer before I went to first grade. I was wearing overalls and in the backyard of my house. I was holding a squirt gun too."

"That is really weird Sarah. Mine and Noah's first memories are so clear, I would have thought yours would be too." They were sitting on the bed in the adjoining room eating room service. Kali was pretty sure there was no food left in the kitchen after Nate placed his order. She had never seen anybody eat as much as he did.

"Apparently I showed up in their yard a month before, the same day you did, completely naked. But the neighbor's dog had gotten out and pinned me down. They heard my screams and the dog barking."

"No wonder you can't remember the day, you must have been scared to death. You probably still don't like dogs."

"Oh no, my parents ended up getting me a puppy a year later, and I got to raise her. I loved her until the day she died. If they hadn't, yeah, I probably would be scared of dogs to this day. As for the memory loss," Sarah stopped talking and just stared at Kali.

"What?" Kali gently prompted.

"I think I would have been terrified if I remembered. Wasn't it awful for you? Waking up naked in the back of the cop car?"

Kali tilted her head and decided to give Sarah a much more serious answer than she had ever provided to anyone other than Noah. "I wasn't scared. I was cold, and I knew the man who had gotten into the car with me was good. I was already in the car when he got in. I was kind of sleeping. Dad explained how he had to unlock it."

"Then what happened?"

"I just woke up, and I was cold, it was winter in Chicago. He got in, and I remember him saying something to me, and me responding. I understood him just fine. Then he spilled his coffee and said something else and it took me longer to understand, but after I did, I asked for a blanket. Then he started to yell words, but he wasn't mad and I wasn't scared. I knew he was good."

"Can you always tell?"

"Tell what?"

"Tell when someone is good or not?"

"No. I was only ever able to do it with Dad the first time. But there was no doubt in my mind, it was a soul-deep knowing. This man was someone good, someone I could trust. There was no fear."

"Why was he yelling?"

"He'd spilled his McDonald's coffee onto his lap. He was swearing in Polish. So it's how I ended up asking for a blanket and his breakfast sandwich in Polish. Trust me, if there was someone scared in the patrol car that night, it was him, not me."

"How old do you think you were?"

"They examined me when I was taken to the hospital, and determined I was no more than five years old. God, he was so scared, Sarah." Kali put down her fork, the baked potato losing its flavor. "He carried me into the hospital and never once left me. He called my mom and she came to the hospital as well. I didn't know her, but I knew she was important to him. You could see the love."

"Could you feel it? Like you feel things with Noah?"

"No, the only time I've ever been able to feel anyone's emotions has been with Noah. I've never had the ability before."

"I don't know if I have the ability, but I definitely get a sense of what's wrong with someone when they come in and need care. It's stronger with children. It's one of the reasons I'm drawn to trauma care, so often a case will come in where they can't speak for themselves, but it's almost like I can spend some time with them, touch them, and I almost always know what's wrong." Sarah was whispering so quietly Kali had to lean in to hear her.

"Do you have some kind of healing powers?"

Sarah let out a big laugh, ruining the quiet moment. "Girl that would be crazy."

"Sarah, don't you think other doctors, I mean people who have a real affinity for healing, can sense things with their patients?" Kali watched Sarah's brow furl as she thought about what Kali was saying, then her expression lightened, and she gave her a bright grin.

"You know when I was in medical school, there were two different doctors who talked about getting quiet and letting themselves get in touch with the patient. One just flat out said he could feel where the blockages were with the patient. He had tenure, and came from Berkley, so it wasn't surprising."

"Is it what you do? Find blockages?"

"There might be swelling in the abdomen, but I can trace it to the liver, or the kidney. I just know where the real problem is. I have a higher clear rate for my cases than other doctor. When I go in to find the underlying problem of a symptom my first guess is almost always right."

"Dammit, I told my Dad and Noah you were special!" Kali grabbed Sarah's hand where it was lying on the little room service cart. "Stop looking at this like it's a bad thing, or something you need to hide." At Sarah's wry glance, Kali laughed. "Okay, maybe you shouldn't shout it from the rooftops, neither of us needs more of a spotlight on us. But still, your ability is something to be treasured."

"Kali, of course I'm damn grateful I have it. I shoulder check other doctors out of the way when I think there is a case where I'd be more effective. I know this ability is a gift, but I can't help but think we're from some other planet and once somebody realizes what I can do, they will come and get me and put me under a microscope."

Kali felt the sincerity of Sarah's words.

"Ah Sarah, I think you are blessed with an ability other healers have, you're just more in-tune with it like the two teachers in med school. I bet if you spoke to some of your other colleagues, *really* talked to them, they all have some sense of what is going on with their patients."

"If you think I'm going to talk to my co-workers about this Whoo Whoo shit, you have another think coming." Sarah rolled her eyes, making Kali laugh again. "So you don't think this is some kind of special mastery we have? You think this is a normal human sense maybe hopped up on steroids a little bit?"

"Something like that. Noah has the ability to sense and find things. It's like the natives in the jungle who can track down predators. But, maybe even more than that."

"Oh, you just think he's all that because you're in love," Sarah said in a sing-song voice. Kali laughed again. Sarah was a crack up.

"I don't want to jump your bones, and I think you're pretty damn special!"

"What do you mean you don't want to jump me, I'm fiiinnnneee."

Kali fell back on the bed and laughed at the ceiling. This woman was good for her, why hadn't she ever taken the time to meet her before, like she had with Alfred. Just that fast, she stopped laughing.

"What is it girl?"

"I was thinking about Alfred."

"Alfred Hawley? Yeah, Dan told me what happened, but he probably lied. What was the true story?"

Kali sat up straight on the bed again, and looked across the cart to where Sarah was sitting on the other double bed. "You know I was kidnapped, right?"

"And those same bastards tried to kidnap Alfred." Sarah got up and pushed the cart out of the way, it was obvious neither of them were going to be able to eat any more.

"Actually there are at least two different groups out to capture us. The ones who kidnaped me are different than the ones who kidnaped Mai. Therefore, we're not sure who was behind the attack on Alfred."

"Holy shit." They sat on the beds across from one another. Kali tried to think of something to say to lighten the mood, but couldn't come up with anything, so she plowed on. "The people who have Mai want to start a breeding program. They think we're special and our genes will make Uber babies."

"Fuck Girl! See, I told you I didn't want to stand

out!" Sarah jumped up in agitation and started pacing the room. There was a knock on the adjoining door.

"Come in."

Nate poked his head in.

"You ladies all right?" Behind his trademark grin his voice held concern.

"Can you come in and help explain the two groups we're dealing with?"

"Come in and talk to two beautiful ladies? Twist my arm." Nate closed the door behind him and pulled up the desk chair he barely fit in.

"I'd like you to start from scratch. I'll assume everything Dan told me is bullshit, and discount it. I hate believing there is more than one group of people out to kidnap Kali and me."

Nate ran his hand through his short cropped brown hair. "Sarah, you have to remember, they aren't specifically targeting you and Kali. They would target anyone who appeared twenty years ago. This isn't because of the person you are."

"Nate, you're not making me feel better. Just tell me, okay."

Kali watched the big man struggle for words for the first time. It was clear he somehow wanted to soften the blow for Sarah. "Tell her Nate, she's tougher than she looks."

"Okay. We still don't have a bead on the group that took Kali. They were obviously concerned with where she came from, it's why they tortured her for so long."

"You were tortured? My God, it wasn't in the papers, not that starvation isn't torture. Are you okay?" Sarah jumped from her bed, and Kali was wrapped in warm arms.

"It's okay, I'm okay now. It was tough for a while."

"Anyway, like I said, we don't know what group it is. We're still trying to track them down. We have another team searching for them. The organization that kidnapped Mai and was targeting you wanted you for a breeding program. They think they can make super babies. Based on you, Mai, Alfred, Niko and Kali it's obvious the *found* are extraordinary, and this organization has people bidding to use your ovum and sperm to mix with theirs to create what they consider a superior race.

"They're fucking Nazi's," Sarah spat out. "You wouldn't think they'd want my black eggs."

"Mai's Vietnamese. This group isn't the racist group. The splinter group out of Idaho wanted you all dead because you were different. They intended to blow up your hospital," Nate said.

"Dammit, did you have to tell her that?"

Sarah looked at her in shock, then turned to Nate. "Truly, there was a third group wanting us dead?"

"But we got them all, they're no longer a threat," he said encouragingly.

"Just how many people hate us, or are after us? And why now?"

"I think it's because you have all started to become known in your fields."

"Except for me," Kali joked.

"Dammit Kali, would you please stop with that shit?" Nate said forcefully.

"What are you talking about?" Sarah demanded. "You are amazing, I've been keeping track of you for years. You graduated three years early. Now they are planning on making you a principal in one of the largest school districts in Chicago. You would be the youngest principal ever. I'd say you are outstanding in the educational field."

Kali stopped to really think about what Sarah was saying, and realized she was probably right.

"So Nate, do you think there are even more groups?"

"No, Sarah, I think that's it," Nate assured her. Lie, definitely a lie, Kali felt it clear as day. She watched the relief spread across Sarah's face. Nate gave her a quick glance, and she realized he might know she was able to pick up on people's feelings. She didn't feel any distress, just a little amusement. She really was growing to love Noah's teammates.

CHAPTER TWENTY-ONE

"Don't you dare lie to me Nate. He hasn't called in and neither has Riley. None of you know where they are." Kali was livid. She was a grown woman who deserved the truth. This was the man she loved, the man she was going to marry, and he was in trouble.

"This isn't uncommon, Kali. Things happen in the field, and we all end up going off the grid for a while, it's the nature of our work."

"When you're in the fucking jungle. Not when you're in Dallas." She was no longer livid, she was past furious, and moved on to terrified. She watched as Kota packed his duffel, and Sierra's fingers flew over two keyboards damn near simultaneously.

"I'm going with you." Everybody stopped and looked at her.

"I beg your pardon, Ma'am?" It was probably the most words Dakota Blackthorne had spoken to her since he had apologized at their first meeting.

"I'm going with you. You need to find him. Don't you want to use all possible tools?"

Kota looked at Nate.

"Of course we do Kali it goes without saying," Nate assured her.

"I've got a lead on them. One of the partners of the Rixitron Corporation just filed a flight plan to Cancun. For all intents and purposes it looks like a holiday," Sierra said as she continued to scan her monitors.

"There you go Kota, you and I are going on a fun trip to Cancun together."

"Kali, you're not going anywhere." Kota watched the byplay between her and Nate, as he continued to pack his duffel bag.

"You're not listening. I'm connected to Noah. I might not be able to find things like he does, but I sure as hell can pinpoint his location. He better not ever think about cheating on me." Kali said, and Nate barked out a laugh.

"I want that ability, can you teach me?" Sierra called out from the corner.

"Ma'am this is a hot zone. I don't need a civilian going with me, it will slow me down." He was finally looking her in the eye, this was a very good sign. "You have no idea how bad things can get."

She lifted an eyebrow, and he had the good sense to backtrack. "You're right. Of course you know how bad it can get. But things are going to move fast, and I can't afford to be worried about you when my focus needs to be on retrieving the Lieutenant and Riley."

"I get it Kota, I really do. But how much of an advantage is Noah to you when you're on missions?" Nobody spoke. "Nate, tell me the truth." She emphasized the word truth.

"He makes a huge difference."

"Then so will I. Kota, I promise, if you tell me I am becoming a liability, I'll hole up someplace. But I think you'll find I can help. Noah is my world, I wouldn't put him in more danger. You have to believe me." She watched as he looked from Sierra to Nate. It was obvious they worked as a unit.

"Sierra, get two reservations," Kota relented.

"Already did."

Kali had never been someplace so humid. She and Kota had a cover, they were boyfriend and girlfriend, and they had to walk down the steps from the airplane. He led the way, making sure she didn't have a miss-step. Her throat tightened, because she knew it would be the exact thing Noah would have done.

As soon as they landed, Kota turned on his phone. Sierra downloaded information about a compound the Rixitron executive, Abel Trent, owned on the western tip of the island. It was closely guarded. She got them reservations in the honeymoon suite at a luxury resort close to his home, and a Range Rover was waiting for them at the airport rental agency.

"How far is it to the resort?"

"First we're going to one of the hotels in the city, and you're going to the spa, Sierra has it all arranged."

"What? We need to get to Riley and Noah."

"No, I need to get some supplies, and you need go to the spa."

"It makes no sense, let me go with you." He was driving through a congested part of the city filled with taxi cabs and drunken tourists.

"Look Kali, I don't think anyone is watching us, but in case they are, we need to make this look plausible. You going to a spa makes it plausible. You promised to follow my direction, well this is what I'm asking you to do. This is the first thing I've asked and you're already giving me shit?" He cut his gaze away from the traffic to glare at her. Kali slunk in her seat. He was absolutely right.

"I'm sorry. I wanted to help. But if you could tell me why you want me to do something, instead of dictating to me it would help."

"I keep forgetting you aren't in the military. Yeah, I'll try to remember."

"Here," he handed her his phone with all of the information Sierra provided about her reservations. Then he pulled up in front of the hotel, reached over and gave her a hug. She stiffened, and he whispered her in ear. "Relax, you're Noah's woman. But we're lovers, so play the part." She hugged him got out of the car to go to the spa.

Four hours later, Kali sat in the lobby nervously waiting for her *lover*. When he arrived, she watched as women looked him up and down in appreciation and she longed for Noah. She couldn't feel him at all. She prayed she would be able to when they got to the resort. Kali remembered how she had clearly felt him when she had been in the adjoining room and he had been angry and frustrated. She immediately recognized Noah's energy. She'd been stunned, scared...overjoyed. Now she needed to focus, and make sure she could feel him from a distance.

"Hey, you sure are concentrating hard on something." She hadn't even noticed Kota dropping into the seat next to her.

"Are we ready to leave?"

"Yeah. It just looked like you weren't doing so well, so I thought we could just sit here for a few minutes." Kali looked sideways at the man. He picked up her hand and held it. She saw him stare at the scar on her wrist, his mouth grim.

"I really don't remember you doing anything to hurt me, Kota," she said in a low voice.

"It's not that. I just know Noah's going to hand me my ass when he finds out you're here."

"Yeah, probably." Every time Kota did something to pretend they were a couple it made her long for Noah. *Please let him be okay.*

"Can you really help find him?" He was scanning the people in the lobby.

"If I didn't think I could, I wouldn't have insisted on coming. I don't want to be a liability. I want him safe and sound. This isn't an ego thing or a girlfriend thing."

"Good," he said, squeezing her hand. "Let's move on out."

* * *

When they checked into the resort, Kali noticed Kota had an extra suitcase, but the thought immediately fled her mind when she heard the desk clerk checking them into the honeymoon suite. Dammit, it was something she hadn't considered and she should have.

Kota was easily able to manage their luggage and still hold her hand all the way up to their room. In no way was he coming on to her, but the whole situation made her feel awkward and weary.

She stumbled. Her cheek exploded in pain.

"Kali."

Blinking she saw Kota was holding her against the corridor wall. Had he hit her?

"Kota, what happened?" She'd been walking down the hall and the pain came out of nowhere, like a fist to the side of her head.

"You tell me. Let's get into the room first." He picked up the one new suitcase, and wrapped his arm around her, leaving the other bags in the middle of the hallway. He moved quickly down the corridor to their room and got her to the bed.

"Let me get our other suitcases. I'll be right back." He rushed out of the room, and Kali jumped off the bed and went to the bathroom to examine her face. She was flushed. Did she see a little bit of a red mark? She couldn't tell. It felt like she had been hit. Hit. Noah. She'd been thinking about him, trying to tune into him, and he'd been hit. She grabbed Kota by the front of his shirt as he came through the door.

"It was Noah, he was being hit, it's what I felt."

"Use your inside voice Kali."

She realized she had been practically yelling.

Kota closed the door and gently pushed her onto the bed, crouching in front of her. "Okay, you could actually feel Noah?" She could see the excitement in his eyes, and it matched her own.

"Yes. I could. He's in trouble, he was being hit."

"It's okay Kali, its good news. He's alive. He's conscious, those are two good things." Kali looked into Kota's dark eyes, and realized the man was right.

"We've got to get to him." Kota got up, pulled out his laptop and phone, and had Sierra on the line, while booting up the laptop. Kali sat on the bed, leaned against the headboard and closed her eyes. Tuning out Kota's voice, she focused on Noah.

Chapter Twenty-Two

He needed to give Riley another day. He knew there wasn't a chance in hell he would fail to find and hide the woman and child. The parents had done a good job of keeping them safe on the Navajo reservation in New Mexico, but they didn't understand the resources the Rixitron Corporation had at their disposal. What truly baffled him is why Seth Natani would have gone on a long term undercover assignment when his woman was pregnant, it made no sense. Seth was *found*, Noah expected him to have better protective instincts where his woman and child were concerned.

"Are you paying attention to us?"

Spittle dripped down the side of Noah's face. He didn't blink, he just stared forward at the beige wall.

"Tell us where Sarah Johnson is. Tell us what you were looking for when we found you in our offices. Who got away?"

Noah grunted in agony as he was kicked in exactly the same place as before, toppling him forward. He was unable to break his fall because his hands were tied behind his back. At least his chin hit carpet, it could be worse, remembering a time in Eastern Europe.

"What the fuck are you smiling about?" Another kick.

"Fuck." Noah's rib cracked. Not good.

"Not smiling now, are you asshole? Tell us who got away."

Noah stayed down. One more kick and he knew he'd pass out, it's what he needed. He needed to buy time. He felt the toe of the boot prodding the spot they just kicked.

"Ahhhh..."

"Tell us. Where is Sarah Johnson?"

One more kick you asshole. Come on. This pain could stop anytime now as far as he was concerned. One more kick.

He pressed in harder. "What did you find in the office?"

"Nothing." Dammit, he hadn't meant to say anything. The man pushed in more, Noah was seeing stars. *Good.*

Noah?

"Tell us where Sarah is." He was pressing and twisting with his toe. Noah let out a gasp. Blackness was beginning to edge around his vision.

Noah can you hear me?

"Are you listening? We want to know where Sarah is. Who was with you? Where did he go?"

Are you all right Noah? We're coming to get you.

"Tell us what we want to know!"

"Fuck you!" One last kick.

Noah! No!

Darkness.

"Riley isn't with him. He's in New Mexico." Kota gave her a strange look, and then he got on the phone to talk to Sierra. She hurt and could barely make it from the bed to the bathroom. Luckily Kota was looking at the laptop and talking on the phone so he didn't notice.

She desperately wanted them to go after Noah…now! But she saw how determined Noah was that this woman and child be protected. How could she not put their needs first? When she could finally stand up straight and breathe she went back into the room and listened to the conversation. Sierra was on speaker along with Nate.

"How about Noah, does Kali have a bead on his location?"

"I'm here Nate."

"Are you okay Kali? You don't sound so good." Sierra's voice came through the line.

"Are you hurt? What's wrong Kali? What happened?" Sarah's questions were clipped and to the point.

"I'm not hurt. I'm just feeling the effects of Noah's pain. He was beaten."

"Ah fuck," Nate and Kota said in unison.

"Kali, Kota told me you said Riley was in New Mexico. I can't figure out why he didn't call in. It doesn't make any fucking sense," Sierra sounded completely frustrated.

"All I know is there is a woman and a baby Riley is supposed to protect, and they are on a reservation in New Mexico. Noah keeps thinking he has to hold on for just another day." Kali heard her voice break. "What does it mean? Does he mean he gets to die tomorrow?"

"Oh honey, no. He's stalling before he kicks ass and breaks out."

"He's in bad shape, Sierra," Kali said to the voice on the phone trying to reassure her. "I think they broke his ribs when they were kicking him."

"Ah fuck," Nate and Kota said again.

"Kali, how are you feeling this? Are you really so connected you can feel it when he is being kicked?'

"Yes," Kali answered Sarah.

"Kota, is Kali looking physically well or is she manifesting symptoms?"

Dammit. Kota immediately came around the desk, and pulled her arm away from around her waist.

"Sarah, she's wincing when I move her arm, and she's hunched over."

"Kali, are you just psychically feeling his pain,

or do you think you have sustained injuries?"

Kali had been afraid to lift her shirt in the bathroom. She did so now, and she and Kota looked at her side, and she twisted around to view her lower back.

"Sarah, there is a distinct red mark in the shape of a boot on her lower back. She's lightly bruised."

"Palpitate the area."

Kali let out a hiss as Kota probed the area. It hurt. But not nearly to the extent she had felt when she was connected to Noah, and she explained it to everyone.

"Jesus Kali, it's amazing," Nate said.

"It's scary," Sarah said. "But we can use this to our advantage. Kota, let's try to determine how badly Noah has been hurt, and where. Have Kali lay down on her good side." Sarah walked him through the quick examination, and she agreed it was likely Noah's liver and kidneys were fine, but he probably had bruised, fractured or broken ribs.

"He's had worse, and still managed to fight his way out of more dangerous places than some mansion in Cancun," Kota assured Kali as he pulled down her T-Shirt. He went over to his kit and got her some ibuprofen.

"Take these, and try to get some rest."

"Are you kidding? We need to go and get him."

"Kali, one, its daylight, it's not the right time to go. Two, you're not going. Three, I've got some reinforcements who will be here in a couple of hours. Then we'll be going."

"Who are the reinforcements?"

"I'd rather not say."

"Mercenaries? You're trusting mercenaries? Are you out of your mind?"

"Kali, do I have to remind you again?" This time Kota sounded angry, and Kali couldn't blame him. What the hell did she know?

"How are you going to pinpoint his location once you get to the house?"

"I'm not going to have to Kali, the lieutenant won't be waiting around to be rescued, and he will probably take out some of those assholes by the time we arrive."

Truth. Kali relaxed. The man in front of her, who had turned from pseudo boyfriend to scary soldier told her Noah, her man with the broken ribs, will probably fight off his attackers. She was going to hang onto Kota's belief like a lifeline.

"What do we do now?"

"We wait. It's what we do almost all the time, it's a waiting game. We'll also check in with Sierra and see if she has any clue why Riley went missing. It makes no sense for him to have gone to ground. We always back one another up."

Kali tried to sit against the headboard to see if she could get in tune with Noah, but it was too uncomfortable, and she couldn't reach him. It was like she was hitting a blank wall. She assumed it was because he was unconscious. Finally she stretched out on the bed and tried to get some rest.

"Thank God!"

"What?" Kali tried to focus, it was tough. She looked around the strange room. For one brief moment seeing Kota scared. Then she remembered who he was and why they were there.

"Riley finally called in."

Kali sat up and gasped. If she hurt this much, she couldn't imagine what Noah was feeling. "Where was he? Why hadn't he called?"

"One of the thugs from Rixitron was headed out west to get the mother and baby. He hopped in the trunk of the guy's car, and he almost immediately got into a wreck."

"Oh God, is Riley okay?"

"Yeah, he is. It just wasn't until they got the car towed to the impound lot he regained consciousness, and it took him awhile to get someone's attention so he could get out. The damn thing was crumpled up solid. He was damn lucky to get out and still be able to stand."

"Where did this happen?"

"Right outside of Denton," Kota explained.

"Why hadn't he called?"

"Poor bastard cracked his cell phone as he was getting into the trunk. It was useless. It was all kinds of *Murphy's Luck*."

"So how soon before he'll be back in Atlanta?"

"He's not going to Atlanta. He called in to arrange for a helicopter from North Texas to New Mexico. He doesn't think he will beat the guy there, but he's hoping he'll have a better shot of getting people to cooperate with him than the bastard from Rixitron. You and Sarah are his aces. Well, you *were*, now just Sarah."

"What do you mean?"

"He plans to use Sarah with the baby's mom, the same way we used you with Sarah."

"I hope with better results. Who is this mom and baby anyway?"

"Riley and Noah found records of the baby's father, Seth Natani, he's *found* as well. He was raised by the People."

"The People?"

"It's what the Navajo call themselves. He was raised by the Natani's on the Navajo reservation in New Mexico. He's with the DEA and been on assignment for almost a year now. No one has seen or heard from him since then. He left his woman, Annie Newman with his parents, and she's given birth to a daughter, who is five months old. According to Riley, the Rixitron people want the baby really bad."

"I don't get it. Is it just because the baby is the daughter of a *found* man?"

"It has to be. What Riley can't understand, what none of us can understand…where the hell is the father?"

Kota was right, Kali couldn't imagine anything

keeping Noah away from her and their child.

Kota's phone vibrated, and he looked down. "Okay, I'm on. You'll need to stay up here. Remember, this place is a fortress. This is where all the movie stars come to get away but you need to stay in this room." He picked up his vest and the lightweight gym bag he had filled with weapons.

"Kali, you know how to use a gun, right?"

"Cop's daughter. Need I say more?" She held out her hand and he gave her an automatic pistol. She looked it over and made sure the safety was on.

"When will you be back?" She realized it was a stupid question as soon as it left her mouth, but it didn't stop her from wanting an answer.

Kota turned from the door, walked over, and gave her a hug. "It's going to be all right. We'll be back soon." Then he was gone. Kali went to the window and gazed at the beautiful black velvet night sky, and prayed Kota was right.

Chapter Twenty-Three

Noah heard voices down the hall. The carpet was soft under his cheek, and he could swear the duvet cover touching his forehead was silk. Who the hell kept a bloody prisoner on the floor in such a classy bedroom? He moved his legs and arms. No limbs broken. Definitely a plus…maybe a broken rib or two, but he was going to tell himself they were cracked. Therefore, he should be able to blow this little dollhouse easy enough. There was the fact his hands were tied behind his back. Every time he tried to pull the rope apart, it sent shards of pain up through his torso straight into his skull. Fuck.

Noah.

This time instead of pulling, he used his fingers to examine the knots, and found them slippery with his blood. He might be able to use it to his advantage. He worked at the knots for long minutes, finally loosening one, and untangling another. Maybe, just maybe it was enough. He yanked hard, a red hot poker of fire shot upwards through his ribs, then his brain and he passed out.

Noah, wake up.

He heard voices coming closer down the hall. He pulled at his bindings one more time and they ripped apart. He was up and beside the door in less than a second. The door opened, and he pulled the first man in by his head and twisted, hearing a satisfying pop before dropping him to the floor. The second man was bringing up his arm with a gun, when Noah kicked the man in his chest. He grabbed the discarded gun, and stood on the man's neck until he passed out. Checking the hallway, he was satisfied when he didn't see anyone else. He closed and leaned heavily on the door, hissing as he tried to take a breath around the fire in his chest.

It had taken less than a minute, and thanks to the thick carpeting, it had been done very quietly, but Noah still wasn't taking any chances. He realized the voice he had been hearing in his head was Kali, which meant she had to be near. Not only was he trying to save his own ass, but now he had to take under consideration she was being held in this same location.

"Kali," he whispered. "Where are you?"

Talk in your head. I can hear you. I'm about three miles away. Kota should already be there with help.

Tell him not to come. I can get out on my own.

Too late, I'm sure he's on the premises already. Do you even know how many people you're up against?

He was not going to have this argument. *We're in Cancun, right?*

Yes.

Get in a cab, and get to the airport.

I will do no such...

The sound of gunshots rent the night. Noah heard feet pounding above his head.

Kali, I hear gunshots. Things have gone wrong, Kota would have planned to come in silent. You've got to get out of there. Promise me you'll get into a cab and go to the airport. I want you on US soil.

I will, I promise. Stay safe.

Hearing the truth and conviction in her words allowed him to focus on the sounds around him. He bent down and made sure the second man was still unconscious, then pulled the gun from the shoulder holster of the dead man.

Opening the door a little, he saw no one in the hall. To the right were stairs and he headed in that direction. By the time he made it to the first landing it sounded like he was back in the jungle during a full firefight, and then suddenly silence.

"If you tell me where he is, I will let you live," Dakota said in Spanish. Noah huffed out a laugh and immediately regretted his sense of humor. He was pretty sure everything was under control, but he was cautious as he peeked around the balustrade. There was Kota with a knife to the neck of a man who looked like he was going to piss himself.

"Downstairs, he's downstairs." Kota dropped

the thug onto the floor, and turned to another man. "Watch him." He raced towards the stairs, and Noah leaned out to show himself.

"What took you so long, I've been waiting for you to show up since the first bullet rang out," Kota said as he grabbed Noah's arm and wrapped it around his shoulder. "You look like shit man. What, you can't take a beating like you used to?" Kota doubled timed him up the stairs, and Noah fought back groans, trying to connect with Kali again, now he knew the fighting had ended. He couldn't reach her.

"Did you get everybody in the compound?"

"Nope, a helicopter got away."

"What about Kali, is she safe? You left her alone man." If he could have taken a swing at Kota, he would have, but he didn't have the strength. Shit, maybe the ribs were actually broken.

"I left her in the honeymoon suite of Toledaga Resort. Nobody gets in or out of there without proper ID. You can be damn sure you're not getting anywhere close to the honeymoon suite without your security codes and floor access cards. Your woman is safe."

"No she's not." The pain got much worse. "I heard the bullets flying, and I know it's not what we ever plan during an escape."

"No, Lieutenant. It was the damn helicopter. When I saw them heading for it, I had to try to stop them."

"You did the right thing," Noah assured his

man. "But as soon as I heard gunshots, and I realized Kali was alone, I told her to head to the airport."

Kota's face tightened. "Dammit." They both started running faster towards the door, the other men following them. There was a driver waiting in the Range Rover. Kota all but threw Noah into the backseat.

"Back to the hotel?"

"To the airport," both men yelled in unison.

Kali thought she was going to throw up. The cab driver drove like he was drunk, and the smells of the city weren't helping. The windows were rolled down, the air was humid, and she smelled sewer mixed in with sidewalk carts of meat and cigarette smoke. But mostly it was knowing Noah and Kota were in the middle of a gunfight and she was running away. They could be dead for all she knew. She couldn't get any sort of connection with Noah and it was killing her. Tears were dripping down her face, and the cabdriver kept looking at her in the rear view mirror instead of focusing on the road.

She'd left the laptop and everything in the hotel room for Kota. She'd called Sierra, who said to stay on the line with her, but even *that* connection died. Kali hoped when they got to the airport she could pick up a signal again. But more than that, she prayed her connection with Noah would be reestablished.

"Lady, we're here." Grabbing her meager little carry-on case, she paid the driver. Once inside she saw she had a text from Sierra—there was a ticket in her name to Atlanta. She tried calling Sierra, but all circuits were busy. Tired, she tried to smile at the reservation clerk but knew it was a failed attempt.

"Passport." Kali opened her purse, cognizant of the people behind her who were waiting.

Kali!

She dropped her purse and twirled around. He was here. Swiping her purse off the floor, she pushed past the people in line, and scanned the crowd for any sign of Noah or Kota. Then she darted towards the glass exit doors.

No. Stay inside. Stay around people.

Kali stopped so suddenly a man bumped into her. He apologized in Spanish, as she almost doubled over from the pain of contact.

Where are you? Are you all right? He didn't sound all right, he sounded like he was in agony.

Noah's hand brushed along the side of her ribcage, his other arm snaking around her holding her in place back to front. He nuzzled her neck and whispered in her ear. "You're in pain too baby and it's killing me, what happened? How did you get injured?"

It took everything she had to remain upright, knowing he was in no shape to hold her weight.

For the second, or was it the third time that night she felt tears falling down her face.

"Noah, I was afraid they were going to kill you."

He kissed the side of her jaw moving ever closer to her mouth. "I have a woman to come home to, I'm always going to make it back, Kali, always."

They both hissed in pain as she turned in his arms and carefully reached for his lips. Noah's flavor burst across her senses, it was the taste of homecoming. Could she be anymore blessed? He took control, his tongue sweeping inwards, invading her soul.

"Guys, we have minutes before we have to be on a plane to get the hell out of here."

It was like the voice came from a long ways a way. She thought she recognized it.

"Guys." Noah started to stroke her hair. Fingers snapped at her ear and she jerked back.

"What the fuck?!" Noah glared at Kota.

"We have to get the hell out of here. We still have people on the loose, remember?" Kali looked up at Noah and saw determination.

"Kali, we need to leave. It's still not safe, Abel Trent got away."

"Who?" she asked dazedly.

"The fucker from Rixitron who set us up."

"Well he can't get far, it's an island, right?" Kali asked.

"He was able to transport me without a passport to a foreign country. I'd say the guy has resources."

"Walk and talk people, walk and talk." Kota herded them towards the ticket counter. The three of them put down their passports. Sierra had somehow worked magic and got them all in the same row, despite their last minute purchase. Kali could feel Noah's pain with every step he took, despite the fact he tried to muscle through. When they got on the plane the stewardess knocked into him with the beverage cart, and Kali's knees buckled, Kota caught her.

"What the fuck?"

"She can feel your pain, Noah. She's bruised in the exact spot where you're bruised, cracked or broken." Kota insisted Noah take the seat by the window, then Kali sat in the middle and he took the aisle.

Kali breathed through her nose, fighting down nausea. How the hell was Noah even upright? When she asked the question, Kota snorted with laughter.

"I've seen the lieutenant continue fighting for three days with a concussion and a broken wrist."

Noah, picked up her hand, and started rubbing circles on her wrist with his thumb. "How can you even ask Baby, after everything you've been through? You survived the fires of hell, and came out the other side, this is nothing in comparison." He brought her palm to his lips and breathed a kiss into it. "Go to sleep, if you can."

"If you will, I can Noah." His injured ribs were

on the other side, so he pulled her against his side, cuddling her close.

"Sleep Kali, I'll be here when you wake up." She breathed in the scent of the man she loved, and tumbled into unconsciousness.

Chapter Twenty-four

"Her ribs aren't cracked. Yours are. Now hold still why I tape you up."

"How do you know, you haven't taken x-rays." Noah liked Sarah before she had tried to tell him Kali was fine. Obviously Sarah was a quack.

"She only has minor bruising. She doesn't hurt at all, when you're not moving and hurting. Watch. Kali, can you come here for a second?" Kali came over from where she was talking to Sierra. It was the first time she hadn't hovered, and it was only because he practically shoved her away.

"Is he okay?" she asked Sarah anxiously. "Are you okay Noah?" She touched the tape going around his chest. He reached up to hug her and winced. She gasped.

"Stop it Noah. You're the one who hurt her. Now lie back down." Sarah couldn't possibly be right, he looked between the two women. Kali so soft in his arms, and Sarah looking like a commander in the Navy. He reluctantly released Kali and slowly lowered himself to the hotel bed. It did feel good to be horizontal. The whole time he was moving he saw the tension forming lines bracketing Kali's mouth, and he glanced at Sarah who simply lifted an eyebrow.

"Kali, come lie beside me." All thoughts of pain fled as the woman he loved nestled beside him.

"Now both of you get some sleep. Let the others on your team take care of things for a while."

Sarah turned off the light, leaving the room in shadows as she closed the adjoining room door behind her.

"You really don't hurt?"

"Noah, don't you remember how it was when I was being shocked?"

God he was an idiot. He moved the arm of his good side, and pulled her closer, breathing in her clean scent. "Can you sleep Kali?"

"Can now…" Her words already slurred.

He kissed the top of her hair and toyed with the silky strands. He soon heard the even breathing of her sleep. Now she was sleeping, and the pain in his ribs abated, he had time to think clearly. He knew his team was focused on helping Riley, and his quest in New Mexico, which was great. But he wanted to think through what those fuckers were trying to ultimately accomplish.

He knew Sierra ran an intensive background on Abel Trent and found anomalies in the guy's financials. He had millions stashed in off-shore accounts. When he and Riley had been rifling through the offices at Rixitron, he realized how big an operation they were dealing with. Denton was one small branch, but Rixitron was a huge conglomerate, and Trent was one Senior VP who seemed to have a hell of a lot of leeway. Could he have that much autonomy without others at the company knowing? Sure Kali was asleep, Noah reached over to the nightstand and picked up his phone to do some research. He intended to know everything there was about Rixitron before the night was over.

"Fuck. Fuck. Fuck."

The words were loud, the pain was bright. "What's wrong, Noah?" Kali asked. The door to their room slammed opened.

"Lieutenant!" Nate had his gun drawn. Sierra and Kota were behind him, both had guns in their hands as well. Kali gripped her side which was hurting. Noah was off the bed and striding past his team to the other room. Sarah walked where Kali was still struggling on the bed.

"Give yourself a minute, Girlfriend."

"What just happened?"

"Looks like your man might have had an epiphany."

"How long were we sleeping?"

"About four hours. Riley's in New Mexico. He's found the Natani's, but they still won't tell him where the woman and child are. I like them, they protect their own." Sarah grinned, her teeth flashed white lighting up her beautiful face.

"I can't imagine my parents ever giving up my location," Kali said as she gingerly swung her legs over the side of the bed.

"Before we go into the other room, I want to take a quick look at your side, okay?"

"Do I have a choice?"

"Nope." Sarah pulled up Kali's shirt and palpated the area. "I still can't believe this bruise. Look, you can see the actual imprint of the asshole's boot, just like you could on Noah." Sarah traced it, and Kali's hand followed Sarah's meeting in the middle of the yellowing bruise. A buzzing sensation rushed from Kali's fingers up her arm, causing her to shiver.

"Sarah did you feel that?" Kali looked up into the wide eyes of her friend.

"It was a vibration, wasn't it?"

"Yeah." They reached out and clasped hands. Nothing.

"Well never mind. Let's get back out there and hear Noah's big revelation. It can't be anything bigger than you feeling and taking on his wounds. Thank God you didn't actually sustain a fractured rib too." They both reached out at the same time to pull Kali's shirt down over the bruise, their hands touching, brushing against her hurt flesh. This time the pulse of energy was so strong there was no mistaking it.

"Sarah, stop. Look at my bruise." Where their hands were touching the bruise, it was fading away, and Kali's normal white flesh was revealed.

"What in the hell?" Sarah drew her hand away, and put her eye up close to visually examine the area. "Kali, this makes no sense."

"Yeah, and me actually getting psychically injured *does* make sense? Sarah, touch me again. Obviously you can heal me."

"I've never been able to heal anyone before."

"Well before Noah, I've never taken on somebody's injury either. It has to have something to do with being in touch with other *found*. No pun intended."

Sarah giggled, and pressed her hand gently over Kali's bruised flesh. It tingled a little, and Sarah lifted up her hand. There was a slight lessening of the discoloration, but not like the area transformed moments before.

"I don't understand," Kali said looking down at the area.

"I do." Sarah grabbed Kali's hand. "Put your hand over mine." She again lightly applied pressure to the spot, and Kali covered Sarah's hand. This time there was a distinct vibration, a heat, and then it stopped. They lifted their hands, and the bruise had completely disappeared.

"How do you feel Kali?" She stood up and bent side to side.

"I feel great." She grinned. She reached over and gave Sarah a big hug, then ran to the door. "Noah, come here," she said as she opened the door. All four occupants of the room looked up as she called out.

"What's wrong?"

"Nothing. But Sarah can heal you. Come in here." Kali felt Sarah touch her shoulder.

"I might as well show everybody. We don't need any secrets among us."

She was right. Kali stepped aside. This was the first time Kali had ever seen Sarah look nervous, usually the young doctor was in total control. Nate noticed as well, because he immediately stepped up.

"Are you okay, Sarah?"

"I'm fine," she said giving him a wan smile. She turned to Noah. They had been sitting or standing around Sierra's computer set up, and she motioned him toward one of the beds. "Can you lie down? I think it would be best."

She unwound the bandages from Noah's ribs, and within minutes not only was all the horrific bruising gone, but by his ability to move pain free, he and Sarah were convinced his ribs were knit back together. Once again, he needed to put his hands over Sarah's. But the healing worked.

"So can you only heal other *found*?" Sierra asked.

"I don't know." Sarah looked a little lost.

"How the hell would she know, Sierra?" Nate all but growled at his teammate.

It was awfully interesting how protective Nate was of Sarah, Kali thought.

Isn't it?

She smiled at Noah. *When do we get to go back to the other room, now we're both healed?* She asked her soon to be husband.

"Sarah, I ended up with a cut in Cancun, do you want to try healing it?" Kota asked.

Kali and Noah both looked over at Kota, they didn't know he had been injured. He pulled off the jacket he was wearing and pulled off his shirt, an angry gash showed on his bicep. It was obviously a knife wound.

"Why the hell wasn't your coat cut?" Noah demanded.

"Not my coat." Kota grinned. Noah laughed, and Kali realized Kota probably stole it from someone in the mansion to cover his wound.

Sarah went over to Kota and placed her hand on his wound. Nothing happened. "Kali?" Kali came over and placed her hand over Sarah's. Everybody watched in amazement as the wound slowly looked less angry, and after ten minutes it had pulled together and scabbed over.

"It's fucking amazing," Nate breathed.

"Itches though," Kota complained. Sierra hit him on his good shoulder.

Noah, Kali and Sarah looked at one another. Kali wished she could feel happy about this.

Chapter Twenty-Five

Riley finally called in again with his status. He had a lead on Annie Newman and on Seth Natani, the baby's father. Annie had gone into the desert with Seth's grandmother. Apparently the grandmother had a very old home that had been in the family since the early 1800's, and after a certain point it was only accessible by horseback. The grandmother was known to the community to have the second sight and knew Annie and the baby would be in grave danger if they didn't go into hiding.

"Sakuro pulled in some favors and managed to speak to Seth's DEA task force leader. He's so deep under cover they haven't heard from him in three months. The last they heard, he was in Florida. He's one of their best operatives. Whenever one of their men have been uncovered, they were assassinated, their head left on the local police station's doorstep. So they're sure Seth is still alive."

"Are they getting any information from him?"

"No, but three of Lobado's shipments have gone wrong. The DEA's confiscation rate is at an all-time high. They know someone very high in Lobado's organization has to be coordinating things, and they think it is Seth."

"How much longer before they pull him out."

"They can't, they're not sure he's still in Florida, or if it's safe to pull him out."

"So meanwhile Annie and her baby are in danger from Rixitron, and he could be killed at any moment. That's just great," Sierra said with disgust.

"I'm going to see if I can get a lead on Trent. I owe the bastard." Riley said.

"How are you doing after your night in the trunk?" Nate asked.

"I'm fine, but I think I'm going to be avoiding elevators for the foreseeable future."

They talked a bit more about how to track down the man in New Mexico, and Sierra told the men her ideas for hacking into Lobado's organization. As soon as the phone was disconnected, Noah let out a huge yawn and Kota snickered. Nate laughed while Sierra found something fascinating to look at on her computer screen.

"What's so funny?" Sarah asked, Kali who just blushed.

Noah couldn't help it, he laughed and grabbed Kali's hand and headed for the door. "I'm really tired, and Kali needs to tuck me in, Sarah." Even with Sarah's dark skin, Noah could tell she was blushing. "Good night." He hustled Kali down the hall to the room they had shared, was it just two nights ago?

It took him two tries to insert the room key into the slot. He glanced over at Kali, her eyes were hot with passion. God, he needed to get her inside the room. The door opened, but when she took a step toward the open doorway, he shook his head.

What? Why.

Let me just check the room baby.

He peered down the hall and nodded when he saw Nate standing outside the other room, watching. He gave Kali a hard kiss before leaving her in the corridor, and went into the hotel room. It took him less than a minute to ensure it was safe. When he opened the door, Kali was standing there looking dazed and needy. He reached out and brushed the back of his fingers against her flushed cheek, relishing her soft flesh.

"Come inside baby." He watched aghast, as one lone tear trickled down her cheek. "What's wrong Kali?" His voice and mind cried the question at the same time.

She staggered against him, into the room.

"Kali, tell me, what's wrong? Are you hurting again? Do I need to get Sarah?"

"No, I'm fine. I've just been so scared. I've never, been so scared." More tears.

"Baby, I'm so sorry, I didn't mean to scare you. It's the last thing I wanted to do. I'm giving up my commission, going forward it's you and I. We're going to have a nice boring little life, raising our family."

"How can we with people after us?"

Noah knew he couldn't answer the question. All he could really do was reassure Kali they were together and she was loved. That he could do.

Sending a quick prayer of thanks to Sarah, he bent down and picked up the woman who had become the center of his world, and gently placed her in the center of the bed. She gazed at him in wonder, like she was seeing him for the first time all over again.

"You're here, you're really here," she said as she cupped his face.

"Yes baby, I'm here." For the longest time, they stared into one another's eyes, seeing their future. Eventually heat began to expand, and languid touches started, who began he couldn't say. He pulled her shirt over her head, and divested her of her filmy bra, ensuring she was healed. His touch was tentative over the spot recently bruised.

"No. I'm fine. See?" She took his hand and pressed it tightly against her warm flesh, when she arched up, he grabbed it worried he hurt her.

"Noah, your touch arouses me." He slowly smiled. His Kali had been healed. "Now you, let me see you."

Noah yanked his shirt off revealing his smooth even brown flesh, and she pushed him over. He allowed her to straddle him, enjoying the feel of her warm core nestled against his waist. "You are healed," she said in awe.

"I don't know Kali, I think further testing is required," he smiled. His hands reached down the back of the waistband of her loose jeans and cupped the succulent curves of her ass. "Let's get you out of these."

"Only if you get out of yours, after all, fair's fair." Her eyes shimmered like gemstones, but she was smiling. He rolled her over, and once again was able to pull her pants off without even unbuttoning or unzipping.

"You need to eat more."

"I need to buy clothes that fit."

"You need to eat more. Nate will teach you." He was out of jeans, and rummaging through the nightstand. He had the condom packet in hand when he felt her insecurity hit him. Dammit. "Baby, you're beautiful, but I worry about you. I've seen pictures of you before you were taken, you know this isn't a healthy weight for you, that's all." He grabbed her hand, and had her circle his cock. "Could I be this hard, if you didn't do it for me?"

The slow smile and sense of satisfaction had a bead of pre-cum leaking from the head of his penis, and she dipped down and licked it up. "Fuck Kali, you're killing me here."

"Noah, you've been mine all my life and I almost lost you." Her hand trembled.

"Baby, I was fine."

"No. No lies." Eyes the color of sapphire looked

at him, and he tried to untangle the thoughts and feelings in his own heart so he could explain it to her. He rolled over, and pulled her down on top of him again, he loved it when her slight body covered his. Breast to chest, heart to heart.

"Can you feel me?"

"Always."

"Please baby, really look inside, really look, I'm begging you." For long minutes they lied there, so close.

"I see, Noah. I see your confidence, I see your abilities. You're extraordinary. You are capable of more than the others, but you're still human. You can still die."

"I can die crossing the street." He traced soft patterns down her back feeling every prominent vertebrae, cursing the people who tortured and starved the woman of his heart.

"Now, baby, look again. Look at what I see when I think of you in danger. I know you're strong and capable too, but look at yourself from my perspective, as someone I would normally be sent to protect." Her skin was so soft, up and down. He dipped even lower, to the small of her lower back, and then cupped her firm buttocks. She was so warm and smooth, so fragile, so his.

"How can you possibly see me as fragile after what I endured?" She kept her head resting against his neck, her confusion clear.

"Oh baby, I have never doubted your strength, and I never have questioned your will or your courage. But they wanted you alive. If someone wants you dead, you're dead. That's what scares the fuck out of me. Someone wants me dead? Someone wants my team dead? Well, they're the ones who will end up dead."

"I'm still going to be scared for you. I'm going to worry when you cross the street, because you mean the world to me. But okay, maybe I won't worry as much as I have been." She licked the side of his neck like a kitten.

Spreading her legs so she straddled him, her moist heat pressed was against him. Only slightly moist, but he planned to fix that. "Lift up."

"Hmm?"

He coaxed her into a sitting position on top of him, smoothing his hands down the sides of her nipped in waist until he had a hold of her hips. Then he easily lifted her up. "Noah..." she squeaked.

"Right here," he assured her, as he placed her right where he wanted her, close to his lips. Was there ever anything as gorgeous as seeing the flushed parted folds of Kali's sex displayed for him?

"You can't."

"Watch me."

She struggled to get away, but she was no match for his strength, and he kept her still. Long languid strokes of his tongue soon had all of her attempts to leave his embrace flying out of her head. He felt her pleasure like it was his own. It was his own, only softer. He reached around and brought his fingers into play, lifting the hood of her clit so he could suckle the little nub, and those soft waves turned into the kind of frantic pulses of need he was used to.

"That feels. Oh. Please, some more. Noah!" He licked. He sucked. He bit. She whimpered. She thrashed. She screamed.

She slumped over, but despite her languor she quickly scooted down so she could kiss him. "I like how we taste," she whispered. She did, he felt her rush of pleasure at their combined flavors and he was close to exploding, and then she felt that. They were starting the loop of sensation, where their thoughts and feelings were merging into one luscious feast of need.

"Fuck me now, Noah. Fuck me hard. I need to know we're together, and we're both alive." He went to roll her over, but she stopped him. "No, from behind this time, with me on my knees, I need you to grind yourself into me."

His head swam with the image, and in seconds her ass was there, and he spread her wide, seeing her soft wet sex, and plunged deep. They both cried out as they experienced one another's pleasure. With each plunge and pull their feelings entwined, multiplying the effect of ecstasy. When they came, they shouted, unclear where one ended and the other began.

Chapter Twenty-Six

Kali was really nervous about meeting Admiral Nelson Sakuro it was almost like meeting Noah's father or grandfather. When she said as much to Sarah, she just laughed.

"Girlfriend, it could be a whole hell of a lot worse."

"How do you figure?"

"You could be meeting the boy's mother." Kali swallowed, she hadn't considered that. She and Sarah were in the room down the hall that she had been sharing with Noah. Sarah deemed it the Love Shack. They actually were working on shielding.

"I don't want Noah to always be able to read me," Kali complained.

"Of course you don't. There are going to be times you're going to want to beat him over the head with a frying pan, and you'll want to be able to sneak up behind him to do it," Sarah said with a straight face.

"Actually I was thinking more about surprising him on birthdays. Or the times when I was overemotional about something, and I just needed to work it out myself, and I didn't really need him rummaging around through my psyche."

"Okay, I guess your relationship dynamic is a little different than mine."

"How many boyfriends have you had?"

"Boyfriends? I've had lovers, Kali. I haven't had a boyfriend since I was in high school."

"Horse pucky, I saw you blushing when Noah was dragging me off to the Love Shack."

"That's because the man was obvious about it, but all right. I've had three lovers since high school, and one boyfriend in high school who I never…well…you know. What about you?"

"Just the one before Noah. I was a late bloomer."

"I had six brothers who chased everyone away. I didn't have a chance until I went away to college, but I made up for lost time," Sarah grinned. "Speaking of which, what's the four-one-one on Nate?"

"Nate?"

"You know, junk food boy? The one who could bend me to his will and bend me in every other direction as well?"

"From what Noah has said, everyone is single. They haven't felt comfortable being in harm's way and putting their family through that kind of worry."

"People in the military do it all the time."

"Yeah, but this team is an elite force, and they have all volunteered for the riskiest assignments. Noah's resigning now we're together."

Sarah let out a low whistle. "So you guys are going to be permanently permanent."

"Yep, babies and grandbabies."

Sarah came over and wrapped her arms around Kali. "I'm so happy for you."

"I can't believe it. I feel like a part of me was missing all my life and is now back in place," she said, hugging Sarah back.

"I hope one day to find someone like that, but in the meantime I think a dalliance with a junk food addict sounds like a real plan."

"Dalliance, sure, Sarah." Kali might have been trying to work on blocking Noah, but it didn't mean she wasn't picking up on some of the vibes coming from Sarah whenever she talked about Nate.

"Enough about the big guy, let's talk about the admiral. Why do you think he'd risk coming here? It has to be big. He had to make sure he wasn't seen by a lot of people to get here. It must be pretty important if he wanted to see all of us in person."

"I would have been fine if he didn't want to see me in person," Kali mumbled.

"Yeah, I bet." Sarah laughed as there was a knock on the door.

"It's me, Sierra."

"Showtime, Girlfriend." Sarah hooked her arm through Kali's.

Noah had a bad feeling. Yes, everything sounded good, and his team was excited to be getting out of the cramped quarters of the hotel, but it didn't feel right. Another shoe was going to drop, unfortunately he didn't know where or when. But he knew it would drop. And another thing making him antsy was t for the last hour he couldn't feel Kali. She'd told him what she'd planned. She wanted to work on blocking him, putting up shields so to speak. Made sense. Hell, he had already been surreptitiously doing the same thing, only he'd been an asshole and not told her. They needed their privacy. But still, he *wanted* to be able to reach out and feel Kali. He didn't like being cut off from her. After only three days of practicing, not being able to feel her presence was like losing a limb.

He breathed a sigh of relief when the three women came through the door, and then he did a double take when he realized how nervous Kali looked. Sarah motioned him over. He put his arm around Kali, and Nelson Sakuro walked across the room to greet Sarah and Kali.

"Ladies, it's an honor and privilege to meet both of you. My name is Admiral Nelson Sakuro, and I cannot express how deeply I regret people from the Navy have been involved in trying to cause you harm."

Noah watched as the admiral's patented charm

once again worked wonders. They might say promotions were entirely based on merit and performance, but it was bullshit, they were also based on your ability to play politics, and Nelson Sakuro had that in spades.

"It's not your fault Admiral. Noah has told me how much you have done for him, and the *found*. I know you are doing everything in your power to stop these people."

Sakuro could let go of Kali's hand any time now, Noah thought. Nate knocked into his shoulder on the way to the mini bar. He looked up and his friend gave him a knowing grin. He flipped him off.

"And you Dr. Johnson, we intend to get you back to practicing medicine as soon as possible." Sarah and Kali both stiffened, waiting for the admiral to say more, but he didn't.

We didn't tell him about Sarah's new abilities, or about our ability to communicate.

That's good. I don't know why, but that's good.

Noah turned back to the area housing Sierra's computer monitors, allowing Sakuro to talk to Kali and Sarah. Nelson was his godfather. He loved the man like he did his grandfather, and he knew he had only the best of intentions...but it was the fact he was so good at politics that made Noah wary of telling him everything. His team had followed his lead beautifully. No one divulged any information other than what Noah provided. Dammit, Noah liked knowing exactly who the bad guys were. All the gray was driving him insane.

He looked up from the computer screen. Nelson Sakuro was a good man, there was no question in his mind. The man's heart was in the right place, but he swam with a bunch of sharks, and looking at Kali, Noah bring himself to trust Sakuro with the information about Kali or Sarah.

"Well, I guess now everyone is here, I should actually tell you why I came."

Nate had pulled in the chairs from the other room. Everyone was huddled in around the small desk area.

"Rydell found Mai and brought her home."

"That's wonderful," Sarah clapped her hand over her mouth, tears welling up in her eyes. Nate put his arm around her. "How is she?"

"She's pretty upset," the admiral answered.

"What did they do to her?" Kali asked in tremulous voice. Noah went to Kali. He hated hearing the despair in her voice. They didn't have to be connected for him to know she was reliving the hell she had gone through at the hands of her captors. She rested her head on his chest, unable to look at the admiral.

"She said they did nothing. In fact, according to her, the time she spent with her captors was the most enlightening time of her entire life. She told us she learned more about her real self and what she was meant to be and do. She felt like it was a homecoming. She resents the hell out of Dave Rydell for taking her away."

"What?" Sierra shouted.

"You've got to be shitting me," Nate said with disgust.

"Who were these people? Wasn't it Rixitron? The same people Dan was working with, the same people holding me hostage in Cancun? How did they talk their way out of kidnapping her in the first place?" Noah's questions came out rapid fire.

"When we recovered her, she was staying in a penthouse of the One Hotel in Taiwan. She was alone. Dave said he tracked them down to a clinic in Taiwan. He was positive it was where she had been held for the last week, but when he got there, it was an empty room. "

"Where did he think she was for the previous three weeks?"

"Mainland China. He has no idea why she was brought back to Taiwan."

"How did he find her at the penthouse?"

"Apparently she woke up, found herself there alone, and called down to the front desk asking for someone named Mr. Phuong, when they couldn't find someone by that name staying at the hotel she got very agitated. Eventually the authorities were called and then her parents. They contacted Rydell who came and got her."

"Is there a Mr. Phuong working for Rixitron?"

"No."

"I don't understand," Sarah said.

"The best Dave can figure is she was taken and brainwashed. She's convinced she spent time with Mr. Phuong who supposedly explained to her she had been taken from her real parents as a young child, and Phuong was working to reunite them."

"Did he explain to her why they were taking so damn long to come out of the woodwork?" Kali asked bitterly.

"According to Mai, it was Phuong's job to deprogram her before she could be reunited. Mr. Phuong said her supposed real family knew how poisoned her mind had been by the people who had raised her, and the education they had forced upon her."

"That makes no sense. Mai is becoming one of the most accomplished violinists and mathematicians in the world, she knows better than to believe such nonsense. Why would she buy into something like this after just one month?" Sarah was in tears, working her way up to sobs, which also didn't make sense.

Noah, it would have been her too.

"Rydell is out of the picture. The Taiwanese government brought in specialists to work with her. They're good, we've checked them out. Unfortunately they're neuroscientists, not specialists in brainwashing techniques."

"So do you have any good news for us?"

"Yes, I do. You're going to move operations to California."

"Pardon me Sir, but we can't go to San Diego. We don't know who is rogue."

"I didn't say San Diego, now did I Chief," Sakuro rounded on Sierra. "I said California.

You're headed for the strawberry fields. I want you near the John Wayne Airport, in case you need to fly out. It'll put you close enough I can check in regularly without anyone being the wiser and…"

"Disneyland," Nate cried, coaxing a giggle out of Sarah.

"Rixitron is headquartered there," Noah stated.

"Give the man a cigar." Sakuro gave him a grim look. They realized this was not going to be a short or easy assignment.

"Where are Kali and Sarah going to be located?"

"I'm going with you."

Noah hugged Kali close and looked at Sakuro. He didn't like what he was feeling from the man.

"Son, you know they are going to be after Ms. Wachowski and Dr. Johnson. You and your team will be the best people to protect them."

"Keeping them far away and under wraps will be the best way to protect them," Nate growled for Noah.

"Son, do you want to explain to me how your ribs got healed?" The room got so quiet the air conditioner sounded like a 747 taking off. "Noah, I saw the footage from the Atlanta airport security cameras. You and Kali were both injured. Your ribs were obviously fractured if not broken. Now they aren't. Between the three of you, you can speak eighteen languages. You Noah, can find things that can't logically be found, and Kali, you could probably teach a gorilla to speak aloud. Dr. Johnson, if I had to bet, healed these two. We don't need any of you under lock and key, we need everyone working together to fight these motherfuckers. As a matter of fact, I'm working to get Niko brought over to the states. We know he's a target, so he might as well make himself useful."

Sarah was the first one to fidget. "I don't…"

"Shh, you don't have to tell him a thing," Nate said.

"No she doesn't. None of you do. But I know you. You've worked as a team for over six years. It's obvious Kali isn't going to leave Noah. Sarah, I'm sorry, I know you just got roped into this goat rodeo, but I think you're stuck."

"Don't listen to him, you're not stuck."

Noah watched as Sarah looked at Nate for reassurance.

"Sarah, Nate's right, you're not stuck, the choice is yours to make," Noah assured her. "But you are a target. I think for the time being you're safer with us."

"I have to explain this to my family, I can't just drop off the face of the planet. Despite my phone calls, I know I've probably scared the hell out of them. What do I tell them?" Once again she looked to Nate.

"We'll go with you, we'll help to explain."

"Oh yeah, just what I need. A bunch of Navy testosterone explaining to my six brothers how I'm the target of a multi-national conspiracy, and you're the guys going to keep me safe. You won't live to finish the explanation."

"Ah, Sarah?" Kota started.

Noah watched as she looked at the man who had been sitting quietly near the window.

"Yes, I know. You all are big strong warriors, but my brothers have been watching over me all of my life, they would die for me. There is no way they are going to let me leave with you."

Noah, Nate and Kota exchanged glances. "Young lady, you have a very good point, and that is part of the reason I'm here. Chief Petty Officer Mathers sent me all of the information on not just your brothers, but also your mother and father. You have a very impressive family." The admiral's sincerity was clear.

"Thank you, Sir, I think so too."

"I took the liberty of contacting your father this morning, and meeting with him. I explained the situation to him, and he invited us to your house for dinner tonight."

Noah worked hard to contain a chuckle as Sarah's eyes widened and Nate winced.

This is going to be interesting.

Noah looked down at Kali, and then kissed the top of her head. *No more interesting than the first time I went to dinner at your house after we started sleeping together. Remember how your dad took me out to the garage to look over the car he was working on?*

The old Bel Air?

Yeah, he really wanted to make it clear if I hurt you, he'd rip me apart.

Kali giggled, everyone in the room looked at them, and Sakuro raised an eyebrow.

Chapter Twenty-Seven

Frank and Lila Johnson's requested they come as soon as possible, because they missed Sarah. Dinner would happen when it would happen, and introductions with the siblings and families could happen then.

After a tearful reunion with their daughter, Kali was stunned to find herself swept into their arms like she was one of their children.

"Kelly Wachowski, we have watched you grow up. You are a gift from God to your parents, just like our Sarah was a gift to us," Lila said as she gave her another hug.

"I kept a scrapbook," Sarah shyly admitted.

"Oh my God, so did I," Kali exclaimed.

"We should have arranged for you girls to meet, but we didn't want to intrude," Frank said, his voice filled with regret. "Then when you were kidnapped..."

"Kelly, we had our church do a prayer circle for you," Lila explained.

Kali's eyes welled up.

"Mom, we call her Kali now. She and Noah remember some of where we came from." Kali, Sarah, and her parents were sitting in the kitchen while the members of the naval team were helping Sarah's youngest brother warm up the grill in the backyard.

"The admiral explained one of the men who rescued you was also a *found* child. He didn't tell us you and he remembered your lives prior to coming here. Where are you from?" Lila asked.

"I don't know."

"Are there many of you?" Frank asked.

"I don't know. I don't know. I don't know." Agony streaked through her temples, and she staggered from the table and fell to the floor. Her head hitting the hard linoleum.

"Kali? Kali, are you okay?"

Noah. Tell them I don't know. Please don't let them hurt me!

Kali!

"What the fuck happened? What did you do to her?"

"Noah, move out of the way."

It hurts so bad, why won't they stop talking? The stink of copper was everywhere. Why couldn't she just pass out? Why couldn't she just die?

Listen to me Kali, I'm here. You're safe. Nobody's going to hurt you ever again.

"Sarah, please do something, the pain is so bad.

I don't think it's ever hurt her this badly before. You've got to help her."

Was Noah crying?

"S'fine." Blood in her mouth. She tried to spit it out, but couldn't make her tongue work. They must not have used the rubber bit in her mouth when they questioned her this time.

"Sarah, she thought she was being questioned. She must have had a flashback to the electro-shock treatments they gave her."

"Jesus, Mary and Joseph, this poor girl was tortured, and our questions did this to her, Frank."

Kali could hear Lila's anguish, but she couldn't move, the pain, the agony was too much, her body wouldn't obey her commands.

"Got it Noah. Try to relax Kali, let me just touch your temples, okay sweetie?"

Kali felt hands turning her head and let out a scream. "Nooooaaaahhhh."

"Stop!"

"Noah, I have to touch her to heal her."

"Let me hold her, if she feels me holding her, maybe she'll know she's safe."

"Aren't you talking to her?" Sarah asked.

"Sarah, she's so confused between now and before. This is the worst PTSD flashback I've ever seen. Just move aside, and let me hold her."

Kali heard the whole conversation with one part of her brain, but it was so fuzzy, it came from one tinny little speaker and couldn't really be heard over the sound of her own screams of pain and pleas to not be hurt. She heard the sounds of the electro-shock machine. Heard as the dial was turned, and it was re-charged to increase the level of shock.

Can you hear the wind?

No I can hear the dial being turned.

You can't hear the wind as it rushes through the grass here in the meadow? You can't hear the song of the meadowlark? Listen Kali. Listen Kalani, can you hear it now?

Yes, Noah I can hear it.

Can you smell the wildflowers?

I can only smell the copper of my blood.

Really? These pink flowers with the yellow centers are your favorite, smell their aroma. Don't they smell nice?

They smell coppery.

I have cookies Nana made. Would you like one? Can you smell them?

Oooooh. Cloves, orange and vanilla. I can smell it Noah.

"Noah, I need to touch her, she's bleeding from her ears. I need to heal her."

"Not yet Sarah, she's still too deep, give me a little more time, or she'll just go deeper and do more damage."

Kali could hear him, his voice was so shaky. She could feel him through the red haze of her pain, and he was in agony. She felt a touch on her head and screamed.

Baby, it's me. I'm just brushing the blood away. Can you feel my fingers?

Paddles!

It's me, Noah.

It's going to hurt, Noah.

No baby, nobody's going to hurt you. It's just me, Noah. Can you open your eyes just a little and look at me baby? I'm here with you. Nobody's going to hurt you.

The lights hurt my eyes, and they'll know I'm awake and it'll get worse. The questions will start and they'll just hurt me longer and make the pain go higher.

I swear to you, I'm here and I'll protect you.

"Noah, the bleeding is getting worse."

Kali, please open your eyes. Don't you trust me?

You're just a dream. It's all been a dream. I need to leave, I need to go away this time.

"Kalani, open your eyes, don't give up on us." Before she left, she needed to reach for her dream. It didn't matter if the pain was going to get worse, not having tried to seize this perfect moment on her way to oblivion would be the true horror.

The light shot straight to her brain stem, causing her to keen in pain.

"Turn off the lights!"

She was wrapped in Noah's arms, she wasn't lying on a metal table.

"Can I touch her now?" It was Sarah's voice.

Baby, are you with us?

"Noah?" It came out as a whimper, her eyes were closed. She couldn't move. She could smell copper, her face was wet. She knew, she just knew it was tears and blood. Had Noah rescued her again? She heard a woman crying.

"Sarah, yes, hurry," Noah answered. *Sarah's going to touch your temples. It's just Sarah's hands, and I'm going to put my hands on top of hers, okay beautiful?*

Okay. She remembered, it was how Sarah healed. *Where was she? What had happened?*

She felt Sarah's small warm hands close over each side of her head. Then she felt Noah's hands encompass her hands. Tingles, immediately changing to sparks, changing to white light and then a tsunami of blessed relief overcame her entire body.

"So good, I feel so good." Kali was slipping away, but remained clearly in the kitchen. She hovered above her body, as it rested and healed. She felt the relief coming from Noah and Sarah so she knew she could safely leave them for a few moments and they wouldn't worry.

Nana, where are you Nana?

"I'm here, Kalani. I've missed you child." She hugged her, such a long sweet hug. She still smelled the same. They stood in her kitchen, holding one another for a long time. Finally parting, they rested against the sink, and stared out the window. Kali wasn't surprised to see a small boy on the tire swing outside in the yard. Of course her Nana had taken in another child to raise.

"His name is David, he's your third cousin."

Kali smiled, wishing she was actually there and could eat a cookie. "Nana, what is my purpose, what should I be doing? Everybody asks, and I just don't know, Nana. What is my purpose?"

"Oh my beautiful child, your purpose is to be you."
"That is not an answer, Nana."
"It is a true answer."
"Why did we decide it was important to go?"

"Their collective consciousness was being brought down, they were warring and many people were chasing wrong goals. There were many people who were pushed aside and forgotten. Their energy was low, but there were so many good people who were also trying to make things right, to push and pull their world towards a higher purpose. The small acts of kindness some people did was helping, so were the larger groups that tried to make a difference, but it still wasn't quite enough. We could see they were going to be at a tipping point, where they would need just a few more people to help with their struggle."

"Help in what way?"

"By doing good, and being good, it lifts up many, many others. It has an amazing ripple effect. Children, with such beautiful souls such as yours, were bound to bring such love and caring to this new place. We knew if you were strategically placed you could make the difference."

"But why someone like me? Oh yeah, I wasn't chosen, I just followed Noah."

"Oh my beautiful child, the elders were so happy when you decided to go, your energy was one of the highest. You bring the gift of light, and lift others up. You were meant to teach. Aren't you a teacher in your other world?"

"You would love the kids in my classes. I learned to teach from you, Nana."

"We have mourned the loss of our chosen children, but we know you are helping your new home and its people. You will turn the tide. Your energy and efforts will make the small and large differences necessary to ensure all that world's people are lifted up and cared for in the coming generations."

"I don't see how, Nana."

"You must trust my beautiful child, you must have trust. Now you need to go. I feel you have found your Noah again. You will have beautiful babies together. Now go."

Chapter Twenty-eight

"Nate tell the next person who opens the door, they are going to lose a limb."

Kali laughed.

"It's about time you came back to us."

She could hear and feel Noah's worry.

"Kali, can you open your eyes?"

She looked up in to her friend's beautiful brown eyes. "I'm fine Sarah, you healed me." She gave Sarah a reassuring smile. She pushed up on her elbows, realizing she was on a bed.

"Lay back down. You need to rest."

"I'm starving. I thought we were here for dinner."

"Amen sister." She looked up and saw Nate standing beside the door in the small bedroom. He was actually leaning against it, and it seemed like someone was trying to open it. Then she heard a persistent knocking. She looked around even further, and realized she was in a room decorated by Pepto Bismal. Noah choked back a laugh.

"Sarah, I'm fine. What happened?"

"Do you remember being in the kitchen with my parents?"

"Yes, we were having a great conversation, and then I…I…"

"My parent's questions triggered a flashback. Noah said you were tortured using electro shock therapy." Sarah reached out with a trembling hand, and brushed back a strand of her hair. "You were bleeding from your nose and ears."

"Sarah, I'm fine. You healed me. I'm just hungry and sorry I scared you and your parents." She sat up, but both Sarah and Noah pressed her back down onto the bed.

"Guys, I want to get up. Seriously, I'm fine."

"You were just on the floor curled in the fetal position, why don't you take it easy for a bit," Sarah coaxed.

"I…"

"Kali you will…" Noah looked at her, his eyes blazing, and she lost it. She pushed both of them away.

"Nate, can you excuse us?"

Nate looked from one to the other, his gaze staying on Sarah the longest, and finally nodded, then left the room.

Kali waited until the door was closed. Nate's voice could easily be heard, telling the others Kali was fine and they would all be out to the barbecue in just a few minutes. Kali relaxed as she turned back to Sarah and Noah.

"I don't think I have ever felt better in my life. I am very sorry I scared you, but you certainly don't need to be treating me like an invalid."

"Kali, you likely had a stroke or an aneurysm." Sarah's voice was grave.

"You *cured* me. Just like you were meant to do."

"Baby, you had a flashback, this might happen again."

"No, it will never happen again. I promise you. I know the answers to those questions, they won't scare me like they did when Frank and Lila asked me." Kali reached out and gripped both Noah and Sarah's hands. She looked from one to the other. "I understand now, for just a brief moment I was allowed to go back, and I know, I know what our purpose is."

"What? When?"

"It was right after you laid hands on me. Noah, I got to visit with Nana, she explained it to me. I also remembered more about the day in the stadium. There were at least fifty of us. And there were three older children, teenagers, they were sent to look over us. They weren't going to lose their memories. Nana told me we are here to help. Somehow our abilities and energies will make a difference in making this world safer and better for the inhabitants today and in the coming generations."

"I'd love to believe that," Sarah said. "But it

sounds like a near death experience to me. That's just a bunch of neurons sparking off in your brain honey, especially when all that trauma was going on."

Sarah's tone and touch was so calm and loving, her patients had to love her. Too bad she was so full of shit.

"Sarah, I need you to really listen to me. I know you don't remember where we came from, but Noah and I do. Somehow with you and Noah touching me, and the beautiful surge of light and energy, not only did the pain instantly stop, but when I was looking down I saw a shimmering glow. I have never felt better in my life, and then I flew out of my body. I soared to the other world and spent time with Nana. Not a memory of an old conversation, but I saw her how she is at this moment, and we spoke. She knew Noah and I were together, that we would have babies together. She explained our purpose."

Kali watched Sarah's face change from an expression of doubt to fear. Both she and Noah wrapped her up in a hug.

"It's going to be fine, Sarah," Noah said in a comforting rumble.

"I know Kali keeps saying a *little* difference, but it sounds like they expected so much from us, and I'm scared."

Kali wasn't surprised to see Sarah eventually calm. Noah had a way about him that made everyone believe and feel better.

That's you Kali, you're as much of a healer as Sarah.

"Hmm." Kali looked up to see Nate glaring at Noah.

"Nate, is something wrong?" Sarah asked. "Oh, my family must be worried about Kali. Let's go you guys. She hopped off the bed." Nate gave Noah a hard look, and Kali watched as Noah returned it with an innocent smile.

Neither Noah nor Nate were smiling. Every other person in the Johnson's backyard was having a fine old time, but he and Nate were leaning against the fence sipping beers, and hating life.

"Did you know two of Sarah's brothers were cops?" Noah asked Nate.

"Yeah, she told me," Nate said grimly. "Seriously man, all this time I've thought we've just been flirting. She's told me about her family. Told me I'd have to go through a gauntlet, I laughed. It was all in good fun." Noah watched as his big friend rubbed the back of his neck and looked at him.

"So what's your problem?"

"I'll tell you what my problem is. The last twenty-four hours haven't been good fun. At least not for me, and meanwhile she's been telling her family I'm some boy-toy she's going to test out."

"Oh, that's got to be going over really well," Noah choked, now realizing why so many testy glances were coming their way from the Johnson brothers. "But in all fairness, weren't you just planning on a little..." Noah was reluctant to put it into words, not when he could see Sarah sitting over at the picnic table looking so pretty and innocent in her white dress.

"What? A shag? A dalliance? A one night stand?"

"Sure, one of those. Isn't it what you intended?"

"That all went out the window when I saw her touch Kota."

"When you saw her ability to heal?" Noah asked.

"No, when I saw her put her hands on Kota. I thought I'd rip his throat out. She's mine. She just doesn't realize it yet." Whoa. Nate wasn't kidding. Noah knew his background. Nate might seem fun and affable, but there were some really dark corners, and when he said he was going to rip a man's throat out, he wasn't kidding.

"Nate, where does Sarah stand on all of this?"

"I don't care. Eventually shell be standing next to me. So now we've talked out my problem, Noah, how about we talk about the fact you have two men trying to talk your woman into leaving you?" Noah felt the aluminum of his beer can crumple beneath his hand.

"Again, why didn't you tell me some of Sarah's brothers were cops? And one was a firefighter? They are all in love with the cop's daughter."

"Hell Noah, they would have been in love with

Kali even if her dad hadn't been a captain in the Chicago Police Department. She's Kali." She was seated across the table from Sarah, wearing a pink dress from Sarah's closet. Something Sarah had probably worn when she was a sophomore in high school, but it fit Kali like a dream. On either side of her were Johnson brothers. Noah had no idea what their names were, they were big and handsome, and were hitting on his woman. The only blessing was she was oblivious. He tried to talk to her again.

Kali?

Isn't it wonderful? Aren't you happy? Doesn't the food taste great? The admiral and Sarah's dad are sure having a great time. Isn't Cyrus a hoot? Did you see the cat?

Kali was higher than a kite. He had remembered being hungry and feeling really good after being healed by Sarah. He'd even compared notes with Kota. Both of them had felt better and more energetic. They decided it was because they were hurting and it was the natural sense of thinking you were feeling much better than before, when really you were just back to normal.

Obviously they were wrong. The healing did something to you. It really did make you feel better. What had Kali said? She never felt better in her life. Noah would bet anything it was more than that. He didn't know what, but he didn't think it was a matter of her being Miss Hyper-Happy-Hungry-Girl. But if the only side effect to come out of this was she would be happy and hungry for the rest of her life, he would give thanks. He watched as she held out her plate for another helping of cornbread and green beans. Then he saw the brother on her right side, slide his hand down her back, and rest it at the top of her ass as he spooned some yams onto her plate.

Noah moved forward, ignoring Nate when he said, "go get 'em Lieutenant."

Noah stood directly behind Kali and placed a kiss on the top of her head, at the same time he put a hand on the young man's shoulder and squeezed...hard. He lifted his head and looked into the man's pained expression.

"Would you mind if I took your seat?"

"No Sir, not at all," he said as he scrambled to get up. Laughter erupted from the table, and Noah sat down next to Kali.

"Noah, did you have a chance to meet Tyler? He's an arson investigator," Kali said indicating the man who had left the table.

"I had a chance to watch his investigative skills, I wasn't impressed."

"We haven't been impressed with him for years," an older Johnson brother called out from further along the table. Noah looked up to see Lila Johnson putting a plate of food in front of him.

"Don't you worry about Tyler, Noah, he's harmless."

Noah slid his hand down Kali's back, feeling much better when it was his warmth touching her. She peered at him, and then rested her head on his shoulder. All of his jealousy smoothed out.

"All of them are harmless," she murmured.

"Sure they are," Noah chuckled. "Harmless was the word I was going to use to describe them. Sarah has quite the family." Noah kept his voice low, and with all the activity and talk going on around them, he hoped they weren't being overheard, still...

Why out loud?

Oh. Its better now, it was too chaotic before. I was having trouble talking in my head, it was getting kind of jumbled, like I was high. Anyway, I heard Sakuro and Cyrus talking. Cyrus is Sarah's oldest brother. He's the task force leader with the Atlanta Police Department. He said he wanted in on whatever the hell was going on, or he wouldn't let Sarah go. He sounded pretty adamant.

Noah looked around the table and saw the man Kali was talking about. He was the one giving Nate the hardest time. He looked to be the same age as Dave Rydell who was in his mid-thirties.

He is, he was an MP in the Army.

Noah had thought he was shielding, but apparently he was broadcasting.

Nope, I think it is a side-effect of the healing. I'm still cranked up. I swear Noah, I am in the zone. I could win at Jeopardy, bake a cake and give you the best blow job of your life. Noah choked on the rib he was eating, and reached for his beer.

When can we leave and have sex? I want a lot of sex. I'm so needy. I'm so wet. Please, can we leave now?

Noah took a larger swallow of beer, and looked

around the table. Everybody seemed to be talking, nobody was focused on them, but he felt like they must be setting the backyard on fire.

Please?

Suddenly, it wasn't just words. It was a feeling, the amazing sensation of Kali's mouth encompassing his cock, her tongue licking up the vein on the underside of tip. Then a picture blasted through his brain of her tied naked and spread eagle to an old-fashioned four poster bed. The beer fell out of his hand, liquid spilling through the cracks of the picnic table.

"Noah, are you okay?" Sarah asked from across the table. "You're looking flushed."

"I'm fine, but I'm still worried about Kali. I want to take her to the hotel. I think she needs to rest." Sarah opened her mouth, but before she could say anything, Kali interrupted.

"Thank you Noah, I do need to lie down." *Under you.*

Chapter Twenty-nine

Why weren't she and Noah sharing an apartment? When the admiral explained he arranged for their living arrangements in Southern California, Kali had no idea they would be so nice. They took over an entire floor of furnished apartments in Newport Beach. She only had one problem with the living arrangements, she and Noah had separate apartments, and Noah hadn't said a word when they were each given their own key. Weren't they going to be living together from now on?

Never in her life was she connected to someone as the night they made love after the Johnson family picnic. It was positively spiritual. But here a week late and a thousand miles away, it seemed like an eternity had passed. What's more, Noah constantly blocked her now. He would politely knock to telepathically communicate with her, and she would do the same, but she could no longer hear him at all. Rarely could she even sense what he was feeling. She knew he had done it on purpose.

She lay down in the beautifully appointed new bedroom and cried.

Her tears were ripping him apart. How could she doubt his feelings? God the night together in Atlanta had been everything. She was everything, and that was the problem. Oh, he intended to keep her forever, she was his. But Sakuro and his plan to have Sarah and Kali in California near Rixitron was both ingenious and the worst fucking thing in the world. Therefore, his team, and now Cyrus, had come up with their own plan.

Noah still wasn't sure how he felt having Cyrus Johnson here with them as part of their team, but he had to admit the man was smart. Sierra had run his background. His record in the Army had been phenomenal, it was no wonder he was a task force leader in Atlanta.

One of the apartments had been converted into a command center. They had briefly considered taking up office space in the bottom floor of the apartment building. The other offices were there, but no one liked the idea of being so far away from Sarah and Kali.

"How are you doing keeping things blocked from Kali? I'm thinking it's working since she looks like shit."

"Great Nate, you sure have a way with words." Sierra sat in front of her computers looking glum. It didn't give Noah a great deal of confidence. Normally she was the one who provided their intel.

"So no leads on Rixitron?" Kota asked from his seat beside the window.

"That's not it. I heard from Riley. He can't find Annie. Not one possible lead. It's like she fell off the end of the world."

"What about the Seth Natani? Any word on him?"

"No, and not looking good at all. Lobado and the gang know they've been infiltrated on the inside," Seirra explained.

"Well, it's a *no shit* kind of thing," Nate said.

"They're chasing their tails. Which is good for us, and good for Natani. He came up with a cover the DEA doesn't even know, but I figured it out."

Noah thought she might buff her fingernails. "Spill it."

"I used a facial recognition program, and found him in this bridal magazine of all places." She turned her monitor and showed them a glossy magazine photo of a couple in a garden, both of them dressed in wedding clothes. There was Seth Natani with a beautiful blonde woman.

"Oh fuck," Nate hissed. "How can the DEA not know? I mean this is a national magazine, right?

"Actually, only women who want to get married read this type of magazine, it's because I had the software cranking for days I was able to find it."

"How did an Indian make himself into a Carson?" Kota asked in disgust. When everyone stared at him, he held up his hands. "Hey, I'm Native American, just saying, I would have come up with a name a little less Anglo Saxon is all."

"This Portia, how is she mixed up in things?" Noah asked.

"Portia, is Portia Benitez of Benitez Shipping, and her father is up to his eyeballs in drug and arms shipping. I don't know about his daughter. I think Seth is a scumbag who couldn't resist marrying a beautiful woman," Sierra said with disgust.

"Did you inform his superiors?" Cyrus asked.

"Nope. There has to be a reason he's not reporting in. I figured I would keep his secret."

"I disagree, I think it should to be reported to his superiors, but it's your op," Cyrus said with a shrug. "Now let me get this straight. We have three different things going on. One of your people, Dave Rydell, was working on a case with a *found* girl in Taiwan, right? Is he coming back here?"

"Nope, he refuses to leave. He is positive the assholes who took her are going to make another attempt, and he's not letting her out of his sight."

"Got it. The second one is Riley—first name or last?"

"Riley Jones, he's in New Mexico searching for Annie Newman. I thought she was Seth's Annie," Sierra said bitterly.

Noah could feel the hurt coming off her in

waves. It wasn't about Riley, it was Seth's betrayal of Annie. Had she been similarly betrayed at some time?

"So what is Riley's plan?" Cyrus asked.

"He intends to track down Annie. Rixitron is after her because she had Seth's baby. They know the baby is the child of a *found*, and are determined to get their hands on her and the child."

"If Annie is so well hidden, why not just leave her alone?"

"She's out there in the desert with Seth's grandmother as protector, it's not good enough, not with the type of people Rixitron put into play. Once Riley has her located we'll be called in and bring them here."

"Got it." Cyrus went to the kitchen area and grabbed a club soda. "So it leaves the assholes after my sister."

"The same—all Rixitron. From what we know, their intent is to create a breeding program and propagate the *found*."

Cyrus slammed down the soda. "That's just sick."

"And it's not everything," Noah reminded the team. "The people who had Kali weren't interested in breeding her, it was all about finding out where she came from."

"I'm sorry Lieutenant, you're right," Sierra said. Nate moved from his spot against the wall and put his hand on Noah's shoulder.

"Just because Sierra didn't mention it, doesn't

mean she isn't looking into it. Go ahead, tell him what you've discovered."

"I tracked down who owned the buildings. I had to go through three shell companies, but I finally found a name. Jade Melling Galleries out of New York."

"How big an operation?"

"Single owner. She's in her fifties, never been married. An artist who hit it big thirty years ago, and then started representing other artists."

"What kind of motive would she have to capture and torture Kali?"

"Absolutely nothing I can see. I'm thinking she's just another link in the chain, but until she comes back from her buying trip in Europe, I can't be sure. She'll be back in two days. I figure one of us can go and question her then."

Noah felt a rush of relief. They were making some progress on Kali's kidnapping after all.

"There's still Niko," Cyrus finished.

"Fuck. Did you have to remind us?"

Nate was not a happy camper. Sierra scowled at Cyrus for the third time that morning. He was definitely usurping her role, Cyrus' talents as a Task Team Leader were obvious.

Noah?

He shut her out, figuring he'd see her after the briefing. He wanted to discuss how to keep the women safe while they were out doing reconnaissance work.

"What's he like?" Kota asked Sierra.

"I can answer," Cyrus said. "Sarah kept a scrapbook on him, like she kept on Kali, Alfred and Mai. He's a geologist, with a degree in mechanical engineering. He's been working to help safely develop the natural gas fields in Russia. His work has been adopted in fifteen different countries including ours. He's saved thousands of lives, and it's helped stop harmful effects to the environment."

"Can he afford to be away?"

"He has to. There was an attempted kidnapping. They sent a contingent of men, damn near a SWAT team, but he's guarded as closely as the Russian President. They massacred those men."

"Couldn't they have left even one alive to question?"

"Apparently it's against policy." Cyrus laughed.

Nobody said it, but everybody was thinking about all the civilians they were going to have to guard.

"What's our plan to keep everybody safe?" Kota asked. "Is Sakuro going to give us anymore reinforcements?"

"He still isn't sure who he can trust. I want to bring in someone from Hawaii," Noah said.

"What about the other *found*? Are there any others who have backgrounds that might be helpful?" Nate asked.

"What other *found*?" Cyrus asked.

"Sakuro explained there were other governments, including America that knew of *found* children who hadn't received public exposure." Sierra explained. "Each of their respective governments kept them under wraps. As the shit hit the fan with Kali, Alfred, and the others they put them under covert protection."

"Is there anyone else we can pull in?"

They all watched as Sierra's fingers flew over the keyboard. "Brice McElyn, SAS from Scotland."

Yeah, he would work, Noah agreed.

"Get him. I've got to go."

"Me too," Nate said. They headed towards the door, Noah in front. Before Nate could make it, Cyrus was in front of him.

"Nate, I think you and I need to have a talk."

"I agree. Let's go downstairs. I need some air."

Chapter Thirty

Kali opened the door knowing it was Noah, because he finally opened up to her. She didn't understand why he had been blocking her, but it hurt.

"Baby, I love you." He swept her into his arms, and carried her back to the bedroom. When he tried to lay her down, she held onto his neck, not letting go.

"You blocked me."

"I had to." His face was resolute.

Letting go she turned on her side, and cried. He was serious, he thought he needed to block her out. She never wanted to lose their connection, but he wanted to sever their ties.

No, Kali, never. But I never want you to suffer like you did when I was in Cancun.

"It was okay when I was lying on the floor in the Johnson's kitchen? Sarah told me your nose was bleeding. She had to heal you too, but that was just fine, wasn't it?"

It's not the same thing at all.

"It is. It either works both ways, or it doesn't work at all. If you block me, I'll work on blocking you. You know what, Noah? After everything they put me through in the fucking little room, I bet I'm even better at it than you are." She watched him wince. Felt his pain. Ignored it. Ignored him. She rolled in on herself.

No baby, please no. He curled up behind her, tucking up close. After long moments his warmth seeped through. He crooned softly in a language she didn't know, and her tears slowed.

"What is that?"

"It's a Hawaiian lullaby, one my mother used to sing to me. You're right love. Forgive me."

He gently rolled her over, and she looked into eyes more familiar than her own. He rested his forehead against hers.

"Let me show you." His thoughts swirled into her mind, a kaleidoscope of memories, thoughts, and feelings. Kali could almost taste his anguish when he realized she suffered his beating along with him. It felt like she was pushing against a steel wall of determination as he made the decision she would never endure such pain on his behalf again. Then there was the fire of his will as he promised he would protect her at all costs as he figured out who was behind her kidnapping, even if it meant doing things to add more scars to his soul.

"No Noah, I'm not going to let you do this," she cupped his cheeks and brushed kisses against his lips. "We're in this together, and you are *not* going to take the law into your own hands."

You're never going to be hurt again. I love you too much. You are my life. He pressed urgently against her, instantly her need ratcheted up, her body blazing to life needing the connection with Noah's mind. Noah felt it too, and his need transmitted to her, raising her higher.

He pulled at the front of her blouse and buttons pinged across the room. She wished she had his strength, but all she could do was thrust her hands under the hem of his shirt. Relief. His hands on her flesh, hers on his, blessed relief. He ripped her bra open, and his mouth was on her breast, sucking, she arched up and tried to grab his hair and realized her hands were stuck under his shirt.

"Noah. Stop." He did, lifting up, but not enough, his hands bracketing her torso. "I need you naked." The words came out so fast they blurred together as one. He understood and got off the bed, as she shed her clothes. No seduction, just a greedy need. She fumbled her zipper twice as she watched his cock pop out of his jeans.

"Kali, concentrate." Then he was on her, naked. Pulling at her jeans, until they joined his on the floor. He shoved her thighs apart. "Fucking gorgeous." Using his thumbs he spread the lips of her pussy. She stretched her legs even wider knowing what was next. The exquisite feel of his tongue lapping at her wet entrance. There was not the slightest unease, his pleasure and her pleasure crashed through her brain, and she cried out in wonder.

Make more noise.

His tongue speared deep. She could taste herself, the flavor, an explosion of spice.

Yes, more noise.

"Need you in me," she moaned

I am in you. Come first.

"Please Noah. I need to be one with you."

An orgasm first, and then I'll fuck you. She bucked against him, grinding upwards. She felt him laugh, his tongue vibrating. So close.

Oh I like this, a how-to manual. She felt his laughter.

Two fingers plunged deep and hooked, as his tongued latched onto her clit and for the first time, brought his teeth into the mix. She hit the stratosphere. Stars.

He kissed her face, and brushed back her hair. *How could it keep getting better?*

You like rougher play than I imagined my love. He gave her nipples a sharp pinch and then drove deep, she moaned filled with bliss and felt his rapture. Drawing her knees up, she squeezed his hips.

He plunged in and out in the strongest rhythm she had ever experienced, and all she could do was cry for more, plead with him to fuck her even harder, and faster, pressing her breasts against him as an offering.

You were made for me.

His mouth dipped and took a nipple and suckled hard, his teeth scraping just right. Her cries were incoherent, but he understood every one of them.

Up and up and up until they achieved the perfect moment transporting them through time and space. Gazing into each other's eyes they realized what they had knew no bounds. Embracing, there was nothing left to be said.

Kali fell asleep secure in the knowledge there never again would be a barrier between her and the man who was the other half of her soul.

She loved coffee. Probably because it was the first scent she remembered. Waking up to it was wonderful. Wait a minute, she hadn't set her coffeemaker.

No you didn't.

Noah. She rolled over and he was sitting on the edge of the bed holding a mug of the magical liquid in equally magical hands.

I heard that.

"I wanted you to. Good morning," she said taking the coffee. Kali couldn't wipe the grin off her face. "So what's on today's agenda?"

"You join the morning briefing and I get my ass handed to me." Noah's hand trailed lazily down her bare leg.

"As the lieutenant, aren't you in charge?"

"When a final decision needs to be made it's mine to make, but we're really a team, everybody has input and a say. Now we even have Cyrus. He's going to realize if you're attending the meetings then the only person who isn't is Sarah. That'll last a nanosecond, and he's going to want her protected from this ugliness. So yeah, this isn't going to be pretty." His hand drifted upwards, and she was having trouble focusing.

"Stop, Noah. This is important."

"Nah, I've been beat up by the team before. Are you finished with your coffee?" He plucked the mug from her hands and put it on the nightstand.

"How long before your meeting starts?" she asked as he nuzzled her neck.

"We have time, it doesn't start for an hour." He easily lifted her to the center of the bed, and then spread her hair so it fanned across the pillow. "You're so beautiful Kali."

"I have to talk to Sarah. I have a plan," her voice didn't come out nearly as firm as she intended. The man was still staring at her breasts. "Noah seriously, go to your apartment. Sarah and I will see you at the meeting."

"Can't go to my apartment." He dipped down and lapped at the sensitive peak of her right breast. She had seconds before all words would be beyond her. She tried again.

"Yes you can go to your apartment, go now."

"This is my apartment. I started moving in this morning." He blew on her nipple, and rolled the other in his fingers and tears leaked out of her eyes. He didn't mistake the reason why.

"We're together forever, Kali."

"Forever Noah. Forever."

"Are you sure this is going to be okay?" Sarah asked for the third or maybe fourth time.

"No, it's not. They are going to hate this. Do you really care?" Sarah rubbed her palms on her jeans. Not for the first time, Kali was blown away by Sarah's beauty. None of the pictures had done her justice. Her energy made her so appealing, even if it was nervous energy like now. No wonder Nate couldn't take his eyes off of her. It was a crap shoot as to who would hate having her in on these briefings more, Cyrus or Nate.

Kali reached for the doorknob and Sarah stayed her hand.

"Wait. Shouldn't we knock?"

"Nope, we start as we mean to go on. We plan to push our way into this whole show no matter what their objections are, so we might as well walk in on them."

Sarah finally nodded.

Kali opened the door and every head turned towards them. The curtains were drawn, and a video was being displayed against the wall over the sofa. It was immediately shut off.

Cyrus pulled back the drapes, and glared at

them. "Do you mind telling me what the hell you're doing here, Sarah?"

"I'm sick of being kept in the dark. But I see it's how everybody is operating," she said with a laugh. Cyrus chuckled. Sarah knew the right way to play her brother.

"You're not part of this, neither of you are. You're civilians," Nate's voice was forged in steel.

"Wrong. We're *found*. We're not *just* the targets, we're eventually going to be the goats you'll stake out to lure them in. Even if we're not, we are coming into some interesting damn skills. We could make your operation a whole lot more successful if we help." Kali kept her voice calm and level, knowing she had no hope of convincing Nate, instead, working to convince everyone else in the room.

"We don't plan on using you as bait," Kota said emphatically.

"You might not plan to right now, but eventually it will be the best case scenario, and I'll be all for it, because I trust you to keep me safe."

Not going to happen, baby.

"It's never going to come to that," Nate said.

"Fine, it's never going to happen, but in the meantime, we refuse to be excluded. This is our lives, what's more, we're all living here together. We refuse to be treated like second class citizens." Kali saw how that remark hit home with everyone.

"So what was on the video you just turned off, was it about Rixitron?" Sarah asked.

"No, it's about Jade Melling. From everything we can tell, she actually funded the purchase of the office park where Kali was held and tortured. We thought her art galleries were just one more false trail, but it looks like this time it is the end game."

"Who is she?"

Cyrus shut the drapes again, and Sierra turned the projector back on.

"Meet Jade Melling. She is one hell of an artist, who happens to own eleven galleries around the world. She also represents some of the most influential artists of our generation." Kali looked at the woman on the screen. She was older and nondescript. There was not one thing about her that stood out, then Sierra flashed to a benefits program where Jade was presenting a check to a hospital. She was on stage with three children, and her entire demeanor changed, she was animated and effervescent. Her interaction with the children was delightful to watch, it was clear she managed to make them comfortable and happy, even though they were on a stage in front of hundreds of people.

"This can't be the person behind my kidnapping."

"We agree," Noah said. "But Sierra has been digging into her financials, and besides the money spent on the office park, there have been many other large withdrawals made and unaccounted for."

"How much are we talking?" Cyrus asked.

"Millions," Sierra answered. "I sent a text to the

lieutenant this morning. We were thinking someone would contact her when she returns from Europe tomorrow, but now I think one of us needs to go to New York and talk to her face to face."

"If you don't think this is the person behind Kali's kidnapping, why are you going to meet with her?" Sarah asked.

"Because we think she's being used, and probably by someone she knows. Meeting with her face to face will shake her up, get her to tell us what she knows," Nate explained.

"Then, I need to go with whoever is going," Kali said looking around the room. Kali's statement was met with silence, and everyone turned to look at Noah.

"Why do you think you need to go?" Noah asked. She felt only support coming from him, support and love.

It's all you'll ever feel.

"If you think she is being duped, then she needs to know what her money caused, the harm it did. It would be best if she hears it from me." Sarah leaned in closer, and took her hand in solidarity.

"She's right."

"Sierra, I guess you're buying tickets again," Kota said.

CHAPTER THIRTY-ONE

The gallery was beautiful. Noah felt out of place. He had expected it to be like one of the many galleries in Hawaii where beautiful, wildly expensive, works of art were sold to tourists in shorts and flip flops. Here in New York, it was like he stepped into an eighteenth century men's club with wood paneling and dark lighting. Hell, to get in they'd had to make an appointment. How in the hell did they expect to sell anything to customers, if the customers couldn't come into the shop and browse at their leisure?

He could feel Cyrus clearly enough to know he thought the same thing. He and Kali joked about it in their bedroom while the appointments were made. The only one who wasn't surprised was Nate. As a matter of fact, when the assistant came over and asked them if they wanted anything, he had immediately asked what kind of champagne they had, and the girl named three different vintages. How had Nate known to ask for champagne? Noah knew he'd grown up well to do, but this was ridiculous. Nate winked at him.

"Ms. Melling is currently on a call. She asked me to seat you in our conference room." They followed the woman into a lushly appointed board room.

"Do you have anything to eat, to go with the champagne?" Nate asked.

"Certainly." Minutes later a tray of cheese, crackers, smoked salmon and pastries were on the table.

As soon as the woman left, Noah leaned toward Nate. "Why didn't you ask for a ding dong?"

"Actually, I'm disappointed they didn't bring in some caviar," Nate said. Noah looked at him, and he be damned but his friend was absolutely serious. They all watched in awe as Nate proceeded to fix himself a huge plate of food.

After twenty minutes, and two plates of food for Nate, Jade Melling finally made her way into the room. She smiled, but she looked like she would have preferred to be home with her feet up.

"Ms. Melling, we're here under false pretenses. We are not interested in purchasing art," Nate said bluntly. They had agreed he would do the talking, since he dealt the New York Gallery scene in the past. Apparently, he preferred them to soup kitchens.

"If that's the case, I'd like you to leave. I don't have time for subterfuge."

"We're here because of your interest with the *found*."

Kali leaned forward, she had been sitting back in the large leather chair, hidden by Noah's big body. As soon as she noticed Kali, Jade froze.

"Kelly Wachowski," Jade breathed. Noah thought the woman might pass out. Bingo. Any question as to her involvement flew out the window. Cyrus stood by the door of the conference room, to ensure they weren't interrupted.

"Ms. Melling, I think you have some explaining to do," Noah said in a deadly tone. It took everything he had not to block himself from Kali. He wanted to kill this woman, and he didn't want Kali to feel his rage, but he had promised.

"Noah," Kali said, her hand on his forearm.

"No Kali, she's responsible for you being kidnapped and tortured. She's going to be held accountable."

She shivered, this was not the man she knew. When she looked around the room, she saw the same look on all the other men's faces.

"I'm so sorry," Jade Melling said, as she placed both hands on the conference room table. She reached towards Kali, and her expression anguished. "I never thought you would be taken. Jared told me we needed answers. He promised he would find answers for me." Tears dripped from the older woman's eyes. Fury emanated from Noah and the others, but Kali felt genuine sorrow coming from Jade Melling.

"I don't understand. Can you explain why you had me kidnapped?"

"It was never my intention. I gave Jared the money he said he needed. I read all the reports, I knew you had no memories of where you had come from, and I knew you weren't lying. But Jared convinced me he had resources and methods at his disposal to get the answers."

"Do you know what he did to her?" Noah slammed his hands onto the table, causing Jade to jerk in her seat.

"Of course I know about the kidnapping and the starvation. I can never forgive myself. I can't. Please know it was my grief because of Joey. I wouldn't have done this, except for Joey."

"It wasn't just starvation," Noah's voice was a roar. He went to grab Kali's arm, and at the last moment, touched her gently. "Baby, show Ms. Melling your wrists?"

"Who's Joey?"

"Who in the hell cares? Show her your wrists." He picked up her arm where it rested on the table, and pushed back the cuff of her blouse. "Do you see this scar?"

Jade Melling blanched. "Yes," she said, in a quavering voice.

"This is where Kali tore at her bindings to

escape the electro shock therapy they gave her. The pain was so bad she ripped her flesh down to the bone. They thought she would be blind and brain damaged when we found her."

"No, no, God no. Tell me it's not true," the woman begged. She rocked back and forth in her chair, frantically looking around, then she ran for the trash can and threw up. Kali wanted to go to her, but this was the woman who was ultimately responsible for her pain and suffering. Still, she couldn't help herself. She grabbed some napkins, and went to the kneeling woman.

"Don't touch me. You can't. If it weren't for Joey, I would have turned myself in when I realized you had been kidnapped."

"Did you have information on where to find her?" Cyrus demanded.

"I couldn't get ahold of Jared. It was as if he disappeared from the face of the Earth."

"You still could have given a name, stopped funneling him money."

"I did. I didn't give him one red cent after Kelly was kidnapped. I closed the account. I…I…" She burst into tears. "I can't believe I was…" She fell to the floor. Each man in the room stared at the woman. Kali looked at them with disbelief.

What do you expect?

Kali tried to lift her.

Leave her.

"Help me." She looked around, still nothing. "Please." Finally Noah relented and motioning Kali aside, helped Jade to the chair she had vacated. Kali gave her a napkin from the table. Jade wiped her mouth with a trembling hand.

"Who is Joey?" Kali asked quietly.

"Joey Mirelli?" Noah asked?

"Yes, he's my Godson."

"We thought he died."

"Who's Joey Mirelli?" Cyrus asked.

"He's one of the *found*. He was identified by the US government years ago. But we thought he was killed in a car crash with his parents eighteen years ago. What happened, Ms. Melling?"

"He suffered extensive brain trauma. I've brought in every specialist from around the world. But they haven't been able to figure out what's wrong. The brain trauma he suffered, isn't significant enough to account for the reason he never progressed past the age of seven. It has to be because he is one of the *found*."

"And that justified torturing Kali?"

"No. Of course not. God no. You have to believe me, please believe me." She grabbed another napkin off the table, and shoved it against her face, trying to stem her tears.

"Then what the hell were you thinking?" Nate demanded.

"Jared told me he had a way to help Kelly recover her memories. I read all the accounts of Kelly, Sarah, Niko, Mai and Alfred. Not one of them had any memories of their time before coming here, but Kelly was closest to where Joey was found. They even looked alike..." Jade started sobbing again.

Noah, she doesn't know anything, and she feels such guilt.

She fucking well should feel guilty!

"Where did you meet this Jared?" Cyrus asked.

"He found me. I was visiting Joey. He said he was coming to visit the patients in comas. He felt his methods could assist them."

"What methods were those?"

"He had different holistic methods, where he would put headphones on them, and provide massage therapy. They seemed to respond. I saw one patient move their feet. Another patient blinked. He was making real progress."

The men exchanged glances.

"Anyway, I asked him to spend time with Joey, to see if he could make any headway with him. He knew right away Joey was special."

Of course he did.

"They spent hours together. Even though he wasn't supposed to, Joey finally explained how he was found in the woods behind his parent's estate in Boston. He was playing in the snow. He was having a grand old time playing in the snow."

"They were Senator and Mrs. Scheffield. Their estate was closely guarded, and damn near impenetrable."

"Yes, Sofia and I were sorority sisters. I was staying with them that day. I ended up being Joey's Godmother. I was the only other person on Earth who knew his story, until he told Jared. In all those years at Rosewood, he hadn't told a soul."

"Jared sounds like a peach," Cyrus said.

Jade's tears dried up, and now her tone was steely. "I should have known from the beginning he was a charlatan. He kept saying he had to spend time alone with Joey, it should have been a red flag."

"Yes it should have," Cyrus said, no give in his voice.

"When he confronted me saying Joey was *found*, I was so stunned."

"How did he find out Joey was *found*?" Cyrus asked.

"Joey told him. Like I said, he is basically a seven year old boy, still his parents and I had drilled into him he couldn't discuss this. He needed to say he was adopted. He always told everyone he was adopted. Jared was the first person he talked to about being found in the snow. Jared continued to probe until he got the entire story from Joey."

"Then what happened, Ma'am?" Cyrus prompted, in full cop mode.

"He started using the techniques he had used on the coma patients. Bio Feedback and massage therapy. He suggested mild shock therapy, but I was appalled. I said of course not."

Kali shuddered.

"He assured me it would be the mildest form of shock, like used by a massage therapist to stimulate nerve endings in the lower back and neck, but I said unequivocally no."

"Good. But then he told you something else, didn't he?" Cyrus probed.

"It's when he told me it was the reason Joey hadn't progressed. Not because of any organic problem with his brain, but because of something to do with his being one of the *found* children." She paused for a long time, obviously lost in thought.

"And then?"

"He said we needed to talk to another one of the *found*."

"I'd extensively researched all of the *found* children. I knew none of them ever recovered any of their memories from where they had come from, they were all like Joey. Jared said Joey was a special case, and all it would take was some deep questioning and hypnotherapy of a high functioning adult to regain their memories..." Jade's voice trailed off.

"Ms. Melling, why Kali?"

"Jared said we needed to contact the *found* who most closely resembled Jared. That was Kelly."

"And you believed him." Cyrus just shook his head.

"He said the kind of equipment and neuroscientists would cost in the hundreds of thousands of dollars. I told him money was no object. As soon as I said that, he started talking about the research hospital he wanted to set up for coma patients. He had been talking to other parents at the facility. Of course I said he could have funding for that as well." She looked around the room, obviously pleading with people to understand the decisions she had made.

"Why was everything done in secret?" Cyrus demanded ruthlessly.

"Secret?"

"Shell corporations."

"Shell corporations? I don't understand what you're talking about. I set up a fund for him. Of course we didn't want to use my name, because it might be connected back to Joey. It's imperative to keep Joey Mirelli dead. We were going to use my mother's maiden name for the hospital."

"Why?"

"I knew eventually the *found* would become targets, they were different. It was bound to happen. As much as Sofia and the Senator intended to keep Joey's origin a secret, eventually it would leak. So this was one more way of keeping his secret forever."

The woman was right, Kali thought. The hate group from Idaho was a perfect example of people wanting the *found* dead.

"Well, he duped you again Ms. Melling, he used three different shell corporations to purchase a business park in Indiana where Kali was held."

"Why would he purchase such a large piece of property to keep one woman?"

"It's one of the many questions we'll ask the son of a bitch when we finally catch him," Noah ground out.

"I have to know, what did he do to you Miss Wachowski?" Jade asked in a whisper.

"I only met him once. He had this woman…this sadist named Tara, who kept me in a tiny cell, and only took me out to strap me to a table where they applied higher and higher dosages of electro shock therapy. I wanted to die the pain was so bad." As she told Jade, she remembered, and tears rolled down her cheek. Nate handed her one of the napkins from the table. Noah pulled her into his arms.

"She was almost dead when we found her," his voice was gentle as he talked over her head.

"Now you know about Joey, will you take care of him when they take me away?"

Kali whipped her head around. "What are you talking about?"

"I need to be arrested."

"You definitely aided and abetted after the fact," Cyrus concurred.

"Cyrus, she didn't know what Tara and Jared were doing to me."

"She knew Jared was behind your kidnapping and she didn't come forward. She is culpable," Cyrus' voice had no give.

"He's right, baby."

"Miss Wachowski, I can never make up for what was done for you. I deserve to go to prison. All I ask is you look in on Joey. I'm begging you. Will they allow me to continue to pay for Joey's care at his facility? Will I be allowed to explain things to Joey?"

"Couldn't there be another way of handling this Cyrus?" Nate finally spoke up.

"What in the hell are you talking about?" Cyrus asked angrily.

"Couldn't Ms. Melling help us put Jared behind bars, and therefore cop a plea or something?"

"You've watched too many TV shows," Cyrus said with disgust.

"Please Cyrus," Kali said. "She was only guilty of trying to help her godson."

"How in the hell can you say that, Kali? You almost died. She was fine throwing you to the wolves, doing anything she needed to save him. She turned a blind eye. In my book that's worse. You don't get to say you're a good person and have good intentions, but then let someone else do shitty things on your behalf. It's un-fucking-acceptable."

"He's right Ms. Wachowski. Just don't take this out on Joey, I'm begging you. Let me explain to him I'm going to be leaving him. It'll confuse him too much if I just leave him like his parents did." She started to cry again. So did Kali.

"Cyrus, we have to get our hands on Jared, he's not going to stop. Melling is our best bet. We need her. You've got to cut her a deal," Nate said.

"She'll work with us, even if we don't cut a deal, won't you?" Cyrus asked.

"Of course, I'll do whatever I can to stop that man."

"Please Cyrus, we can't let her go to jail," Kali begged.

"Kali, it won't be up to me, it will be up to the DA. However, if she cooperates I suppose there might be some leniency."

"I don't need leniency."

"It won't be your decision to make either," Cyrus said in an icy tone. They spent the rest of their time asking Jade Melling question after question about Jared Spellman until finally they had a lead they could work with.

After the long interview, Cyrus and Nate left for California on the red-eye to work on the lead. Jade's assistant arranged for her driver to take her home, and Noah and Kali went to their hotel. They agreed to meet at the facility in Rochester the following morning.

Chapter Thirty-Two

"I'm nervous."

"What's there to be nervous about, love?" Noah asked, as he held Kali's hand. God she looked beautiful the red sweater. Her face had filled out a little. Nate had been sharing treats with her, and Sarah made her finish every meal they ate together.

Climbing the stairs they approached the sliding glass door of the Rochester Center for Long Term Care. Everybody decided not to tell Sarah about Joey, she would have been on a plane in a heartbeat. Nobody truly knew what her capabilities were, and first Noah and Kali wanted to meet him. They were taken to a room with large windows and scattered with tables and chairs.

"This is our Visitor's Lounge," their escort explained.

When they looked around it was obvious there were family members visiting with patients, many of whom were in specialized chairs. Noah saw some traumatic brain injury patients, and realized they were likely vets.

"Noah?"

He looked into her concerned blue eyes.

"It's nothing, baby."

She kissed him on the cheek.

God he loved her.

"Kelly? Noah?"

He saw Jade sitting at a table with a blond man. As they got closer, Noah realized there were Legos scattered all over the table.

"Thanks for coming. Joey, this is Kelly and Noah." Joey didn't look up, he was struggling to put something together that looked like a spaceship. "Joey?" Jade's voice was firm. He finally set down his toy and looked up. Suddenly Noah was back in time, in a stadium, briefly looking into the eyes of the boy. Joey's eyes widened.

"I know you," he said, pointing at Noah. Then he turned to Kali. He grinned widely. "Kali!" He rushed around the table, and grabbed her in a big hug.

Kali's eyes were as big as Joey's. She turned to Noah, and then Jade. "I know him." She hugged the big blond man, and they continued to hold one another.

"Kali, do you want to play Legos with me?" Joey asked. Noah picked up the box, and noticed it was for children ten and above. He, Kali and Jade only occasionally helped, instead watching to see if Joey would improve with the building project. He continued to look at the box and find pieces to put together as he talked about playing outside, running races and wrestling with his pet dog in a long forgotten time.

"What about your parents?" Jade asked.

"They died in the wreck, don't you remember Jade?"

"I mean in the time before," Jade probed.

"Oh, my Mom and Dad were sad when I had to leave. Remember Kali, they cried with your Nana. But they said it was good too. I cried too. But I knowed it was good."

Noah watched as Joey grabbed Kali's hand. "Thank you for helping me remember Kali. And you too Noah. Are you going to stay with me? I want you to be my friends forever." Noah watched as a tear dripped down Jade's cheek.

"Joey, what have you been doing since you've been here? Aren't you bored?"

Now that was an interesting question his Kali had asked. Noah watched as Joey tipped his head to consider it.

"Yes, it's boring here. It's like I can't think sometimes, like I'm mostly just playing in my old room waiting for something. I've been waiting for a very long time. Do you like my spaceship?" he asked, holding up the toy.

It was perfect.

"It's really nice," Kali said.

"You can have it. Can I go back to my room? I'm tired now," he said looking at Jade. She looked at

Joey, and nodded. She had been staring at him in wonder for the whole conversation. He walked around the table and gave her a kiss.

"When will I see you again? Can you come back tomorrow?"

"Do you want me to?"

"Yes. Can Kali and Noah come too?" He looked at them shyly.

"We'll be here," Noah assured him. It was so disconcerting to hear such boyish questions coming from a grown man.

As soon as Joey left, Jade turned to them. "I can't believe it. I've been bringing him more complex toys every time I visit. I brought that one today because I knew you two would be here to assist him, and I thought it would help pass the time. There is no way he should have been able to do even a quarter of the work, let alone most of it."

"I think as we meet and interact with one another it has a multiplication effect. I've definitely seen it with Kali and me, and then when Sarah joined us, I noticed it even more."

"But…" Jade stopped herself.

"But what, Jade," Kali gently prompted.

"Even with Joey? Do you really think it will work with him? I hoped. I hoped so much. He is the most loving soul I know. He deserves to have a full life. He deserves it. Nobody, and I mean nobody, deserves it more." Nothing could or would justify what had happened to Kali by Noah's way of thinking. But after meeting Joey,

Noah understood why this woman would be working so hard to give him the life he was clearly meant to have.

They agreed to meet the following afternoon so they could have dinner with Joey. It worked out great, because Noah had plans to keep Kali up late, so she would need to sleep in.

I heard that.

Let's see if you can see the pictures in my mind. He teased as they walked into the warm autumn air. He liked how she cuddled up against him on the way to the car.

Noah always reached for her hand, every single time, and it made her heart warm. She wove her fingers through his, once again amazed at the difference in size. The man was huge!

Well thank you, baby.

Be good.

I thought I was good. Remember last night? Remember this morning?

"Noah, I missed you. I needed my friend, I'm so glad you rescued me." Looking at his beautiful brown eyes and black curls, her heart melted. She intended to keep him forever.

"I like the idea of being a kept man." He squeezed her hand gently, that was Noah, always aware of his strength, sharing it with her, making her feel loved.

"You'll always be loved." He kissed her, right on the steps of the facility as doctors and nurses walked past and Kali couldn't have cared less. She was still floating when they walked into the Visitor's Lounge. Jade and Joey were waiting for them. Joey's smile split his face, and he yelled across the room.

"Kali! Noah! What took you so long?"

An older woman looked up and yelled at him in a foreign language. Joey looked crushed. He waited until Kali and Noah came to him. "Am I really a monkey?"

Kali realized the man was serious, so she answered him seriously. "No Joey, you're not a monkey, what makes you think that?"

"She said I was." He pointed at the woman who was leaving out the double doors. "A baboon is a monkey, right?"

"She was speaking Russian," Jade said. "Joey never learned languages like the rest of the *found*."

"Was he ever exposed to foreign languages when he lived with his adoptive parents?" Noah asked.

"No, only English. Then nine months later he was here. He was in a coma for a little over a year. When he woke up he was still the same age." Jade turned to Kali. "I read accounts you and Sarah learned languages and I brought in people who spoke French, Spanish and Korean, but he never learned."

"No, I never did, but I understood her." Joey

looked thoughtful, then he once again brightened. "Can we go outside for a walk? Can I hold Kali's hand, Noah?"

"Sure Buddy." As they walked around the grounds it was clear Joey was friends with everyone who worked or lived at the center. But as time went on, other things became disturbingly clear as well.

"That's Trisha," he said pointing to a hospice worker who was pushing a man in a wheelchair. Minutes later he pointed to a doctor. "That's Dr. Michael. He was...he was making Trisha feel uncomf, uncomfor," he stopped to glare at the doctor who immediately started walking the other way. "Dr. Michael is a weasel. I told him to stay away from Trisha, or I would hurt him like Trisha was scared he would hurt her." Joey didn't have the look of a child on his face now, he looked like a man who was taking care of the defenseless.

"Joey, why didn't you come and talk to me?" Jade asked.

"Nobody wants me to tell you things. I need to keep their secrets, Jade. I just listen most of the time, but sometimes they need help. If I can, I help them. It was easy with Dr. Michael, he was just a bully. You can't let bullies win, or they will bully another person and another person and another person."

Kali realized the rules of the playground really were often the rules of the adult world as well. They kept walking, Joey swinging her hand as the sun started to sink.

"Hello Joey, is this your family?" An older man with his leg in a brace was raking the leaves. Joey pulled Kali over to meet him, but he was careful not to disturb the piles of leaves already stacked.

"Mr. Issa, this is Kali. Kali what is your last name?"

"Wachowski."

"Mr. Issa, this is Kali Wachowski, we have been friends for a very long time. This is my godmother, Jade Melling, she is a wonderful artist. This is Kali's boyfriend Noah." Joey asked specific questions about Mr. Issa's health and pain levels with his leg. It was obvious the man considered Joey a confidante, but was now feeling very uncomfortable discussing those same things in front of others.

"Joey, please, spend time with your family. This is fine. I am fine." He reached to grab Joey's arm, to better make his point, but his leg gave out. Joey caught him before he fell.

"Mr. Issa, you work for a hospital, we should talk to the director. You shouldn't be in this much pain. "Let's get you inside."

"Dont rahatsız Lütfen," he said waving Joey away.

"Don't be silly, you're not being a bother."

When the old man continued to speak in the other language, so did Joey. A long conversation ensued, and finally the old man threw up his hands.

"Fine, take me inside." He turned to Jade. "All

these years, I didn't know your godson was Turkish." He turned back to Joey. "You're a good boy Joey Melling."

"My name is Joe Mirelli, and you're a good man and a good friend." Joe held out his hand. Jade burst into tears. Mr. Issa understood the importance of the moment, and responded in kind.

"Mr. Joe Mirelli, I am honored to make your acquaintance," he said as he solemnly shook the blond man's hand.

"I will be following up to make sure you've spoken to the center's administration."

"Evet, I mean yes, I suppose you will," the old man smiled. "I will talk to the chief of staff in the morning."

Apparently satisfied, he turned towards everyone. "My thinking is finally getting clearer."

Kali saw tears well up in Jade's eyes. Joey, Joe she mentally corrected herself pulled Jade into his arms and started to speak low into her ear. Finally she stopped crying.

Kali leaned into Noah's side. He immediately put an arm around her, and they watched the miracle that was Joe Mirelli.

I remember him. Do you?

Yes. He was my age, I remember playing with him and his dog. It was a collie. I don't remember him telling me he was going. How do you remember him?

I saw him at the stadium. He had such a big smile on his face. You could tell he thought this was going to be a great adventure, and look what happened.

Noah, maybe this was exactly what was supposed to happen. Kali snuggled even closer to him, happy as he pulled her in for a heart melting kiss. When they finally broke apart it took a moment for her to become aware of her surroundings. When she did, Joe was looking at them both. Once again he wearing a big smile, like life's adventures were just beginning.

At dinner, Joe peppered them with questions. He asked about anything and everything. At one point Kali's sweater rode up and he saw the scar on her right wrist.

"How did you get that?"

Kali wasn't going to tell him, but Jade explained what had happened, including Jared's involvement. She didn't explain the torture in graphic detail, but instead said how there had been bad people who hurt Kali for information and Jared had been the boss of them.

"Jared is an evil man. I hated him and I only spent time with him because you asked me to Jade."

"Did he hurt you, Joey?" Jade gasped.

"No, he wouldn't hurt me, he wanted me to like him, because he wanted your money."

"Joe, you sure had him figured out," Noah smiled. "Is there anything else you can tell us? We're trying to find him."

"Sure. He was always talking to his girlfriend on the phone. Her name is Ashley, and she lives in Las Vegas. You could talk to his wife, but he would always avoid her phone calls."

"Do you know the girlfriend's last name, Joe?" Noah asked.

"One day when turned off his cell phone because his wife kept calling, she called the front desk and they said an Ashley Hayes was on the phone for him."

"What about his wife?" Kalie asked. "Or anyone or anything else you can remember." They questioned Joe, and it became clear Jared felt totally comfortable speaking in front of Joe as he would have in front of any young child. Obviously the man didn't have much exposure to children and the fact they were actually sponges who absorbed everything.

He thought Joe was damaged Kali.
Well then he's an evil idiot.

Noah's deep laughter warmed her heart. She loved it when she could make him laugh, and the people around them would wonder why he was laughing for no reason. But Joe didn't look surprised, as a matter of fact, he looked at Noah, then at her, and gave her a knowing smile. All this growth in one day was phenomenal.

"I think his brother was even worse, you should find him," Joe said suddenly.

"What?" Kali and Noah asked in unison.

"Jared's brother. He came and visited me one time. He scared Jared, I could tell. He lives in the Catsfins. His name is Aaron, he had a different dad, so he had a different last name he said was better than Jared's. His name is Aaron Price and he lives in the Catsfins Mountains."

"Joey, do you think he could have said Catskill Mountains?" Jade asked.

"That's it," Joe nodded decisively. "I got gill and fin messed up."

"Joe, we have to go. We have to find Jared, and you've been very helpful."

"Noah, will you make him go to jail for what he did to Kali?"

"You can bet on it." Joe stood and shook Noah's hand, then he turned to Kali and gave her a hug. "Will you come to visit me again?"

"Joey, I think before the year is out *we're* going to be visiting *them*," Jade said linking arms with her godson.

Kali figured it would be more like another couple of weeks.

I think you're right, beautiful. Now let's get a move on.

Chapter Thirty-Three

They hadn't been able to track down information on Aaron Price, it was like he had disappeared. Yes, he had a residence in the Catskills, but he moved without a forwarding address about the time of Jade Melling's first donations. Sierra was able to find information on Jared's Vegas girlfriend. Supposedly she was now cohabitating with a Gerald King, but Noah would bet the farm it was Jared Spellman. Unfortunately, Ashley Hayes and Gerald King were on a cruise in the Mediterranean. It was time to focus on the Rixitron problem.

"I still can't believe everything that went on with Joey." Sarah said as she spooned another helping of mashed potatoes onto Kali's plate.

"I'm full."

"You ate about seven hundred calories. Try again, slim." Sarah made an eating motion with her fork and Kali scooped another bite of the potatoes.

"They are good," she smiled.

"My brother can cook."

Noah watched as Kali really started to dig into the food.

"Kali, there's something you haven't fully considered. If you marry Noah, your name is going to be Kali Wachowski-Kukailimoku, if you marry me, it would be Kali Wachowski-Johnson, and I cook."

"Can it Johnson. She chose me. What did you make for dessert?" He looked around the table and wished Rydell and Riley were there as well. He liked Cyrus, but it wasn't the same as having his team.

"I made apple brown betty."

"What's that?" Everybody turned on Noah.

"Seriously Noah, you haven't had it before?" Sarah asked. When he shook his head, she rubbed her hands in glee. "Oh, you're in for a treat. "Brother, is it warm?"

"Sister, I wouldn't serve it any other way."

When the warm crusted brown sugar and apple treat was put in front of him everybody watched as he took the first bite. "This is great, Cyrus. I'm sorry Kali, I think *I'm* the one who's going to be marrying Cyrus, and I'm not hyphenating my name, I'm just going to be Noah Johnson."

He loved to hear her laugh, and watch her eat. She had no idea the way she could seduce him with just her lips around a fork, or her smile. She always thought she was only passably pretty, because her skin was so light, and her light hair blended with it.

She didn't realize how the pink of her lips, the blue of her eyes, and the blush of her cheeks made her a study in contrast he could stare at for hours.

"Noah, are you all right?"

"What, baby?"

"You haven't heard a word I said," she whispered.

"Tell me again."

"Have you heard from Dave, have they told him anything about Mai's condition?"

"So far they haven't told him anything."

I'll tell you more in our room. He had to get her alone. He got up from the table and reached for Kali, satisfied she had eaten all of her dessert.

"Cyrus, as always, it was a great meal. Tomorrow night I'll cook." There was a round of groans. "Okay, I'll order take-out."

"Chinese," Nate said hopefully.

"Anything you want," Noah said as he gently tugged Kali towards the door. "We'll see you in the morning for the briefing."

As soon as they were out in the hallway, Noah had her up against the wall, his lips stealing kisses. When she wrapped her arms around his neck, he had what he wanted. He pulled them away he slid her arms so they pressed against the wall of the hallway, arching her high taut breasts against his chest like an offering. She moaned in supplication, and he licked her collarbone, trailing ever downwards to the "V" of her t-shirt, it had been driving him wild all through dinner.

"Someone might see," she said in a breathy voice making his cock even harder.

"Everybody knows not to come out the door."

"But…"

He pushed his knee between her legs, tight against the crotch of her jeans, and slid it up and down. As she cried out he thrust his tongue between her parted lips. Back and forth he rocked her. He couldn't get enough of the flavors of cinnamon, apples and Kali. Please God, he couldn't hold on much longer, and finally her nails ground into his hands and she shuddered her release. He held her still, sandwiched between the wall and his overheated body. When he thought he could move without doing permanent injury to his dick, he slid one arm around her waist and the other under her knees picking her up.

"I can walk."

"I like carrying you." He had no choice, he had to keep her as close as possible, it was a biological imperative.

She was dizzy, and it seemed to get worse, better, and more intense the longer she was with him. They twined together, mated. Tears pricked her eyes, and she gulped in big breaths of air, trying to get ahold of herself.

Don't try, I'm right here with you.

He pushed their apartment door closed and had her on the couch before she could respond.

Clothes went flying in every direction. Names called with frantic need. At the exact moment Noah's perfect lips touched her nipple she arched up to meet him. Just as she was about to ask for a certain touch, his fingers slid through her folds, and she knew to bite his neck hard enough to make him groan.

Truly joined, in sync, they knew each other's thoughts before they were thoughts. They were parts of the same whole. His other hand helped her undo his jeans so she could unleash his cock, and then he was spearing inside her.

Pleasure swamped him, her, them. She was tight, he was thick. He was hot, she was wet. The friction was sublime. They flew high, so high.

"So what couldn't you tell me in front of the others?"

"Dave has decided to break in and talk to Mai. He doesn't trust she's being told the truth about what happened. He thinks she has been kept in the dark about her brainwashing."

"What is the correct procedure?"

"She should be with her parents, her adoptive parents. She needs to be reconditioned. She needs to see these people love her, and what she was led to believe is wrong. It will take time, but it's what needs to happen. Dave thinks they haven't told her anything."

"Why wouldn't they?"

"He doesn't know, but he thinks the Taiwanese scientists have always wanted an opportunity to do experiments on Mai, and now they have a legitimate excuse to do so. It's suspicious they haven't let the Zhang's even talk to their daughter since her rescue."

"I didn't know that. Her parents have to be frantic."

"They are, and they have begun a public campaign to get her released. They are making it sound like she is a political prisoner. It's a good tactic. She's been high profile since she was *found*, but when she first played the violin publically at age ten, she became an international sensation. Then the mathematics? Well, she's Taiwan's rock star. The idea Mai Zhang is being held prisoner will not go over well with the public."

"No, I suppose it won't."

"What's wrong?"

"Nothing."

Baby, please share.

Sometimes I feel less than…

They had been having hot chocolate on the couch, and he plucked her mug out of her hands, pulling her into his arms, and across his lap. She cuddled. He liked how she always did that now.

"I've been noticing some things, at first they were kind of subtle, but I really noticed it when we were dealing with Jade." She was silent and still, just listening to him. "Remember how Jade really didn't understand how Joe could be assimilating Turkish like he was. She was really struggling when I tried to explain." Kali didn't bother to deny it, and he liked that, there was no false protests to protect his feelings. She understood he was a big boy.

"Also, let's talk about your time spent with Nate. Did you notice he couldn't wrap his head around Sarah's healing at first?"

"Sure."

"Out of all the team, Kota took to it first."

"Of course he would, he was healed."

"Nope. It was his background, he's talked to me about his great uncle who is a Shaman. He is very deferential when he talks about him. He already believes in spiritual and supernatural things like healing powers. Then there is Sierra, she was already onboard with you and I being able to speak telepathically. Nate believed we were just in tune with one another." Kali was open to him, so he could listen to her process what he was saying.

"Okay, I agree."

"Nate's one of my oldest friends. I tried to explain to him we were just coming more into our powers at this point in time, and our time spent together seemed to augment those powers. He wasn't having any of it."

Kalie nodded her agreement, remembering back.

"But Kali, you and he had lunch together, just the two of you, and after you explained it to him he seemed to really get it."

"I didn't say anything differently than you, Noah."

"I don't think you did either baby, but I think the difference is *you* said it. I think that's your gift. I didn't think much of it, but after I listened to you talk to Jade, it became really obvious you have the ability to get through to people. It's almost like you can educate them."

She drew back so sharply she hit her head on his chin. "Are you saying I brainwash them?"

"No, not at all. Baby, I'm saying you are able to help people see things more clearly. You have the ability to impart knowledge, to help educate people. That's why you're a teacher."

"I don't buy it. You're saying I'm putting thoughts in people's heads, leading them, ultimately changing their thinking. That's brainwashing."

Noah was getting frustrated. "If I had managed to convince Nate that Sarah's healing was just a natural progression of the *found* abilities, and if I could have explained to Jade how each *found* child was able to assimilate languages in their first few years here, and Joe was doing that now because he had basically been in stasis, would I have been brainwashing them?"

"Well, no," Kali said slowly.

"Am I brainwashing you now as I'm convincing

you on the validity of my argument?" He watched as she smiled. She hit his bare chest. That smile, and her in his shirt was making him hard.

"See, you do have special abilities, Beautiful."

"Making you horny?"

"That definitely heads the list. However, I think your ability to explain and convince people is going to be our ace in the hole, especially when we have to explain things to people like Sakuro's superiors."

"What do you mean? I thought he was in charge?"

"Everybody has a boss. Sakuro hasn't said anything, but my guess is eventually as we go after Rixitron there will be repercussions. Your ability to explain and educate people will be invaluable." He could see and feel her doubt, but as time went on, and they were in more situations where she used her skills, she would see what he meant.

"Kali, in the city of Chicago were there any other teachers with a zero drop-out rate for your grade?"

"There were three."

"How many years in a row did you accomplish this?"

"Only two years in a row."

"Did the other three?"

"No," she reluctantly admitted. He decided to drop the subject. He could feel her considering what he had said. "Are you sure *convincing* people isn't your ability?"

He gave her question serious consideration. "I think it's because we're linked. It's why you could find me. I think because we are paired, I've taken on some of your abilities, and you've taken on some of mine."

"I can *only* find you."

"Just like I can *only* convince you. Maybe this is something we can work at." He could see she was tired. "Come on, let's go to bed. Maybe there is something else I can convince you of." He liked seeing the blush suffuse her face.

Chapter Thirty-Four

"Riley, get your ass back here. If you haven't found her after all this time, then she's safe from the idiots at Rixitron," Nate said in disgust.

"I want Sam, I mean Noah to get out here and help find her." The connection was scratchy but Riley's determination came through loud and clear.

"Why? She's safe. Obviously Seth's grandmother has her holed up so tight nobody can get to her, why should we interfere?"

Nate had a point. What's more, bringing her in, would eventually make her more of a target. Noah wasn't sure how long they could keep this location in Orange County under wraps.

"The grandmother is in her late seventies. The baby is less than six months old, and they had to get to wherever the hell this is by horseback. This is not good. I understand she is hidden from the fuckers, but she is not in a safe place. It's our job to keep civilians safe. I would have thought the child of a *found* would have mattered to you, Noah."

"God dammit, any child matters to me, Riley."

"Don't use the Lord's name in vain."

Noah was about to lose it. But he wasn't sure at who. Riley was making sense.

"Ah fuck," Nate said. Noah looked around the table. Everybody was gathered, listening to the phone, and it was clear Noah would be going to New Mexico. He looked at Sierra, and she looked up from her damn computer and nodded her head. His ticket had been booked.

"I'll be there Riley."

"Has anyone found a way to talk to that motherfucker, Seth Natani?" Riley demanded.

"Not without blowing his cover," Sierra replied.

"Tell me again, why the hell hasn't the DEA managed to notice him?" Nate demanded. The fact Seth married someone else during an investigation while his girlfriend gave birth to his child wasn't sitting well with any of them.

"We got lucky with our facial recognition software," Cyrus said. "I still disagree with your decision not to notify his superiors of his location."

"Duly noted, Captain. But as a member of an organization recently infiltrated, I'm saying Seth had a reason for choosing not to trust his chain of command. We need to respect his decision."

"Or he's gone rogue."

"How do you account for all those tips the DEA has received in the last six months? Has to be Seth. He hasn't gone rogue, at least not when it comes to his duty towards his job," Riley said, through the phone.

"How are we going to tell Annie when we find her?" Kali asked.

"We sit her down with shots of tequila, and we tell her. Then we give her a nutcracker, and let her at him," Sarah said, her voice filled with venom.

"Nah, we give her a knife, a serrated hunting knife, a rusty one. Girl can do a lot of damage with one of those," Sierra said knowledgeably.

Noah winced. Somewhere out there was a man who had done her wrong, but he had the feeling he had paid for it.

"First Noah has to find her. When will you be here?"

"He'll be there tonight, I'm texting you his itinerary right now," Sierra said. "He'll be staying at the same motel as you."

"I'll be waiting." Riley hung up. Everybody looked at one another.

"Shit, he's wound tight," Kota said. "It's a good thing you're going to be there, Lieutenant. This assignment is hitting him hard."

"It's the baby. His father abandoned him and his mother when he was a baby, and he can't stand seeing Annie vulnerable."

"No he didn't," Nate disagreed with Sierra. "His Dad is a preacher. He holds him up on a pedestal."

"That's his stepdad. He's a wonderful guy, took them in, treats Riley's mom like a queen. But Riley never forgot those early years. He had it rough until he was about five."

"It explains why this has become such a personal quest for him," Kali nodded. "I'd wondered."

"I figured it was because he had been stuck in the trunk, and he wanted to make the Rixitron bastard pay," Nate said, with a shrug.

"You really are oblivious, aren't you?" Sarah said shaking her head. She got up from the table. "We're done, right?"

"No, we're not Sarah, we need to discuss Jared Spellman."

"Ah damn, I'm sorry," she said to Kali as she sat back down.

"Sierra, what do you have?" Noah asked.

"Ashley has the worst taste in boyfriends."

"Skip the commentary, Sierra," Nate grumbled.

"They're due back three days from now. Anyway, she has to start her shift at the casino that night, so we should be able to question him at her house or take him, whichever way we want to play it."

"Sounds like it will be me and Kota, since you'll be in New Mexico," Nate said decisively.

"I think you should take me as well." All eyes swung to Kali.

"The last person Jared is going to expect to have questioning him is me. What's more, Noah and I have been talking, I think I would be useful during questioning."

Fuck. Every muscle in Noah's body stiffened to the point of pain. She was right.

"I really think I should be the one who goes," Cyrus said gently. "Questioning suspects is actually one of my job duties."

"Exactly cop, it's why you *aren't* going. You have a badge to protect, we don't want you doing anything to tarnish it."

"Cyrus, Nate's right and so is Kali." There was silence around the table.

"This concludes this morning's briefing," Sierra said.

Noah wanted to follow Kali back to their apartment, but he had to make sure he kept up on everything. He watched as everyone left the conference room, until only Sierra remained.

"What's up, boss?"

"Three things. First, how tight is our security here? Second, has anyone been trying to tap into us? Third, I understand the DEA trying to contact Seth could put him at risk, but what about us? I'm sure you have a plan, what have you thought through in that devious mind of yours?"

"Seth…"

"Let's start with number one."

"I haven't heard a peep. So far our cover as corporate housing for a company out of Delaware is holding just fine. Universal Concepts is a consulting firm that routinely does this type of thing. I would have made us employees of one of the top three consulting firms, but they're like ants, they are all over Southern California, and they might have wanted to be social."

"Okay, so our cover is tight as far as the apartment housing, what about when we start trying to doing some reconnaissance? Have you been able to come up with some decent covers?"

"Security, and I'm not talking the security for a booth or patrols the building, I'm talking the real security that monitors the cameras and takes care of the high end executive needs."

"Don't they have seasoned people?"

"They do, yes."

"But their top security guy is finally going to be offered a job in one of the Caribbean Islands like he has always wanted. Then one of their other guys is going to end up taking a nasty fall, resulting in a broken leg."

"How are you going to guarantee we'll be the replacements?"

"Sakuro is old friends with the head of the agency who supplies security for Rixitron. We just lucked into that one."

"I'll never turn down luck, it's saved my ass too damn often. Now, tell me about Seth."

"I hate him."

"You and every other woman in the room."

"Don't forget Riley, he hates him too," Sierra reminded Noah.

"I wasn't going to be able to forget, now was I? So what's the word, I'm sure you've figured out a way for us to get close to him."

"It's still in its infancy stages. I'll let you know when you get back from New Mexico. In the meantime, you stay safe. I know Riley has counted the Rixitron guy out, but I've checked on him. He's one of their security guys, and he's good. He's former special ops. I'm actually relieved you're going to be there with Riley."

"Got it." Noah left and made a beeline for Kali. Sierra might be worried about Riley, but he was worried for Kali.

He got to the apartment, and Kali was in the kitchen making grilled cheese sandwiches and tomato soup. She knew it was one of his favorites.

"That's not going to work."

"Sex is next."

"That might work." His neck still hurt, every time he thought about her in danger his neck hurt. If he wasn't careful he'd develop a twitch. She turned off the stove, and put the food on the table.

"Nate and Kota are going to be with me. Everything we've heard about Jared says he just got lucky when he kidnapped me."

"He damn near tortured you to death. I'd say he got more than lucky." He gently grasped her hands, pulled her towards him, and rubbed his thumbs over the scars on her wrists.

"Noah, I refuse to live my life in fear. Besides Jared, there's Rixitron. I'm not going to live holed up in this apartment forever. I'm going to go back and visit my parents. So is Sarah. We're taking back our lives. This is the first step." She pulled away, and rubbed the kinks in his neck, hitting just the right spots.

"It's not fair you can read me so well," he said as he melted into her touch.

"Sure it is, because it works both ways." Finally able to take a breath again, he kissed this woman who was his world. He knew Kota and Nate would ensure her safety, and she was right. She was going to be phenomenal getting Jared to talk. But dammit, he wished she wouldn't so Nate and Kota could use a car battery on the son of a bitch!

Chapter Thirty-Five

Sitting in the front seat of the car with Kota, Kali had flashbacks to their time in Cancun. She rubbed her sweaty palms against her black jeans.

"It's going to be fine. Nate is checking the backyard. Spellman doesn't suspect a thing. We've had them under surveillance since the airport, and Ashley left for her job at the casino. He's alone. Nate's just being extra cautious."

Kali understood, but she also understood they didn't know if Jared was armed. She didn't want either man hurt when they went in and confronted him. She knew she was being unreasonable, and she built Jared up to be some kind of all-powerful monster. In her mind, he was the man who controlled her very existence, he was the ultimate monster.

Kota squeezed her shoulder. "We've got this Kali. You don't have to come in. Nate and I will get the information we need."

"No, I've come this far, I'm going in." She swallowed down the bile.

"Okay, but if at any time you need to bail, just say the word." Kota cocked his head listening to the transmitter in his ear. "That's the all clear. Show time."

Kali knew what was next. Kota was going to the front of the house, and Nate was going to the back. When they had Jared subdued, they'd text her to come to the front door. Kota left the car. It wasn't the longest five minutes of her life, but it was pretty close. When she got the text, she made her way leisurely to the door as planned.

Nate answered. "It was easy. Spellman's in the living room. He's not talking. Says we have the wrong guy."

Kali saw him at the airport, she would know him anywhere. He was not the wrong guy. When she walked into the normal ranch style living room, she found Jared strapped to a chair with duct tape. His mouth taped shut.

"That's going to make it hard for him to talk, isn't it?"

"He was doing some impressive yelling, we didn't want the neighbors to hear. I'm surprised you didn't hear him," Kota said.

Jared's eyes bugged out at the sight of Kali.

"Hello Jared. It's been awhile, hasn't it?" She stood over him, and they locked eyes. He stared as if he were seeing a ghost. "Gentlemen, can one of you get me a chair? I think this is going to take some time."

As soon as Kali was seated, she reached over and ripped off the duct tape, satisfaction running through her veins when she saw his bottom lip start to bleed and his eyes water. "Did it hurt?" He didn't say anything.

"It really is too bad you weren't there the day they rescued me," she said.

Still nothing.

The chair they had brought was one of the stuffed ones from the living room, but the chair Spellman was sitting in was one of the more uncomfortable chairs from the kitchen table. The men knew what they were doing.

"Didn't you bring zip ties?"

"Yes."

"Let's use them. I think Jared needs to be reminded why I'm less than happy with his lack of cooperation." Kali pushed up the sleeves of her black sweatshirt and held up her wrists. "You understand why I want to know why this was done, don't you? What possible reason could you have to torture me?" Kali actually felt a pulse of energy, and Jared blinked.

"Tara went too far." *Truth*, he was telling the truth.

"Tara was in your employ, ultimately you were responsible," Kali kept her tone reasonable, conversational.

Jared tensed, but nodded. "I thought she was the right person for the job. She said she understood how to get information."

"You trusted her, and she betrayed your trust."

"That's exactly what happened. I had no idea what was going on."

"I know, Jared. I was there the day when you stopped things. You made her stop."

"I did. That's right. I made her stop what she was doing."

"But in the beginning it was your decision, wasn't it? It was your decision to have me taken, wasn't it? Why would you do it, Jared?"

"It wasn't my decision. I hired Tara. I needed some questions answered. It wasn't my decision. I asked her to get those questions answered, and she went about it the wrong way. It was never my intention you be kidnapped Ms. Wachowski, you have to believe me."

"But I don't believe you. Let's work together to get to the truth. You met Joe Mirelli and realized how special he was. When was that?"

The questions and answers continued for three hours. Kali could actually feel pulses of energy surge through her body at different moments when she would hit on just the right way to phrase a question.

"Did someone make you realize you had something to gain by finding out more about the *found*?" Kali watched as Jared blinked rapidly. Even Kota and Nate squirmed in their seats, which was unusual.

"It was really obvious. Everyone knows you are special. You're not from here. You needed to be studied, and our governments were pussies."

"All of us had physical examinations to make sure we were okay when we were discovered. We are as human as the rest of you."

"You're freaks."

"But it's not what Tara was doing, now was she?" It took everything Kali had to keep her voice calm. The man wasn't making any sense. He was talking about the *found* needing to be studied, but she was tortured and questioned. What the hell was it? Both scenarios made her want to throw up, but one had almost killed her.

"It wasn't my fault, it was his."

"What do you mean, his?"

"I wanted to study your powers. Mai is a freak. So is Niko. You and Sarah are amazingly smart. I wanted to figure out if there was some gene we could splice, something in your brain or your blood we could harness and sell. You were the easiest one to get to. It's why I set up the facility in Indiana, where we could work on you indefinitely." Kali surged to her feet and Kota got up with her. She barely made it to the bathroom in time. She heaved the entire contents of her stomach. For long moments she just rested her crossed arms on the toilet seat.

"We should stop."

She looked up from her knees. Kota's eyes were glittering shards of obsidian. She grabbed some toilet paper and wiped her mouth and then flushed the toilet.

"We're not done. He mentioned someone else,

someone who wanted answers, instead of vivisection. He might not sound as bad, but I want them all stopped. Nobody is getting away with trying to capture us ever again." Kali hated her hoarse voice. Kota pulled her into his arms and just held her. She stood there, and finally relaxed into the embrace, needing the comfort. After long moments she pulled away.

"Thank you."

"Any time, it's part of our service." He grinned. "So you're sure you're up for another round? God knows what he's going to say next."

"We've got Rixitron with a breeding program, and this asshole was basically talking about cutting into my brain. Seriously, how much worse is it going to get?" As soon as the words were out of her mouth, she regretted them. Kota raised an eyebrow.

"I know, I know. I'm knocking on wood right now." They went into the kitchen and she found a bottle of club soda to rinse her mouth and soothe her stomach. Back in the living room, Kota took his seat looking stone faced. Kali sat down and made herself comfortable and smiled.

"How is your stomach feeling?"

"Much better, thank you for asking. How did you feel, I mean really feel when you were putting together your plan to conduct medical experiments on me? I've gotten to know you over the last few hours, this couldn't have felt good. You had to have had a strong reason, what was it?"

"Profit. Pure and simple. If I could figure out what made you different, then I could have sold it to a pharmaceutical company and made hundreds of millions of dollars." Truth, but not the entire truth. She wanted to know the deeper truth, but first she needed to know who was involved.

She needed to know the names of the people who had been willing to experiment on her. Nate had been recording this entire conversation, and even though it would never make its way into a court of law, it would help them track down every last person involved in this fucking operation. The questioning took another hour.

Finally she could ask what she wanted. "But you changed your plans, you didn't bring in the doctors, why?"

"We were saving them for later."

"Why later? You were destroying my brain, the actual thing you needed to make all this money."

"I told you, Tara went rogue."

Truth, but again, not the entire truth. "Jared," she said silkily. "You've admitted to being behind my kidnapping. You've provided all your co-conspirators. I expect you're going to prison for life. Are you sure you want to protect the person who screwed up your perfect plan? The person who turned your multi-million dollar plan into a torture session?" Again she felt the pulse of energy, and she knew she had him.

She wasn't surprised when he named his brother. She was expecting it, after what Joe Mirelli had said, but she had needed the confirmation.

"It was my brother," he spat out. Pure truth.

"Why would he want me tortured?

"He's a crazy asshole." Truth.

"Tara kept asking me questions. Were those questions he wanted answered?"

"Yes, he insisted they were the key. If we found out *those* answers, it would make us rich. Not that he needs the money, he has more money than God. His father left him richer than Midas."

"Where did you come from? How many others are there? Where are the rest of you now? Why were those answers so important, Jared?"

"I don't fucking know. I told you, he's a crazy asshole." Truth.

"Where's your brother now."

"Some place in Deer Valley, Utah. I know his old man kept a place up there."

"What was his father's name?"

"Herbert Price. My half-brother is Aaron Price. Arrogant prick. Thinks he's better than everyone. Keeps telling me everything is my fault, when it was his idea. What an asshole." He definitely believed what he was saying.

"Come on Kali, we're out of here. We need to call the cops."

"Bitch, you're going to jail for what you did to me."

"Are you kidding? She's been in California this entire time. Airtight alibi. This was a home invasion, and you're about to be charged with some heinous crimes. Nobody's going to be blaming this poor victim who is the daughter of a police captain. Do yourself a favor, and go with the home invasion." Nate tipped over the chair with his foot. Then he and Kota went about knocking some of the things in the living room over. It was the mildest home invasion Kali ever saw.

When they got in the car she asked about it.

"It was probably Ashley's stuff. We didn't want to mess it up too badly."

Yep, Kali really liked the group of people she worked with.

Chapter Thirty-Six

Noah hadn't been on a horse since he joined the military. Despite what people thought, there were horses on Kauai. He actually worked a couple of summers guiding tourists on horseback through the lush green mountainsides of the island. It was totally different on the hard packed land of the New Mexico desert. The horses seemed to clomp instead of delicately picking their way along the trail.

"You going to make it?"

"I'm fine, Riley."

"We can take a break."

"We're not too much further, let's finish this."

"Lieutenant, I hate to burst your bubble, but I've been all over this area, and they're not here. I know they're further in the mountains," he said pointing towards the mountains in the vista.

"Nope, they're over there." Noah pointed to a place less than a mile away. "They have a house cut into the rocks."

"Not possible, they said this place has been there since the early 1800's."

"Chief, they're there. If you're not going to believe me, why'd you want me here?" Was he ever this young?

"Sorry, Sir." They rode in silence for the next ten minutes. "Look, I didn't mean to doubt your abilities. I talked to my dad about them. We both believe they're a gift from God. But it's just I've been over this area with a fine tooth comb." It was hard to arch your eyebrow when you were being tossed about like ice in a blender, but he must have managed because Riley bent his head.

"Riley, what is it with you and this girl?"

"What? What do you mean?"

"You know exactly what I mean. This has gone far beyond an assignment. This has become a quest."

"Lieutenant, I'm just concerned. We were together at Trent's office in Denton. You were kidnapped. I know how ruthless these bastards can be. Can you blame me for being worried about a woman and baby?"

Well, when he put it like that, still. "Riley, it's me Noah. Let's cut the crap, all right? We're going to be there in less than twenty minutes, and I want to know what's really going on with you. Do I have a problem?" Again he gave his young team mate a hard look, and he watched as Riley wilted.

"I can't believe she's been abandoned is all. She needs to be taken care of, her daughter needs a daddy. I'm not volunteering for the job. I don't know her. I'm just going to make damn sure she has somebody on her side so she knows she isn't alone. So she knows she doesn't have to decide between a bad or worse option because somebody isn't there to help her." Riley no longer sounded like the youngest member of the team, he sounded like the oldest.

Noah didn't point out Seth Natani's parents and grandmother had already done it by rallying around the young woman. Even though it looked like Seth had abandoned her in the worst sort of way his parents had her back. Riley was determined to be another person she could rely on.

As they approached the rock formation, Noah understood why Riley had missed the shelter. It was a unique, not man made with explosives, instead one rock slid down at one point and provided a courtyard. Someone then cut in a small area allowing people and horses to go in single file. Shit, it was defended well. They'd have their heads blown off when they went in there.

"You found it." Riley was off his horse and at the entrance by the time Noah told him to halt.

"Riley, this is going to take some discussion." Noah got down off his horse, and thanked God he actually worked out, otherwise he would have fallen down. His legs felt like strands of spaghetti. He gratefully leaned against the rock wall and yelled.

"Mrs. Natani, my name is Noah Kukailimoku. I am *found* like your grandson. I was raised on the island of Kauai." There was no answer.

"Annie, this is Petty Officer Riley Jones with the United States Navy, I've come to help you. I know you are hiding from people who are out to capture your baby because she is Seth's daughter. I know Seth has abandoned you, but I can help."

God help him from young men who wanted to help. "Riley, I will do the talking from now on," he commanded sharply.

Riley nodded.

"Annie and Mrs. Natani, this is Noah again. I'm in the Navy as well. There have been different factions trying to either capture or do harm to the *found* for years now. Mrs. Natani, you and your family did the right thing by keeping Seth's identity secret. Unfortunately, these groups are well-funded and they have been searching for us for years. Seth is safe right now because he is undercover, but people at a company called Rixitron has found out about Annie and her daughter, so we need to get her to a safer place."

"Seth isn't deep undercover, if we know where he is," a woman's voice shouted back.

"Annie?"

"Yep, Annie Newman. Seth has obviously moved on, which is his prerogative. My job is to keep my daughter safe."

"My job, and my son's job is to keep our

granddaughter and great granddaughter safe. So how can you prove you are really one of the *found*?"

"Ask me questions only someone who is a *found* child would know. I should know the answers."

"What language did you speak when you were discovered?"

"I spoke Hawaiian—the language spoken to me first." There was a long pause.

"How old were you when you stopped being able to learn new languages?"

"Eleven."

"There's a difference, Seth stopped being able to learn languages when he was nine."

"Let me guess," Noah said, "he was about seven years old when he came to you. I've talked to four other *found* children, they all lost their ability to easily assimilate languages two years after being here." Noah and Riley looked at one another as they waited.

"Did you have a name?"

"Yes. My name was Noah, but my adoptive parents called me Samson, Sam for short. What was Seth's name when you found him?"

"Seth. It was his name, we did not take it from him." Noah heard the censure in the old woman's voice. "Did you dream boy, and if you did, what were your dreams?"

"I dreamed of a stadium."

"What filled your stadium?"

"Other children."

"Come on in."

Noah led his horse through the entryway with Riley following behind.

He stopped short as soon as he got into the open area, it was like he had entered a scene from a photo shoot. Female laughter floated over to him, which made him continue forward, and allowed Riley and his horse to come in as well.

"You were expecting something out of the old west."

Noah looked around at the gracious patio furniture and the baby swing and smiled. The patio had an awning rolled out from the house, and off to the side was a small corral with two horses grazing and room for at least four more. The house was a small adobe style and would blend in with the rocks when someone flew overhead. As a matter of fact when he looked closer, the awning was really made of camouflage netting, so it too ensured the patio furniture wouldn't be seen from the air. After realizing all of it, he looked at the corral again and saw there was a natural rock overhang the horses could be tied under, and the fence could be folded back.

"Does everything meet with your approval?" The older woman asked, her eyes alight with amusement. She stood behind a table set for four people.

"You were expecting us?"

"My son said your young colleague had been pretty stubborn. He felt with your help you would probably find us."

"You seem awfully welcoming. I would have expected a little more caution."

"Again, your young friend is not very discreet. He is also a very sound sleeper. We were able to find out who he was, and who the Rixitron bastard was within the first twenty-four hours they were in town. Then it was just a matter of figuring out everyone's motives."

"What do you mean I'm a sound sleeper? Are you saying someone broke into my room at the motel?" Noah worked hard not to smile at Riley's outraged tone. He was great to have at your back out in the jungle, but apparently he was not a good field operative. He would have to have Nate train him.

"No offense was meant towards you, Mr. Jones."

"Petty Officer Jones," Riley corrected.

"I beg your pardon. No disrespect intended. You have been working to protect Annie and my great granddaughter from the very beginning, and I can't thank you enough."

"If you knew that, why all of the questions?" Noah asked.

"Because we thought there was more to your background than was reported." She sounded like his Hawaiian grandfather.

During the time Noah and Mrs. Natani were talking, Annie continued to sit at the end of the table, quietly sipping her lemonade, and pushing the baby swing.

"Annie, are you okay?" Riley asked, the question bursting from him. It was obvious he had contained it for as long as possible.

"Yes, Petty Officer Jones, I'm fine. Nell is fine. But I do want to leave. Why are people after us, shouldn't they want Seth?"

Riley's face hardened, and Noah finally saw the man he normally served with.

"We think they are after Nell. When we were in Texas, we discovered documents showing they planned on developing a breeding program with the *found*."

"It seems they're a little late," Annie replied calmly.

Mrs. Natani said something in a language Noah couldn't understand, he assumed it was Navajo. He wondered if Nell would have the gift of assimilating languages.

"We need to take you someplace safe."

"We're safe here," Mrs. Natani said confidently.

"We found you," Riley pointed out. "If we could, they can."

"Noah found us with his abilities. They don't have Noah."

"How did you know it was me, Mrs. Natani?" Noah asked.

"Seth has abilities as well. No one has ever discovered my home. You did, therefore you have a *found* skill, like Seth has his skills. These people do not have *found* people, we are safe."

"And if Nell becomes sick? What then?" Riley's

voice held steel, and the baby whimpered. Annie picked her up from the swing.

"They are right, Grandmother. It is time to go. They will keep us safe."

Noah breathed a sigh of relief.

Chapter Thirty-Seven

It was two a.m. when he crawled into the warm bed.

"Noah," Kali sighed.

He gathered her in his arms. They lay together, and softly in the moonlight shared their day. He swallowed down his own bile as she showed him her confrontation with Jared. He saw how Jared explained his plans to experiment on Kali so he could find out secrets to the *found*. Experiments to ultimately result in her death and dissection.

"God, baby, I would have never have allowed you to go, if I had known that was going to happen."

"We both know I'm the perfect person to question someone. I can convince them to talk, and I can discern the truth of what they are saying."

"I don't want you to do this anymore. I just can't stand it."

"Normally this won't pertain to me."

"Shit all of this will pertain to you. All of this pertains to the *found*. All of these fuckers want to breed us, kill us, dissect us, experiment on us, or some other fucking thing we haven't even thought of yet."

"Can we talk about something else?" she pleaded. "Show me Annie and her grandmother."

He was too wound up.

Kali pulled him tight against her naked body and started to caress his back.

"Stop it! I should be comforting you."

"This is a two way street. I've had almost two days to cope with this, you just saw it. You're as raw as when I heard it. Give yourself a moment, and then tell me about it. Annie is gorgeous. I bet all the dark hair and green eyes made quite the impression."

"I know what you're doing, you're trying to goad me into talking about something else."

"Is it working? Noah, I get a little insecure when you spend time with beautiful women."

"Are you kidding me? Kali, you're the only woman I see. You're beautiful." As soon as they stopped talking about experiments, he became conscious of Kali's naked form in his arms and started to get aroused. He pressed his erection firmly against her. He knew he was being played. Kali wasn't feeling insecure, they were past that, but he relished the opportunity to tell her how attractive he found her.

"Does this feel like I don't think you're

attractive? Hell Kali, Nate arranges to bring in powdered doughnuts every day because they know they are your favorite and to watch me suffer."

"What are you talking about?"

"You end up licking your lips to get the powder off, and then you lick your fingers too, when you're done. I can barely stand up from the conference room table when we're done because I'm so damn hard. The whole team sees it, even Sarah. I'm begging you, please don't eat the doughnuts in front of Mrs. Natani tomorrow."

"Really?" she said, with an awed smile.

"Really. You're it for me, beautiful. Why don't you let me prove it to you? Just thinking about you and those damn doughnuts has put me in a mood."

She reached for his cock, as if she didn't believe him, and attempted to curl her fingers around him before he gently grasped her wrist. "No baby, we're going slower."

"I want to touch. I want to taste."

Looking into her eyes, he thought he might drown.

"Me first, we are making a rule tonight, I get to always go first."

"Bad rule." Noah grinned, and pulled her hands above her head, and holding them in one hand. Then he stroked the line of her arms to her rib cage, over to her breast, cupping her fuller flesh, and brushing the pebbled nub with his thumb.

"Good rule," she breathed.

Bending his head he took the turgid tip of her other nipple into his mouth.

"Such a good rule."

He pressed his leg between hers, feeling her moisture coating his flesh. But even more seductive was feeling her slip into that languorous state of arousal, when she started to float and do nothing but be present in the sensations sparking throughout her body. As he felt her response to him, she felt his desire. He yearned to see her, to touch her, to taste her. He needed to conquer her every fear and grant her every wish.

He nipped at her peak making her to cry out in wonder, and pleasure-pain. "Keep your hands over your head, okay, beautiful?" She nodded. "With words."

"Yes, Noah. Always yes."

He slowly moved downwards, stringing kisses and nips along the way towards her mound. Pushing her legs apart, he stared at her sex.

"Noah," she whined.

"Beautiful. All of you is beautiful. See me, read me."

She quieted and he could feel her awe, and she saw his sincerity. The scent of her desire drove him wild, and the glistening shine on her flushed red sex drew him in. All of this arousal was because of him, because of what they shared. He was humbled, he was needy. The tip of his tongue felt silk and tasted honey. He licked delicately, and moved upwards towards the sensitive nub of flesh and with one slight touch he had her jumping.

"Hands up, perfectly still," he said as he pressed down on her soft tummy.

"I can't."

"You will." He felt her reluctance, but also her curiosity and heightened arousal. He angled his arm, so his elbow reminded her to keep her hips pressed down, and his thumb lifted the hood of her clit. Licking the small exposed morsel, he slid two fingers barely inside her entrance, and circled them around and around, mirroring the motion with his tongue. All of the flesh of her sex swelled.

"Noah, I'm so close."

He kept her right at the edge, easily feeling when one harder touch would push her over, and backing off. Long, long minutes he continued as she sobbed and cursed his name. Finally.

"Love me Noah, be inside me."

"Do I love you, Kali?"

"Yes, Noah."

"Who is the only woman I see? Who is the only woman I love? Who is the woman I'm going to grow old with?"

"Me. Kali."

He reared up, and plunged home. Knowing he did it without protection, knowing deep in his soul they were going to conceive a child.

"Yes, Noah, our child, yes, Noah."

Deeper. The friction was exquisite. Kali was his everything. Never was life better, no matter the danger. He loved and he was loved.

"So much Noah, I love you so much," she sobbed, wrapping her arms around his neck and her legs around his waist. Up and up, into each other's minds and hearts and souls.

"I love you, beautiful."

They found their release. As always, together.

Chapter Thirty-Eight

They gathered in the conference room. Mrs. Natani and Annie hadn't been told about the briefings. While Noah was gone, Dave Rydell showed up. He had to report in with Admiral Sakuro, so he came from San Diego yesterday, and he and Kali were formerly introduced. She watched the reunion between the two men. Obviously they meant a lot to one another.

The other man in the room also new to the briefings was Niko Evanoff. Noah and Riley were introduced, and Mathers explained they had a lock on Aaron Price. They finally found the lodge his father built in secret in Deer Park, Utah.

"Okay, let's put together a plan."

After two hours, Sarah and Kali were not happy. After three hours they were furious.

This is a horrible plan!
Baby, this is what we do.

"I don't like this at all. Cyrus, is this the kind of

thing you were doing when you were leading the task force?" Sarah demanded.

"Except for the cool Black Hawk helicopter. Yes."

"I don't think you should do it. I veto. And Kali, don't tell me you haven't been doing the mind talking with Noah, because I know you have."

"I'm not confirming or denying anything."

"Ladies, this is not up for discussion," Nate said.

"He's right, Kali, Sarah. This is how we're going to handle things. It's a normal operation. If you can't handle our operational planning, then you will no longer be allowed in our morning briefings." He was serious, Kali heard it in his voice. She looked over at Sarah and gave her a slight shake of her head.

It seemed like a lifetime since he had been in a Black Hawk helicopter with his team. He was always determined to take out the enemy, but this time he had even more motivation. They harmed the woman who was going to be his wife. What was more, he knew deep in his gut they were never going to stop. He looked around, and saw everybody from the first operation when they had rescued Kali. Dave Rydell, Nate Goodman, Riley Jones, Kota Blackthorne and Sierra Mathers—his team. They would not fail to procure their target.

They set down less than a mile from the lodge. It

was three a.m. Kota was disgusted when he saw there were no dogs patrolling the perimeter and only two guards. By the time they landed, Sierra already disabled all of the video surveillance.

"Before you get too confident, we still don't know what to expect inside," Noah reminded his team.

Everyone acknowledged his words, and then they split up into two groups. Noah, Nate and Sierra headed around the back wall, while Dave, Riley and Kota headed toward the guards. They intended to meet up at the lodge.

The rapid fire sound of an automatic weapon burst through the night. Noah, Sierra and Kota all dove into the snowbank for cover. Long seconds later, another piercing sound of gunfire was heard, clearly from the front of the building. Noah peered up and saw lights were turning on inside the lodge. He could easily see four men through the large windows and French doors as they rushed toward the entrance at the front of the house.

He hit the radio in his ear. "Dave? You, Riley and Nate okay?"

"We're fine."

"Four more coming your way."

"Roger that. Go find the bastard."

Noah signaled to Sierra and Kota the coast was clear.

Finding a darkened room on the first floor, the broke the window, accessing the house. The team had the blueprints of the house memorized.

"He's heard the gunshots, he's not going to be taken by surprise," Sierra said.

"We go together, and back one another up," Noah agreed.

"Let's sweep everything in this wing and save the master bedroom for last. That's probably where he's holed up."

They quickly and quietly made the rounds. Finally outside the large double doors of the master bedroom. They stayed on either side of the archways, and Kota reached low, and knocked. Three shots rang out, blowing holes through the door where a man's head and heart would have been.

"Now!"

Noah led the charge through the door, diving for the floor with his gun raised. Kota and Mathers were on the other side of the threshold with their guns pointed at the nondescript middle aged man standing next to the bed. His gun pointed at Noah.

"Drop it," Noah said with steely determination.

"No," his voice came out calm, nonchalant.

"We will kill you," Noah said, as he continued to train his gun on the man. But he didn't want to kill him. He wanted to make sure this was the last person responsible for Kali's kidnapping.

"No you won't.," the man said confidently. "You want information and I want to see what kind of powers you'll use. I know you're *found* Sam, and I know the *found* have powers. Use your powers, Sam. I want to see what you can do. Impress me."

The man was nuts. What he was thinking must have shown on his face, because the man laughed.

"Oh, another person who thinks I'm one brick shy of a load. I assure you I'm not. I'm actually a genius. I have a strong will to live, and I have remarkable common sense. I *said*, impress me." Now his voice had taken on a steely edge. His gun never wavering.

"Noah, incoming," Dave screamed in his ear.

"Kota! Sierra!"

"We heard." Noah didn't turn around, but heard two thuds behind him. The man in front of him smiled.

"Thank you, Martin. Don't kill them yet. I need them for leverage." Aaron Price's gray eyes gleamed as he looked at Noah again. "Impress me."

Noah didn't know what he could possibly do. He was good at finding things. He could talk to Kali. He was good in combat, but he had led his team into this goat fuck.

"If you don't I will have Martin kill your teammates. I want to be impressed."

He calmed. He had Kali's gifts and she was good at convincing. He could use that. "I need a minute. Can you give me just a minute, Aaron?"

"Don't fuck with me, Sam."

"I'm not, I just need a minute." He pushed like Kali had shown him.

"Fine, you have a minute." The man raised his arm to look at his watch, and Noah shot the wrist of his gun hand. Rolling over he shot the solider in the head who was standing over Sierra and Kota.

He kicked the gun far out of reach of Price, and rushed over to ensure his team would survive.

"Dave?"

"Noah? You made it?"

"Yeah, you?"

"We're good, on our way."

"Need the chopper stat." He strode over to Price and saw his wrist was spurting blood, he would likely lose his hand. Like Noah gave a shit. But he couldn't die. He yanked down a curtain sash and tied off the wound. Aaron didn't make a sound, just looked at him, his eyes glassy, his face and hair dripping sweat.

"I knew better than to take my eyes off you," Aaron Price said in confusion.

"I told you I needed a minute. I *convinced* you to look at your watch."

"Ahhhhh. Very good. You impressed me. Kelly impressed me, with the way she continued to endure. Where did you come from? I need to get there. That's where I belong." He passed out.

"Un-fucking-believable! That's what this was about?"

EPILOGUE

Kali realized she would never have a normal life again. She could handle the notoriety, but the fact she would have to live in a commune was beginning to wear on her. They hadn't told anyone yet, it was still too new, but they were going to have a baby. She wanted the child to experience the joys and freedoms she and Noah had as children. She couldn't bear to imagine they might have to live the first years of their child's life locked up in this apartment building.

Jade Melling and Joe Mirelli came for a visit three months after Aaron Price's capture. Joe's transformation was incredible. Not only was he behaving like a man who had never had any mental issues, he also had a rich tapestry of knowledge and experiences to draw on from his time at the hospital. He might have dealt with it at as a boy at the time, but he had assimilated it as a man.

"Kali and Noah, it is okay for you to leave here sometimes, right?" Joe asked as they were having dinner. They were in the dining room in their apartment with Joe, Jade, Nate and Sarah. Something was definitely up.

Noah answered. "Sure we can leave, we're not prisoners. We just have to be cautious."

"We'd like you to take us sightseeing on the Pacific Coast Highway tomorrow."

"Sure," Kali answered. She loved going to the ocean. She turned to Nate and Sarah. "Do you want to come?"

"Nah, we'll sit this one out," Nate answered.

Something's up, Noah
Definitely.

Joe wanted to drive, but he just got his driver's license and there was no way Noah was letting him drive on the windy roads.

Apparently Joe didn't want to just go sightseeing, he had a specific destination in mind. "Turn here," he instructed.

Noah turned into a drive with a gate in Laguna Beach. Joe jumped out and pushed a code into the keypad and the gate opened. When they got to the end of the drive, there was a woman waiting for them on the front steps of a huge beach house—basically a beautifully appointed mansion.

"Welcome, come in and look around."

"Are you moving here, Jade? That's great," Kali asked enthused.

"We definitely want to come out here more often," Jade agreed. The four of them followed the real estate agent through the house, all four admiring the views of the Pacific Ocean. The agent explained the house had been built by a movie mogul in the thirties, and was on the western tip of a rock jutting out over the Pacific Ocean.

"This is perfect," Noah said. "The way it is situated it's really a fortress. Joe, this is really secure."

"I knew you would think so," Joe said.

When they finished the tour, the real estate agent handed Joe the keys and drove away. Joe turned to Kali and Noah and handed the keys to Kali. She looked down at them. "I don't understand."

"The house is yours. I asked Joe to find something suitable for you since I realized you couldn't go back to Chicago," Jade said.

"I can't take this gift from you Jade, I know you feel guilty, but I just can't take it," Kali said, as she looked at the house, and then at the keys in her hand.

"Fine, don't take the house, you don't have to. I have set up a trust fund for you, it is substantially more than the cost of this house. I did it after I met you in New York. This property only utilizes twenty percent of the funds. You're stuck with the money, you can do whatever you want with it. You don't have to buy the house."

Kali felt like she was in a daze.

"Noah, you've been saying there isn't any place safe enough for us. You said we have to stay where we are."

"This would do. This is really well protected," he said carefully.

"Do you know the best part about this property?" Jade asked, smiling at her.

Kali shook her head. Jade came over and put her arm around her, and then grabbed Noah's hand. "It'll be the perfect place for a wedding."

Kali tried not to have any reaction to Jade's words, but she must have failed.

"Why don't you two walk around the property, get a feel for it, and talk?" Joe suggested.

"Good idea," Noah murmured, pulling Kali gently from Jade's grasp, he guided her toward the back of the house. The backyard overlooked the ocean. He sat on one of the loveseats and pulled her down on to his lap.

"Talk to me. I thought you wanted to get married," he said, thumbing the engagement ring on her left hand.

"Oh Noah, I do, you know I do, but don't we have to get married at a justice of the peace? I didn't think we could have an actual wedding." Kali looked down at his hand holding hers, not wanting to meet his eyes, afraid he'd see her disappointment.

"Baby, it's always been about doing this in a place where we could be private and secure. All

I've wanted since this whole thing started is to keep you safe. I've never meant for you to feel like a prisoner."

"Oh, I don't Noah." Kali looked at him, and released her barriers so he could feel everything. He touched his forehead to hers, and she showed him how loving him brought only joy into her life. The fact they had to live in hiding was trivial when compared to the wonder and beauty their life was now, and would be with the birth of their child.

"Kali, would you like to live here?"

"Could we?" She looked from his beautiful brown eyes to the magnificent view of the ocean and back again.

"Yes, we could. What's more, Jade is right, this would be a perfect spot for a wedding. We could invite all of our friends and family, we would just have to be discreet."

Kali snuggled close on his lap and gently probed. She could feel both his exasperation and his amusement, but she didn't care. She didn't want him doing something just because he felt she wanted it. He needed to be good with the decision too.

"Kali, I'd walk through fire for you."

"You don't have to."

"I would, you're my life, you and our baby. But, I will never do something to put either of you in harm's way, no matter how happy it would make you. Your safety always comes first. Living here, and having a wedding here, is perfect."

"Oh Noah, it doesn't have a meadow, but I would love it if our child could grow up playing in this yard, overlooking the water."

For long moments they sat there, resting their joined hands on Kali's tummy, and imagining the day their baby would be playing on the grass in front of them. The first pulse of energy surprised them, then there was a second. Stunned they looked at each other.

"Kali?"

"Noah, I felt it too!"

"We're going to have twins."

"A boy and a girl," Kali breathed. She stared into Noah's eyes, and realized every dream she never even knew she had was coming true.

BOOKS BY CAITLYN O'LEARY

THE FOUND SERIES

Revealed, Book One
Forsaken, Book Two (coming soon)

FATE HARBOR SERIES
Published by Siren/Bookstrand

Trusting Chance, Book One
Protecting Olivia, Book Two
Claiming Kara, Book Three
Isabella's Submission, Book Four
Cherishing Brianna, Book Five
(Releasing Feb. 10, 2015)

Excerpt from

Revealed

The Found, Book Two

By

Caitlyn O'Leary

Chapter One

"Put on your clothes. You disgust me." Seth was beyond tired, and seeing his wife on his bed, naked and spread for him made his bile rise.

"Carson, I need you, remember how it was?" She tried to entice him by playing with her breasts.

Seeing her gown on the floor, he picked it up and tossed it on top of her. "That's the problem Portia, I don't remember anything, let alone it ever being any good."

"That night together was the best night of my life. It could be like that again if you'd just try, dammit."

"Get out of my room," his voice deadly. Her eyes widened and she scrambled off the bed.

"Fine, but don't think this is the end. You are going to make me pregnant again. Daddy wants a grandchild."

"Oh cut the bullshit, there was never a baby in

the first place. You dragged my ass to the altar under false pretenses."

"Carson, you got me pregnant that night. You believed me before, why don't you believe me now?"

The million dollar question. He knew from the moment he laid eyes on her she was a criminal and likely involved in drug smuggling with her father. He intended to put her behind bars, and instead he had married her to protect his unborn child. A child that likely never existed.

"Get the fuck out, Portia, before I do something we both regret."

She slung the gown over her shoulder and left his room, uncaring if the servants saw her naked or not. His wife was quite a piece of work.

Seth…Carson, whatever the fuck his name was, Hell he was beginning to question his own identity. Yanking at the bowtie of his tuxedo it knotted tighter instead of opening.

"Good, maybe I'll choke." He was sick of living the double life. Finally he pulled, ripping it apart at the seam. "God damn motherfucker!" He did the same with the cuffs of his shirt, satisfied when the cufflinks flew across the room. They were gold with diamonds. Maybe the maids would steal them. "Good for them."

Fuck, he needed to shut the hell up, it was a bad habit to talk out loud. He knew his room was bugged. There was a damn good chance of video surveillance too. Once when Portia was high she said she hoped there was, that it added to the spice.

Not that he would touch her. He warned her when they started this travesty of a marriage it wouldn't be consummated, but she hadn't believed him. Hence the weekly ritual. Sometimes she'd bring in some kind of sex toy, one night he'd found her tied spread eagle to the bed. He didn't even want to know who had helped her into the position.

He pulled off the rest of his clothes, hoping they would tear as well, but they didn't. At least one of his dress shoes left a dent in the wall. They could report he had a temper tantrum for all he cared. It had been an ugly fucking night and Portia was the cherry on top. He needed a long hot shower to erase the stench of the scum he brushed up against.

God, he hoped it would help his headache. Grabbing three ibuprofen and some Rolaids he chewed them all down, praying it would help his head and his stomach by the time he finished the hot shower.

He often wondered if they had audio and video in the shower too, it wouldn't surprise him. Nothing surprised him about these bastards. Had he ever had such a bad headache? It was the woman at the party, she reminded him of his Annie, and then he had to listen to Lobado's men talk about their new source of income. The pulse of pain in his head was so bad his eyes started to water.

What the fuck had he gotten himself into?

Annie reminded herself to be happy. She escaped from the people intent on kidnapping her baby, but all she could focus on was her baby's father. Somehow she managed to drive Seth away. She took out his letter, went to her desk, and pulled out the tape. Carefully she taped the seams where it was coming apart because she had unfolded and folded it so often.

"Annie,

I won't be coming home after this assignment. Things have changed. I have changed. I have decided on a new life. I deeply regret the promises I made to you but will be unable to honor.

I won't defile our time together by speaking of it now, only know this, you are loved.

I am entrusting this letter with my father, so you can tell him if you need anything. I can no longer claim the name Natani, but you will always be cared for by the family of Natani.

Seth"

Annie pushed the paper flat against the desk. She didn't know why she wanted to look at it. The letter had almost killed her when Rafe Natani, Seth's father, had handed it to her almost a year ago.

Seth's parents had found her at her apartment not

far from the college in Farmington, New Mexico where she was spending a lot of her time. She was working on her doctoral thesis in Archeology based on the Anasazi, and using the college campus library.

"Miss Newman, you don't know us, but we're Seth's parents. Would you allow us to come in?" Everything dropped away as Annie looked at the middle aged Native American couple on her porch. Dear God, Seth had died on assignment with the DEA. Annie grabbed her swollen abdomen and fell to her knees, staring up at the caring faces of Seth's parents.

"Quick Rafe, let's help her inside."

"Seth, is he? Did he? Did he suffer?"

"Oh honey, no. He's not dead. We're handling this badly. Let us help you. Seth's not dead. He's fine." The Natani's helped Annie into her cooler apartment, and settled her on the couch.

"What can I get you to drink?" the woman asked as she hurried towards the kitchen.

"I don't need anything. Where's Seth? Is he hurt? Is he finally home?"

"He's not hurt. He's not home. My name is Rafe, the woman currently rummaging through your kitchen is my wife Wanda." Annie looked at his hand holding hers over the large swell of her tummy. They both looked up at the same time.

"Am I going to be a grandfather?"

"I'd prefer to tell Seth he's going to be a father first."

"I brought you some lemonade. I also found some graham crackers, I thought they would suit." Wanda sat down on the other side of her husband after handing her the glass and setting the plate on the coffee table. She squeezed her husband's shoulder. "She's so young." She whispered to her husband, but Annie heard her.

"I'm twenty-four."

Seth's mother gave her a long considering look, Annie was used to it. She knew she had a baby face. "Do you want to see my driver's license? I'm actually working on my PhD. I'm going to be twenty-five in three months." She watched as Wanda relaxed.

"I'm sorry honey, I worry for you. I hate to see babies raising babies."

"So do I, but I'm a grown woman, and I want my baby very much. Please tell me why you're here, this is killing me."

"Are you pregnant with our son's child?" Mr. Natani persisted. Annie looked him in the eye, and was struck by the lack of family resemblance between Seth and his parents and then remembered the strange circumstances surrounding his adoption into the Natani home.

"I beg your pardon, but why are you here?"

This time Mrs. Natani spoke. "Annie, we need you to stay strong," she looked down at her belly. "Especially now." She opened up her purse and pulled out a letter and handed it to her husband, who in turn handed it to Annie. "Seth sent us a letter, with this letter enclosed. He said we needed to be here when you opened it."

It was the first time she read those words. She didn't say a word, didn't cry, and showed no emotion. She was used to rejection. She didn't know how she had managed to drive him away, but she had. It was the story of her life, she had done something so wrong her mother abandoned her all those years ago. The first foster home she lived in gave her back after two years.

She took small comfort in the fact he bothered to lie and say he had loved her. She would cope, she always coped, no matter what her age, she coped. Only this hurt a million times worse. But she wouldn't give into the hurt, she had her daughter to think about. She stroked her tummy and murmured reassurance to Nell as she kicked in agitation. Her baby felt her Mommy's upset.

"It's okay, baby girl," Annie crooned.

"We're having a granddaughter, Rafe!" Wanda cried out ecstatically, and Annie burst into tears.

"You need...You need to leave."

"Miss Newman, we're not leaving. May I read the letter Seth gave you?" It fell out of her numb fingers and fluttered to the floor as Annie tried to hand it him. Picking it up, he read the note and then handed it to his wife. Wanda took longer to read it, and when she finished she stifled a sob.

"You're coming home with us Annie," the woman said when she stopped crying.

The rest of the afternoon was a blur. There was

no way on God's green Earth Annie would have thought her apartment in Farmington would be packed and she would agree to move to Shiprock with Seth's parents, but it's exactly what happened. Wanda Natani was a force of nature. Her husband was the steady wind behind the force, just steadily pushing, ensuring everything moved forward.

Annie didn't have to lift a finger. Somehow packers and movers showed up out of thin air within hours of the Natani's arrival. One of the moving men said he would drive her car to Shiprock, which is when she came out of her stupor.

"I'm more than capable of driving."

"We never said you weren't," Rafe smiled easily. Seth had the same smile, and it always meant the same thing, she was going to lose an argument.

"Then please give me back my keys." Annie held out her hand. The whole day was surreal. It was a month before she was due to deliver. Her thesis was a week away from being done, and it felt like her life was over. That kind of thinking was unacceptable. She needed to take control. She had her daughter to consider.

"Sure, Miss Newman, you can drive. But the roads from here to Shiprock are icy. Are your tires studded? We want you to be safe."

Damn, he made sense.

"Annie, you need to call her Annie, Rafe. She's our daughter now." Wanda said as she came up and wrapped her arm around Annie's shoulder.

"No, I'm not, what are you talking about?"

"Don't panic, we're not kidnapping you, this is totally your decision. But know from this day forward we consider you our daughter. We would have whether you were carrying our granddaughter or not. We don't understand the choices our son has made, but he has much love for you, and therefore we have much love for you. You are part of our clan, our family, and our hearts." She studied their faces and read the truth in what she said. For the second time Annie started crying.

"Miss Newman, I mean Annie, please don't cry."

"Hush Rafe, these are good tears. She knows she finally has a home." Wanda pulled her into the warmest hug she could remember.

Annie rode in the Natani's car to Shiprock. When they got to their modest adobe home, the moving truck wasn't there. Instead an older woman was standing in the doorway, looking very elegant in a long caftan and boots.

"Mom. What are you doing here?" Rafe called out.

"A good question, since my son didn't see fit to tell me he was bringing home my granddaughter and great-granddaughter." The woman ignored her son and hugged her daughter-in-law before standing in front of Annie.

"Welcome Annie Newman. My name is Shilah Natani. I am your grandmother." For the second time Annie was engulfed in a pair of loving female arms. This time Nell kicked out, surprising her and the older woman. Shilah broke away, and rested her hand on Annie's belly. "And you little one, welcome. What is your name?"

"Her name is Nell." Annie smiled, loving the fact Shilah treated Nell as an actual person, because in her eyes, Nell was a person, she just hadn't come out to meet everyone yet.

"Welcome Nell, I am your great-grandmother." Annie felt her baby kick in obvious excitement. It was like when she ate a piece of chocolate, or the few times she had gotten lost in a daydream about Seth. Nell was extremely sensitive, just like her Daddy. Tears formed for the third time but she willed them away. She was *not* going to ruin the joy her daughter was feeling at that moment.

"Granddaughter, it is going to be all right. This too shall pass."

Annie looked into the eyes of a woman who though related to Seth by blood, really seemed to be his grandmother. Maybe there actually was hope.

"There is reason to hope. Trust me."

Nell kicked again against this woman's hand, as if she too was telling her to believe. Annie's tears dried up.

"You are right. I am blessed."

"You don't believe it yet, but you will. You are strong my granddaughter. We don't understand everything, but you need to know my grandson loves you."

"I can't Grandmother. I can't hold onto that, it will break me. But I can believe in all of you. I can believe in Nell, and I can believe in myself."

"That's enough for now." Shilah Natani pulled her towards the house, and they sat down while Wanda made hot chocolate. Again Annie felt Nell's pleasure.

"I wonder where the moving truck is, I need to call them," Rafe said as he pulled out his cell phone.

"It's at my house," Shilah stated. "The only room here, is Seth's old room. Annie wouldn't want to stay in it. It's best she stays at my house."

"Mom."

"Shilah…" Wanda started.

"Annie, what do you think of that idea?" the older lady asked as she covered Annie's hand with hers. Why was she so drawn to her? She turned her hand over and grasped it, like she would a lifeline.

"I would love to stay with you Mrs. Natani."

"Please call me Grandmother, or Shilah whatever you are comfortable with."

Annie thought it over. Her mother had abandoned her when she was six. She had never had a grandmother. Again, looking into this woman's eyes was like looking into a part of Seth. Even though he had abandoned her as well, it was like a part of him was still with her.

"Grandmother. I want to call you Grandmother." Nell kicked in agreement, and Annie gave a wan smile, the first smile since reading the awful letter.

"You'll do Annie Newman."

About the Author

Caitlyn O'Leary was raised in a small town in the Pacific Northwest. She has always been an avid reader. Her earliest creative writing endeavors consisted of "ghost writing" exercises where she pretended to be her younger brothers and sister when she did their homework assignments.

Years in corporate America honed her ability to manipulate words by day and at night she read everything she could get her hands on, including many steamy romances.

Now happily married to her long, tall Texan and living in Southern California, Caitlyn has finally found the time to write erotic happily ever afters. She enjoys swimming, traveling, babysitting for her nieces and nephews, spending time with friends and family, and doing lots of "research" with her husband for upcoming novels.

Made in the USA
Lexington, KY
10 July 2017